PR
A ... PERSUASIVE EVIDENCE!

"Ra... ...al thrill... incredible—that's how I would ... .ok. Th... is one of the best books that I have read. I was completely riveted from the first page."
—Romance Reader at Heart

"R. Barri Flowers has written a superb legal thriller. *Persuasive Evidence* will appeal to fans of John Grisham and Linda Fairstein."
—Harriet Klausner

"R. Barri Flowers creates a story that keeps you on the edge of your seat. The suspense builds in *Persuasive Evidence* to master a page-turning story I couldn't put down."
—*Romance Junkies*

"R. Barri Flowers lets it all hang out in this fast-paced mystery."
—Rawsistaz.com

"An absorbing legal thriller, *Persuasive Evidence* is proof of Flowers' talent as an author."
—*Romance in Color*

"Quite engaging with all-around solid pacing, plot and delivery."
—Nubian Circle Book Club

"All the elements of a great mystery book: suspicions, red herrings, evidence and witnesses. If you are into mysteries, this would be the book for you."
—A Romance Review

COULD IT BE?

"I think it scares everybody that such a thing is happening—how could it not?"

"It sure as hell gives me the chills," Vivian said, wringing her hands. "Especially if what they're saying is true—"

"Saying…?" Carole widened her eyes.

"You know, that it's a woman beating those men to death with a bat." Vivian shook her head. "I just can't see it. We can take a lot—but dishing it out like that—"

"Don't believe everything you hear or read," Carole said. "Until they capture the killer, it could be anyone of any race or ethnicity or sex."

Vivian sipped her Pepsi. "Actually, I always thought it was only men who committed these types of crimes."

"It usually is," Carole said.

"But this is different…?"

"Maybe," she allowed unsteadily.

Other books by R. Barri Flowers:

PERSUASIVE EVIDENCE

JUSTICE
SERVED

R. BARRI
FLOWERS

LEISURE BOOKS NEW YORK CITY

*To B.J. and Mother Dearest for
always believing in me, and sister
Jacquelyn and her wonderful family!*

A LEISURE BOOK®

August 2005

Published by

Dorchester Publishing Co., Inc.
200 Madison Avenue
New York, NY 10016

This work of fiction and all the characters within are entirely the product of the author's imagination and creativity; hence, purely fictitious. Any semblance to real persons, places, or circumstances is entirely coincidental and should be regarded as such.

ISBN 0-8439-5562-7

Printed in the United States of America.

Visit us on the web at www.dorchesterpub.com.

ACKNOWLEDGMENTS

I am excited to present *Justice Served* as my second legal novel, following the successful *Persuasive Evidence*. I hope that my fans enjoy the book every bit as much!

I would like to thank all those who have played a part in the publication of *Justice Served*, including my editor, Don D'Auria, and agent, Michelle Grajkowski, as well as the wonderfully supportive staff at Dorchester and my talented critique partner and most loyal person in my life, Miss Maui. I wish to acknowledge as well my alma mater, Michigan State University and the School of Criminal Justice, where I began the path toward a successful and satisfying career as a literary criminologist and mystery novelist.

Stay tuned for my next legal thriller, *State's Evidence*, that's sure to be another page-turner for my growing list of fans!

Yours truly,
R. Barri Flowers

JUSTICE SERVED

Prologue

She hid under the bed, carefully controlling her breathing. She didn't move, not even a twitch. Her pink dress was dirty from the dusty pine hardwood floor, and her pink shoes were scuffed. The curls of her raven hair billowed around her head like a halo. She could see their shoes, moving around as if dancing to a tender love song.

Only she knew it was no dance.

And it was no love song.

She heard the sound of his fist as it smashed against her mama's cheek. Her mama immediately crumpled to the floor like a rag doll, dazed and moaning. Blood ran from a corner of her swollen mouth.

Her mama's face ballooned, her cheek shattered from the blow. One eye was swollen shut, protruding like a golf ball. With her good eye, mother made eye contact with her daughter in a moment of sorrow and sheer terror.

She wanted to help her mama and save her from

him. But the girl knew that she would be no match for his brute strength and drunken rage. In that moment of connection, her mama silently warned her to remain still so that she too would not face the fists and battering he had inflicted upon her.

With all of her willpower, the girl closed her eyes tightly, her instincts telling her that nothing would ever be the same again. Not that she ever wanted things to be.

Not this way.

Not with him.

When her eyes opened, her mama was no longer on the floor. She had been dragged to her feet and thrown onto the bed like a sack of soiled clothes.

"Bitch!" she heard him roar like a lion, hovering over her mama as if her shadow.

Then he hit her again. The blow must have been tremendous, for her mama's dentures went flying across the floor like a bird, landing beneath a chair in the corner. She was pounded several more times. Her mama's bloodcurdling screams had turned to faint whimpers.

Then the bed suddenly sank to the point where she thought she might be crushed or cut by the jagged springs nearly touching her. It was all she could do not to make a sound, though inside she was crying as loudly as she could muster.

He had gotten on the bed with her mother.

"This ain't over, bitch," he spat. "Not by a long shot!"

She listened as she heard him unbuckle his pants.

"I'll show you to smart-mouth me. When I'm done with you, you'll know who's boss, and who ain't nothin' but a damned ugly-ass whore!"

She could hear some rustling noises and heavy breathing and groans—the last coming from him, by the wicked deepness of them. She couldn't bear to think of what he was doing to her mama. But she knew it was something awful. Something that would make her curse him even more than she already did.

When he was finished, she heard him roll over. Moments later he was snoring like a bear, the heavy sound coming from well within his throat, punctuated by labored breathing. She could hear no sounds from her mama, but suspected that she was too afraid even to breathe—afraid that he would wake up and continue hurting her.

The little girl was also afraid. After waiting there paralyzed with fear for what seemed like an eternity, she nudged her way beneath the springs until she was out from under the bed. Her pink dress was covered with dust and blood from where her mama had fallen.

She stood, intent on taking her mama away from him forever. But it took only one look at her to know this would never be. Her face was almost unrecognizable—horribly discolored and at least twice its normal size. Her clothes had been ripped apart, exposing a frail, thin body marred with marks and bruises both fresh and from other beatings he'd inflicted upon her. Her legs were spread wide, blood oozing from between them, seeping onto the sheet like red dye.

Her mama's one good eye was wide open, as if held that way by toothpicks. Whatever life was in her had vanished forever.

Beside her, he lay naked in a drunken sleep, his breathing erratic and uncertain.

She felt the hatred in her build like steam in an engine. This was softened only by the love for her mama and hardened again by her own feeling of helplessness and guilt.

She climbed atop her mother's battered, broken, and bloodied body and lay there with her thumb in her mouth, as if she would be rocked to sleep and would wake up and find that everything was all right.

Deep down she knew that would never be the case. He had seen to that.

She began to hum a song she made up on the spot, somehow soothing her, no longer caring if he woke and hurt her as he had her mama.

After all, she could feel no greater pain, bleak darkness, or emptiness than she felt at the moment.

1

Judge Carole Cranston sat on the bench and banged her gavel. The courtroom immediately came to order on this late July afternoon. She was a no-nonsense judge who wanted only to expedite things as quickly as possible from trial to trial, preferring to be in the comfort of her condo overlooking the Willamette River in Portland, Oregon. It was especially nice at this time of year, she thought, when the summer breeze came in and the sun bounced off the water as if too hot to remain in one place. She was reminded of trips to the Bahamas, where she had fallen in love with Grand Bahama Island in particular. She could imagine herself maybe one day retiring to the Bahamas, Jamaica, or even Hawaii, and drinking in its beauty and perennial sunshine each day for the rest of her life.

Carole returned to the present, realizing that at thirty-five years of age and three months, she was hardly able to begin thinking about retirement just yet. *I wish*, she mused. Not when she had a job to do—no matter how maddening and disillusioning at times—and people who depended on her to dispense justice to the best of her ability.

She turned her espresso-dark eyes on the prosecutor. His name was Julian Frommer. He was in his early thirties, but looked about twenty-one, with dirty-blond hair a bit too long, and a small goatee that looked almost taped under his chin. His navy wool suit did not fit his tall, lanky frame.

"Are you ready?" she asked him routinely.

"Always, Your Honor." He pasted a flirtatious smile on his lips.

But Carole had not even noticed as she turned her attention to the defense. George McArdle, fortyish, African-American, and built like a house, was already on his feet and showing off a three-piece tailored gray suit. His closely cropped dark hair had a slightly crooked part off to the side. He acknowledged her with a twinkle in his eyes.

"The defense is ready to present its case, Your Honor."

She nodded and looked at the defendant. Roberto Martinez—a thirty-six-year-old, muscular, Hispanic construction worker—had been charged with beating his live-in lover half to death. The medical report said that she had sustained multiple fractures, including a shattered nose, broken jaw, broken arm, and broken leg. But she would live. And so would the memories.

Martinez flashed her a crooked grin, as if to say, *It would have been more fun had you been on the other end of my fists*, Your Honor.

Carole glared at him. She could feel the tiny hairs stand up on the nape of her neck. But this was invisible to those before her, who saw only the cool, calm, and collected, attractive judge. Her russet-colored individual pixies curved under her chin and onto slender shoulders, contrasting with a beautiful butterscotch complexion. Beneath the oversize black robe was a tall, shapely body with long, runner's legs.

She faced Julian Frommer again. "You may call your first witness, Counselor. . . ."

It turned out that his first witness, the victim, was a no-show. She was going to be wheeled in from the hospital, where she was still recovering from her injuries. She had apparently had a change of heart and now refused to testify against Martinez. The State's case further began to unravel when it turned out that the only other witness was a known drug dealer whose testimony came as a result of a plea bargain that would keep him from doing hard time.

Meanwhile the defense had produced witnesses who would testify that the defendant was seen at work at the alleged time of the assault. It was a shaky alibi at best that left a window of opportunity for Roberto Martinez to have committed the offense and returned to the job. But given that the victim was unwilling to refute this, the prosecution had little choice but to go along with George McArdle's request that the charges be dropped.

And neither did Carole, though this pained her more than she was willing to admit. The thought that a scumbag batterer like Martinez should get off so easily was disturbing. But then, that was the system for you. Justice often needed help to be dispensed properly.

Looking Roberto Martinez straight in the eye, Carole announced unaffectedly, "The charges have been dropped. You're free to leave, Mr. Martinez."

He favored her with a lascivious grin, gave his attorney a hearty bear hug, and headed for the door without so much as a slap on the wrist.

Growling at Julian Frommer, Carole snapped, "I would strongly suggest, Counselor, that in the future you not waste the court's time—or mine—with a case you were clearly unprepared to make!"

On that note, and without giving him a chance for a lame response, she headed for her chambers, disappointed that another woman beater, who was obviously guilty, had found a way to beat the system.

At Portland General Hospital, Lucie Garcia winced from the pain that racked her entire body. This in spite of the painkillers she had been given. They told her she was lucky to be alive. She didn't feel so lucky.

The Hispanic twenty-three-year-old rolled her large ink-black eyes, as if to ward off danger. Her brunette hair splayed across the pillow, soaked with perspiration. An irregular line of blood had seeped across it from her mouth, which had been cut and was swollen to twice its normal size. A tube was helping her to breathe. Her fractured bones were held together with pins and casts. The rest of her was held together through sheer willpower.

She thought about Roberto. She'd been told he had been released from custody. Without her testimony, the case had gone out the window.

When it came right down to it, Lucie knew she couldn't testify against Roberto. Though she was afraid of him, and the beatings had become more frequent and more violent in recent months as his alcohol abuse grew worse, she loved him. She couldn't help it any more than a mother could help loving her son, no matter what he did to hurt her.

Roberto was the only man she had ever loved. The only one who didn't run away at the first opportunity, or when another piece of ass came into view. For that she was grateful. The rest just came with the territory, as far as she was concerned.

Still, Lucie wondered what awaited her when she got home. Would Roberto take it out on her that he had been in police custody? Would he want her back now that she was badly bruised and broken? And not looking anything at all like the pretty Latina that had captured his attention in the beginning?

Lucie winced again before the sedative began to take effect and she drifted off into a restless sleep. Her last thought was that maybe she would awaken and find it had all been an awful dream.

Deep down inside she knew otherwise.

2

Roberto Martinez was counting his blessings as he sat in the bar getting drunk. He had been staring at twenty to life, according to his public defender. He figured that he'd be lucky if he ever saw the light of day again while he was young enough to be able to appreciate it.

But the devil must have been watching over his shoulder. Here he was out among the living again, and there wasn't a damned thing anyone could do about it.

He thought about his old lady. Yeah, he'd beaten the hell out of her. But, dammit, she deserved it. They all did. Especially when they opened their big mouths too much and their legs too little. It was the only way to keep them in line. All whores needed to be kept in line, one way or the other.

Roberto Martinez finished off his last shot of whiskey before winking at the sweet-looking black broad wearing shades in the corner while imagining what he could do with her, then moseying out of the bar. The night was cool for this time of year and darker than most. Stars seemed to have disappeared, as if relinquishing their place in space for other solar systems.

Roberto had half staggered about a block when he heard footsteps behind him. He turned and saw a tall, stacked, dark-skinned woman with a blond wig of box braids almost on top of him. He remembered she was the broad in the bar sitting all by her lonesome at the end of the counter. Only she was without the sunglasses, so he could see her eyes. They were deep, dark, enchanting. Just like the bitch herself.

"You looking for some action, honey?" she asked in a voice that sounded vaguely familiar.

He studied her. She had on a tight red dress that hugged every curve of her statuesque body, red gloves, and stiletto shoes. She was obviously a hooker. *Why the hell not?* he thought salaciously. It wasn't like his old lady was at home waiting to greet him or anything.

He grinned. "Yeah, I'm looking for some action, baby. How much will it cost?" In his mind he figured she was worth maybe twenty. Twenty-five if she was real good to him.

"Keep your money," she said curtly. "Let's just say I'm in a generous mood tonight."

Roberto regarded her uneasily. Was this some kind of a setup or something? Were they trying to get him back behind bars? Trick him into doing something stupid on account of what he did to Lucie and getting away with it?

"You ain't a cop, are you?" he asked tentatively.

She placed a hand on her rounded hip. "Do I look like a cop to you, sugar?"

11

Roberto grinned again. "Not like any damned cop I've seen," he had to admit.

"Then why are we wasting time here jawing?"

He felt at ease again. His libido was admittedly in need of a quick fix.

. "Yeah," he said. "Why are we? Your place or mine?"

"Neither. In there." She pointed.

He looked into the darkened alley. It was hardly the ideal place to get laid, he thought. But who was he to argue? He could get his rocks off just about anywhere.

"Lead the way," he told her.

He followed the whore to the back of the alley, where she leaned up against a wall and urged him on.

"Come and get it, big boy," she teased.

Roberto could hardly contain himself as he rushed toward her. He noticed only at the last moment that she had picked up something with lightning-quick speed and swung it hard at his head. He felt the impact as his skull cracked, sending him to his knees. The pain cut through him like a sharp knife.

"How does it feel?" she asked him, a suddenly wicked edge to her voice. Before he could even think past the pain, much less respond, she struck him again with what he now suspected was a wooden bat. This time it connected across his back, smashing into his spine, paralyzing him. "Does it feel good, asshole?"

She swung the bat like an all-star baseball player, landing flush against his right cheek, dislodging his jaw and most of the teeth on that side of his face.

"Isn't this what you like to do to women, Roberto?" she spat, clubbing him across the top of the head, crushing his skull. "Well, how about a taste of your own medicine, you bastard!"

She swung again and again, each blow shattering another part of him, sending blood, bone, brain, and body pieces flying everywhere.

By the time she was finished, he was long dead. But it didn't matter, for she received great satisfaction to see to it that even in death he would never be whole again. Just like the lover he had beaten to a pulp.

She tossed the bloodied bat atop the corpse. Then she removed her wig, gloves, dress, and shoes. She put them in a duffel bag and slipped on some jeans, a sweater, and tennis shoes, leaving Roberto Martinez's remains to rot like raw meat.

3

The narrow alleyway had been turned into a crime scene as police rummaged through a Dumpster for evidence, while technicians gathered everything they could as standard procedure in a murder investigation. Portland Police Bureau Detective Sergeant Ray Barkley recoiled as his stone-gray eyes gazed at the mangled body with more than a few pieces missing. It was the third time in the past five months that a male had been beaten to death with a bat in the city—the weapon left each time courtesy of the assailant, as if to make a statement.

Ray Barkley had been in homicide for the last ten of his twenty years on the force and thirty-seven years of life. Since then he had seen just about everything there was to see. But now he suspected he was seeing something entirely new. What it was he wasn't quite sure. Except that it scared the hell out of him.

And most other brothers he knew. Or for that matter, all men who usually thought they were invincible.

Until now.

"Looks like someone's having one hell of a time bashing skulls in," remarked his partner, Detective Nina Parker. At thirty-four, she was a short, but imposing, fit, and tough-as-nails sister who had once briefly been his lover—until they both realized it was a big mistake mixing business with pleasure. They had used each other to get over bad marriages and rotten luck in the relationship department. In the end, they worked through the sexual attraction and rediscovered what it meant to be friends off the job and partners on the job.

"Yeah, tell me about it," grumbled Ray, rolling his hand across his shaved baldhead. Clad in his usual cheap, on-the-job dark suit and penny loafers, he was six-four and sturdily built, though admittedly having slacked off somewhat of late with the weightlifting and aerobics. A night-black mustache accentuated his square-jawed oak complexion. "On second thought, don't. I can see for myself that it doesn't pay to be the wrong dude at the wrong time and place these days."

"Who says it was the *wrong* dude?" Nina sneered, her blond-streaked brown Bantu knots bouncing against the broad shoulders of her olive gabardine blazer. "Or the wrong time and place? Seems to me that whoever did this knew exactly what man to go after, when, and where!"

It was an observation Ray could hardly dispute. Which made it all the more frightening. It suggested that specific men were being targeted. But by whom?

15

He looked at the corpse again. Clearly the perpetrator had battered him long after he was dead. Just like the others.

As if to say death itself was not enough to release the rage felt by the killer.

"We got a name yet?" Ray asked of the deceased, eyeing Nina.

She pulled out a notepad from the back pocket of tight black chinos.

"Name's Roberto Martinez," Nina said. "Lives on 8652 Andover. The killer never bothered to take his wallet, money, or anything else, as far as we can tell. Not that he had all that much to take," she added. "Unless you consider twenty-five bucks and a ring that was worth maybe half that as a king's ransom."

"The man didn't have to be a king to deserve a better fate than what he ended up with." Ray flashed her a deadpan look and glanced at the victim. "Roberto Martinez. Why the hell does that name sound familiar?"

"Maybe because a Roberto Martinez was recently charged with assaulting his girlfriend . . . Lucie Garcia—"

"Yeah, right." They'd both heard the call come in about the domestic disturbance—the type of call that had become so commonplace in Portland that many in the department considered them more nuisance cases than crimes. He imagined they would have to be taken more seriously as the body count continued to rise.

Ray took a hard look at the face that was so disfigured it was hard to imagine it was human. "You think this is the same Roberto Martinez?"

"Let me put it this way," Nina responded sardonically. "Just this afternoon all charges were dropped against Martinez, and he walked."

"Just like that?" Ray cocked a brow.

"Just like that."

"How?" As if he had to ask. It happened all too often in domestic violence cases. Reluctant victims and some reluctant police and prosecutors still saw domestic violence as something that belonged in family court, not criminal court.

"Girlfriend refused to testify," Nina informed him. "Need I say more?"

"Looks like somebody's already spoken for the girlfriend," he said, taking one final look at the badly assaulted remains. "Loud and clear."

Ray signaled the team from the medical examiner's office that they could take the body. He had seen all he cared to of it for the moment.

During the drive back to the station, Ray sat in the passenger seat while Nina drove their department-issue late-model dark sedan.

"So what are we looking at here, a vigilante?" he asked, but already knew the answer. The first two victims had recently been charged with abusing a woman, but had managed to beat the rap without having to do time. Shortly thereafter they had been found in much the same fashion as this latest victim.

Nina flipped him an obvious glance. "You got a better idea? It's clear someone's decided to create the justice that doesn't seem to be coming from the system."

Ray's nostrils flared. "Hell, just what we need—

some bat-wielding do-gooder, battering batterers. What's next, rapists being raped to death?" The thought made him twitch.

"You've got to admit, there's a certain irony to the manner of death chosen by the killer." She rounded a corner sharply. "Don't get me wrong, Barkley: I'm definitely not in favor of people taking the law into their own hands. Especially like this. But let's face it; there hasn't been nearly enough attention paid to domestic violence in this country. If nothing else, maybe this will turn some heads."

"Let's just hope they're not turned by hard-swinging bats," he said humorlessly.

Nina stopped at a red light, giving him the full attention of her soulful eyes. "I think our killer is a woman."

Ray had reluctantly come to the same conclusion, though he still found it hard to accept. Women were not usually cold-blooded killers, in his experience. Not like men. Furthermore, virtually all serial killers were men. As well as spree killers. Psychotic killers. And even spousal-abuse killers.

But this was different, he thought. It was hard to imagine a man beating to death other male woman beaters. At least, it was harder to imagine than a vengeful woman who had probably reached the breaking point after years of physical and psychological torment and decided to take out her frustrations on any man labeled an abuser and not fortunate enough to have been locked away.

"Well, whether female or not," Ray said firmly, "this person is a walking time bomb, waiting to go off anytime the opportunity strikes."

"We actually found something we can agree on,

Barkley." Nina gave him a wry smile. "What a concept."

"Ouch, that hurt." He doubled over as if in pain.

"Good," she said with a pleased chuckle. "I'll sleep a lot better tonight."

Ray glanced at Nina's profile. Tiny moles dotted her cheek like freckles. He still found the sister attractive, he thought. Maybe too much for his own good.

For an instant he felt a trickle of desire, but quickly extinguished it like a low flame. Whatever chemistry still existed between them, it was best left to doing the job. Anything else would only complicate a good working relationship—something neither of them wanted or needed.

Not when there were far more pressing matters to attend to.

4

Carole carefully watered her weeping fig, Aglaonema, and ivy plants, treating each like family. She had always loved plants ever since she was a little girl, reading about and growing different types in the backyard garden. There was something about nurturing plants and watching them sprout to life that fascinated her. They were not prone to human frailties that could destroy their soul through misuse and mishandling.

The doorbell startled Carole, who had been in deep concentration. She put down her watering can and went to the intercom, thinking half comically, *Now, who on earth could that be disturbing me and my darling plants?*

She pressed the talk button.

"Yes, what is it?"

"It's me. Stuart," the husky voice said simply. "I need to talk to you, Carole."

"It's kind of late," she noted, annoyed.

"Yeah, I know. I promise I won't take up much of your time."

Carole thought about it for a moment before relenting and pushing the button that unlocked the door downstairs to her condominium. While waiting for him, she took the chance to make herself a bit more presentable. She tucked her three-quarter-sleeve stretch blouse back into her cropped pants and stepped from bare feet into some flats. At five-nine, she had inherited her height from her father, while the metabolism that gave Carole an hourglass figure with almost no body fat came from her mother, along with steady exercising and a sensible diet.

In the bathroom she wiped away dirt that had somehow ended up on her high-cheekboned face. She decided to keep her pixies tied in a ponytail, seeing no reason to make it seem like anything other than a purely social call.

That was what you called it nowadays when an ex-lover paid you an unexpected and not particularly desirable visit at night, wasn't it? she mused.

Carole had dated Stuart Wolfe off and on for about a year, having met him when she was a prosecutor and he a criminal defense attorney. It was hardly a match made in heaven, but they gave each other something they both needed at the time—a warm body to cuddle up to on cold, rainy Northwest nights, and a pleasant dinner companion when one was called for.

It was Carole who had decided it wasn't what she wanted. Or more that *he* wasn't really what she wanted. Stuart had acquiesced to her desire to end their relationship, but insisted on remaining friends.

She had agreed, recognizing that it was not unreasonable and perhaps even desirable. For she had few friends, and even fewer people she could trust.

She padded across the bamboo hardwood flooring, then unlocked and opened the door.

Stuart stood there in an Italian designer sage-colored suit that fit snugly on his six-one, solid frame. A flowered ebony silk tie was loose around the collar of his ivory shirt as though he couldn't decide whether to keep it on or not. He was forty years old but didn't look it. His unblemished fudge-colored skin tone was a perfect match for closely cropped Cimmerian hair and sable eyes. He pasted a hesitant smile on his handsome face.

"Hey," he said softly.

"Hey." She waved him in.

"So how's everything with you?" Stuart asked while sizing Carole up as they stood in the spacious living room with its warm, muted gray coloring, French provincial furniture, and African decorative art, along with her array of plants.

"Everything's just fine, Stuart." Carole turned her body away self-consciously, as if he hadn't already seen all of it. "How about you?" She was mildly curious about this unexpected visit.

He placed his hands in his pockets, as though looking for change. "Oh, hell, I don't know. I suppose things could be better. All right, a lot better."

"Things could always be better," she said rather impatiently. "Maybe you should just tell me what you came to talk about, Stuart."

She had a good idea that it had something to do with his new wife. He had married her five months ago, after knowing her for only a few weeks. The suddenness of the marriage had surprised Carole. At first she had felt a twinge of jealousy, as if he had somehow betrayed her—them. Just as quickly she had come to her senses, realizing there was absolutely no need to be jealous. Their relationship had ended a long time ago. He deserved to be happy with someone else, if not her.

Only it appeared as if he was anything but, Carole thought. She had found herself more often than not in the undesired role of being his marriage counselor, as if she qualified. But as his friend she did what she could to offer him sound, practical advice. At least, she believed that was the case.

Stuart licked his lips. "You know, I could really use a drink, Carole." He hesitated. "Or would that be asking too much?"

It was, she told herself honestly. Particularly when she wasn't much in the mood for company. *Or at least, not someone who is no longer in my life and bed*, Carole thought.

But she said in an understanding tone of voice, "No, it wouldn't be. You want a beer? Wine? Brandy . . . ?"

She knew that he liked them all, at one time or another. Which was probably why she kept the choices on hand for such an occasion, preferring wine herself.

"Beer sounds good, thanks."

"Be right back," she told him, and went to the gourmet kitchen.

Carole glanced at its state-of-the-art appliances, custom-made maple cabinetry, hand-set slab granite countertops, and ceramic tile flooring. She grabbed a cold beer from the Sub-Zero refrigerator, then poured herself a glass of pinot grigio before rejoining her uninvited guest.

Handing him the bottle, she asked directly, "What's going on, Stuart?"

He gulped down the beer as if dying of thirst, then creased his brow. "Vivian's pregnant," he said sullenly.

Carole decided to skip the perfunctory congratulations, considering it was obvious that the brother wasn't looking for any. "Isn't that what you've always wanted?" she questioned.

At least, it had been something he had often talked about when they were seeing each other, Carole mused. But she had not wanted to bring a child into the world, not believing she was mother material. Some things never changed, she thought.

But maybe they had with Stuart. Was he now singing a different tune?

"Yeah," he said, his eyes cast downward as if shamefully. "It is . . ."

"Then what's the problem?" She gazed at him. "Or am I missing something here?"

Stuart looked up. "She wants to have an abortion."

"Oh, I see." Carole wasn't sure exactly where to go with this one. She didn't know how she would react if pregnant; only that it was an extremely personal choice—one that should ultimately be left to the person having the baby.

I'd certainly want to be the master of my own body under those circumstances, she told herself.

"What should I do?" His lower lip quivered. "What shouldn't I do?"

"Talk to her, Stuart," she advised him. "Tell your wife exactly how you feel."

"I have," he muttered. "It doesn't seem to do a hell of a lot of good. She can be a stubborn bitch when she wants to be."

"Maybe you aren't saying the right things?" Carole suggested, though she was admittedly uncertain whether there were any magical words to keep a determined woman from aborting her unborn child.

"I'm not sure what they are anymore." Stuart scratched the tip of his broad nose. "I love her, Carole, and I don't want to lose her—or our baby. But if she goes through with this, I swear . . ." He shook his head mournfully.

"You should try counseling," she recommended. "Both of you. And I mean *real* counseling." *Not the counsel of a judge, friend, and ex-lover like me.*

"Will you talk to Vivian?" Stuart blurted out, as if the question refused to stay put in his mouth.

Carole widened her eyes at him in disbelief and a bit of anger. "And say what? I'm hardly the one to lecture someone on the merits of having a baby."

Stuart twisted his face. "Just tell her how much it would mean to me," he pleaded. "If anyone can—"

She cut him off sharply. "Don't even say it, Stuart. I will do no such thing. The last person in the world your wife needs advice from is your ex-girlfriend. I'm sorry, but you'll have to figure out this one all by yourself."

He flashed her an icy glare, then quickly thawed out. "I'm asking you as a friend, Carole. Not an ex-lover." He sighed. "There's no one else I feel comfortable enough with to even broach the subject. You know what I'm saying?"

Carole felt the pain he was going through. She knew it took a lot for a brother to break out of his shell to ask anyone for anything. Especially some-one who had, in effect, sent him into the arms of an-other sister. She wondered if he was really asking too much of her? Or was she merely making it harder than it had to be?

"I'll think about it," she told him as a compromise.

Stuart broke into a grin, as if he had locked her in. "Thanks, Carole. I owe you one."

You may owe me more than that, buddy, she contem-plated.

He put his arm around her, and Carole immedi-ately recoiled, shaking him loose like a snake that had encircled her and was about to release its venom.

"Don't," she said with snap, hitting him with the brown heat of her eyes.

He blinked in surprise. "Hey, I'm sorry, baby. Didn't mean to—"

"I know." Carole took a deep breath, realizing she had overreacted. "Don't worry about it." She hoped he would leave it at that.

Stuart sighed. "Well, I guess I'd better be going then."

She forced a tiny smile. "All right."

He returned it just as artificially, and they both headed toward the door.

"By the way," he said, facing her, "in case you didn't already know, that guy—Roberto Martinez—was found beaten to death tonight."

"Roberto Martinez . . . ?"

"The asshole you told me about last week who was going to trial for beating his girlfriend half to death." Stuart raised a brow. "You even suggested he might be able to use a good attorney like me. Apparently the lawyer he had was more than sufficient, considering he got him off, and was probably a lot cheaper too. Though little good it did Martinez, as it turns out."

"Yes," Carole said with a nod of her head, "I remember now. Roberto Martinez was released because the prosecution's case was simply too weak." She paused. "I guess with my heavy caseload, it's hard to remember all the sickos who come through my courtroom."

"Well, this is one less sicko to see in the future," Stuart said. "Someone saw to that!"

"I'm sorry to hear about Martinez," she said in a sincere voice.

"So am I. It's about the third time this has happened in the past few months. Seems like there's someone out there hunting down men accused of abusing their women."

Carole stared at the notion, sipping her drink. "If it's true, I certainly hope the police get the party responsible. The last thing we need is to have some damned vigilante taking the law into his or her own hands."

"I'd say it's too late to avoid that," Stuart said flatly. "It's already happening. Stopping this killer is a whole different story."

Carole showed Stuart out, locking the door behind him. She turned on the stereo and moments later began listening to a Norah Jones CD. Curling up on her Normandy sofa, she finished off the wine. She thought about Roberto Martinez. As far as she was concerned, scum like him got everything they deserved, including a painful death.

Now maybe the victim of Martinez's fists could

somehow regain her dignity and get past what he did to her and would have continued to do, had not an avenging angel come forward and meted out a personal form of justice on the batterer.

5

Nina Parker had known she wanted to be a police-woman since she was five years old, which was her earliest memory of her father as a cop with the Detroit Police Department. When the family moved to the Pacific Northwest after her father retired, she kept her own dream alive, entering the police academy in Portland at twenty-one. By the time she was twenty-five she had been on patrol, done vice, and gotten married and divorced.

She had been a homicide detective for the last seven years, the past five teamed up with Ray Barkley. Even now, after their affair she still had some feelings for the brother, Nina conceded, but vowed never to allow them to show or to interfere with the job. In her mind such feelings were always there for ex-lovers, even if kept in their proper perspective as a thing of the past.

She glanced at Ray as they took the elevator to the third floor at Portland General, where Lucie Garcia was being treated. He was already staring at her as if she had toothpaste on her mouth.

"Sure you're up for this?" he asked, as if in doubt.

"Are you?" she challenged him, knowing that each liked to go one better than the other in testing their mettle and fortitude under fire.

"I can certainly think of better things I'd like to do with my time than having to tell a battered woman that her abusive boyfriend was beaten to death." Ray blew his nose with a handkerchief. "But someone has to do the dirty work. Looks like the onus is on us."

Which meant, Nina knew, also asking Lucie Garcia questions regarding her possible knowledge regarding Roberto Martinez's violent death. Even if he got his just due in theory, in the real world it was still murder, and someone had to be held accountable.

They entered the room and saw a nurse tending to Lucie, who appeared in bad shape, with numerous injuries that would keep her in rehab for some time to come. The detectives showed their identifications to the nurse and Lucie, verbally introducing themselves.

The nurse, a stout, white woman in her fifties, gave them a stern look. "Can't this wait?"

"Afraid not," responded Ray tautly. "It's important."

The nurse eyed her patient. "I'll be back shortly." She waddled out of the room.

Ray and Nina exchanged glances before she took the lead. "I'm afraid we have some distressing news for you . . ." Nina began.

Nina wondered just how distressing it would truly be, given that Martinez had really done a number on her. Surely Lucie could do without being used as Martinez's personal punching bag? *If any asshole ever laid a hand on me, I'd kick his ass from here to kingdom come,* Nina thought. But she had read that many abused women tended to have a loving attachment to the abuser that belied the abuse itself. Was that the case here?

Lucie regarded the detective uneasily, clearly in physical discomfort. "What happened?" she mumbled instinctively.

After a sigh, Nina said dolefully, "Roberto Martinez is dead." *As in never coming back to hurt you again.*

Lucie put a shaky hand to her swollen mouth. "Dead? Roberto?"

"He was found in an alley," Ray informed her. "He'd been beaten to death."

Lucie seemed in a state of shock, almost disregarding her own condition. "Oh, Roberto!" she cried. "My honey. You can't be dead. Who would want to hurt you?"

"Do you know of anyone who would have wanted to kill Roberto?" Nina gazed down at the victim of abuse.

Lucie's eyes flooded with tears. "No. Roberto was not a monster!" she exclaimed. "He never really meant to hurt me."

Nina looked at Ray. He shook his head slightly in frustration and dismay. They had seen it all before. Complete denial, even after what the bastard had done to her. She still found a way to be in love with him, as though he truly cared for her.

"Could someone you know have wanted to avenge what happened to you?" Ray narrowed his eyes at Lucie Garcia.

31

"No one I know would ever do such an awful thing," she insisted in an uneven tone.

"So you're saying Martinez had no enemies that you know of?"

Lucie hesitated on that one. She suddenly seemed to have trouble breathing. As if on cue, the nurse raced in. She put an oxygen mask over Lucie's lop-sided face, and then snarled at Ray and Nina.

"I think you've asked enough for now! I want you to leave. She has to get her rest."

"Whatever you say." Ray snorted. "But we may need to see Ms. Garcia again."

"Not until she's physically up to it," countered the nurse. "Which could be quite some time . . ."

Nina looked at the patient, having little doubt that a long recovery, both physically and emotionally, would be needed.

Out in the corridor Ray asked Nina, "So what do you think?"

"I think she loved the creep and would have jumped into the ocean if he'd asked her to." Nina drew her thin, arched brows together. "Whoever murdered Martinez was *not* acting with Lucie Garcia's consent," she said with near certainty.

"Maybe not," he allowed. "But the killer sure as hell was acting on her behalf. Same as the other battered women who found their problem of being knocked around solved with the death of their alleged abusers."

Nina sighed. "I'd say we have our work cut out for us," she feared. "This woman vigilante—if it is a woman—is obviously not going to lie out on the walkway for us to nab like a drug-addicted hooker. She's in no hurry to get caught. Not when she feels she can rid the streets of Portland of the Roberto Martinezes, if not the world."

"That's where it starts to get scary." Ray bristled. "There are too many damned potential targets this person can go after. And we have no idea what triggers the attacks, per se."

"We know at least one thing that does," said Nina ominously. "Domestic violence. Hitting a woman, or any female, is not smart. Especially these days."

Nina considered the implications of her words on the local community. She wondered how many others had to die before the men who abused their women started to get the message, and the killer was stopped.

I don't even want to speculate, she thought. But that didn't stop her from doing so anyway, with frightening possibilities.

6

The sun shone brightly over Portland, its heat bringing the temperatures in the city to near ninety degrees. Inside the medical examiner's office, air-conditioning did little to block the effects of the warmth or the smell of dead, rotting bodies. Ray and Nina did their best to ignore both as they entered the examination room that held Roberto Martinez's remains.

Standing precariously above him was the medical examiner, Dr. Clark Terris. In his late fifties, he looked like the perfect Santa Claus, only with dark red hair and matching beard. Wearing a stained lab coat and plastic gloves, he greeted the detectives like houseguests.

"Glad you could make it."

Ray frowned. "Not like we had much choice, Doc." As it was they already had a pretty damned good idea what had killed Roberto Martinez, if not who. But they had to make it official.

Terris removed the gloves and set them beside the covered corpse. "He died from massive blunt trauma to the head, simply put," he said. "Just as the other two victims did. His skull was crushed like an eggshell; right jaw fractured in a dozen places. There were other fractures as well, including multiple ones to his vertebrae, but most came after he was already dead." He clawed at his own bushy beard. "It's all in the report."

"Tell me, Doc," Ray asked for the record, "do you think a woman is capable of inflicting such damage?"

Terris looked at Nina beneath thick brows, as if using her to consider the matter. "Of course," he said. "Especially if she was mad enough—and I don't mean crazy, though that also can't be ruled out. It helps her cause if she is using an object like a bat that can make almost anyone seem like Hercules."

"You find anything on the victim that we can use to nail the killer to the wall?" asked Nina.

She suspected that, as with the earlier victims, the perpetrator had left no real clues tied to the crime. That is, aside from the bat itself, which had no fingerprints or other identifying characteristics other than those belonging to the victim.

All three bats left behind at the murder scenes were wooden, the same model and manufacturer: Jefferson and Company. They were made in North Carolina and sold across the country, mainly to high schools and colleges. A number of local stores also sold them, as well as mail-order catalogs. The investigation into the bats had thus far gotten nowhere. It seemed that there were no unusual amounts purchased recently either locally or directly from the manufacturer. The consensus was that they had been purchased inconspicuously at different stores, maybe even out of state.

Terris confirmed Nina's suspicions. "Only some blond hair fibers from what appears to be a wig," he answered. "And clothing fibers that may or may not belong to the killer."

"Thanks for your help," Ray told him routinely.

"No problem," Terris said. "It's my job." He paused, then added with a catch to his voice, "Let's hope I don't have to make a habit of this type of autopsy. Don't believe everything you hear about medical examiners having thick skin. Personally, I prefer victims who died of coronary failure. Less stressful on the eyes and stomach."

Ray got the gist. If they did their job Terris wouldn't be left with the mess to clean up. "Believe me, Doc," he said in a controlled voice, "if we could have solved this case yesterday, we would have."

He looked at Nina and they left.

Once outside they headed toward the car. "Are you okay, Barkley?" Nina asked, concern in her voice.

Ray shifted his muscular frame her way. "Yeah, I'm fine," he lied. *Never was too good at dishonesty*, he thought.

"You don't look so good, Ray," she noted. "Sure this case isn't getting to you just a bit?" She squinted from the sun's rays beating down on them like a spotlight. "Men having their brains being bashed in like that can have a sobering effect, even on people trained to deal with it. Or is it the thought that a woman could be responsible for the killings that's left you on edge?"

He sighed. "All right, so maybe this one does have

me spooked. But not the part that a woman might be behind it. I don't like serial-killing bastards of any sex playing judge and jury."

"And you think I do?"

He raised a brow. "To be honest, Parker, I think you may be finding this just a little satisfying— under the circumstances. Brutal men getting their just deserts, and all that crap."

Nina stopped on a dime and peered at him. "Give me a damned break, Barkley, will you? This is Nina you're talking to. Your partner, remember? And we go back deeper than that. I want this son of a bitch as much as you do. I'm not going to stand here and tell you I'm in favor of assholes beating up their wives and girlfriends till they're black, blue, red, and hospitalized, if not on a cold slab. But that doesn't mean I want them brutally murdered as payback."

Ray nodded respectfully, thinking, *Guess I had that coming*. He was ashamed that he had challenged her commitment to this case. The reality was that she was the best damned partner he'd ever had, and always aboveboard in her professionalism. But he wasn't about to tell her that.

Not today anyway.

"What do you say I buy you lunch?" he offered instead.

Nina rolled her eyes. "I don't know about that, Barkley. Sounds like a bribe to me."

He smiled. "So arrest me afterward."

She showed him the pearly white of her straight teeth. "Don't tempt me, honey," she teased him. "I just may take you up on that."

He didn't doubt it for one minute.

7

"Where to?" asked Ray, his gaze centered on Nina behind the wheel. They had just chowed down on some soul food and now he felt like he was about to burst.

"Criminal Court Plaza," she intoned flatly. "Seems as if our dead dudes have one thing in common. Each had a date in Judge Carole Cranston's courtroom prior to death, on charges related to domestic violence against women. Trouble is, in every instance, insufficient evidence or some other luck of the draw got them off the hook. At least temporarily. Seems as if their sinful ways caught up to them. . . ."

Ray drew his brows together skeptically. "You think someone attending court proceedings may be making sure these batterers don't get away scot-free?"

Nina jerked her head in his direction. "Hey, it's worth checking out," she said defensively. "Unless you've got a better idea?"

"None that I can think of at the moment," he admitted truthfully.

The Criminal Court Plaza was part of a renovated downtown structure that included the jail and district attorney's offices. It was adjacent to the Portland Police Bureau Headquarters and near the city center.

Judge Carole Cranston was presiding over a case when they walked into Courtroom 1A. The detectives sat in the back as the sharply dressed young female prosecutor hammered away at a juvenile defendant on trial for murder being charged as an adult. On several occasions Judge Cranston hammered down her gavel, the tone of her voice keeping control of the proceedings.

From where he sat, Ray couldn't help but be more than a little impressed with the lady. *How about* really *impressed,* he thought. He hadn't been in the judge's courtroom before, but had heard she was a tough, no-nonsense sister who could more than hold her own with any male judge in the criminal court. What he hadn't been told was that she was also drop-dead fine, and younger than he'd imagined. Whether she could help them or not on this case remained to be seen.

Just after the judge announced a recess, the detectives approached the bench. The judge barely seemed to notice them during the commotion of people moving about. To Ray it seemed as though her mind were elsewhere, as if she had drifted off to sea. She somehow seemed ill at ease in her black robe. If she were not a judge, he thought, he could well imagine her being a Wall Street lawyer. A college professor. A hotter-than-hell actress. Or maybe a tough-as-nails newspaper reporter.

Even a super lover, crossed his mind.

When they reached the bench, Nina cleared her throat and said, "Judge Cranston . . . ?"

Carole looked down disinterestedly. "Yes?"

"I'm Detective Parker, and this is Detective Barkley."

"Detectives," she said politely.

"We're investigating the murder of Roberto Martinez," Ray told her.

Carole lifted her eyes in recognition of the name. "I see." She spoke levelly. "Why don't we go into my chambers?"

"Please sit down," Carole directed her guests, having removed her robe to reveal a Dolce & Gabbana aquamarine silk suit over black leather ankle-strap pumps. She watched the detectives sit in cranberry Maltese chairs on the other side of a square glass table with a cherry-wood border. She then sat across from them in a high-backed oxblood leather chair.

A quick regard of her visitors told Carole that the female detective was an attractive sister in her mid-thirties with luminous brown skin and a petite, athletic body beneath a dark gray blazer and matching pants with a coral cowl-neck sweater. She thought that the Bantu knots looked nice on her. The male detective, wearing a brown suit, was in his late thirties, tall, bald, and solid in build. His skin tone was caramel and went well with a chiseled face. He had intriguing gray eyes with gold flecks, and a not-too-thick mustache tapered neatly at the corners over an incredibly sexy mouth. All in all, she thought he was a good-looking brother, who was probably married or had sisters falling all over him as a single man.

Only in meeting his eyes did Carole realize the detective was appraising her as much as she was him. This caused her a slight bit of discomfiture as she turned her gaze to the female detective, while thinking, *Make a mental note not to stare too obviously, unless you want a dose of your own medicine.*

"So how can I help you?" she asked equably.

Nina squirmed in the chair. "We're not certain really, Judge Cranston," she admitted. "Roberto Martinez is the third man to be found beaten to death in the Portland area in the past five months. Each victim had been charged with domestic assault and spent time in *your* courtroom before being released on technicalities or insufficient evidence."

Carole strove to remain calm. "I'm not sure I understand what you're getting at." In fact, she did, and was not amused.

Ray leaned forward. "Could be, Judge, that someone—perhaps a court spectator—has decided to use your courtroom and the outcome of these cases to punish the freed men they believe were let off too easily."

Carole repositioned herself unsteadily. "Well, I don't know if I can be of much help to you, detectives, since I have little control over who decides to sit in on my cases."

"Maybe your staff could provide us with a list of the court personnel and others," he suggested, "such as reporters who are regulars in your courtroom?"

"Yes, I can do that," she reasoned. "I'll have my assistant fax the information to your office."

"Fine," said Ray, content to leave it at that.

But Nina had other ideas. "Judge, if you don't mind my asking, I was wondering what your feelings are on these men being released? I mean, many might say they're getting out of the system prematurely."

Carole took a steadying breath, sharpening her gaze at the detective. "If you're asking me if I believe they were guilty, the answer is yes. But, as a judge, my hands are often tied as to what I can do to keep them from walking."

"How about as a private citizen?" asked Nina boldly.

Carole took umbrage to the question, which sounded almost like she was being accused of something, but answered it nevertheless. "I'm not sure I like the tone of that, Detective," she made clear. "As a private citizen, I'm bound to uphold the law just like any other member of the community, irrespective of my personal feelings."

"We wouldn't expect anything less," Ray intervened, before this got out of hand and he and Nina both ended up doing deskwork for the rest of their careers. He gave his partner a hard look, then stood. "I think we've taken up enough of your time, Judge Cranston."

Carole nodded at him, feeling a slight stirring of intrigue about the detective, if not his female counterpart.

Nina rose, her mouth tight. "If you happen to think of anything that might be helpful in our investigation, *Your Honor*, please let us know."

"I will," Carole promised politely, while seething inside.

"By the way," added Nina, "we suspect that the person we're looking for might be a female."

* * *

In the corridor Ray glared at Nina. "What the hell was that all about?"

She stood her ground. "It's not like I was accusing her."

"It sure as hell sounded like it to me."

"Ease off, Barkley, okay?" Nina held his gaze. "So I wasn't ogling all over the sister like you were. My apologies!"

"What's that supposed to mean?" Ray tossed at her, as if he didn't know.

"It means I have no interest in getting in her pants," she retorted bluntly, "like a certain someone I know."

"You're way out of line here, Parker!" He felt his blood boil and his mind churn—even if his libido *was* admittedly in high gear at the prospect of getting to know the judge on a more intimate level.

Nina sighed thoughtfully. "Forget I said that."

How could he? "Maybe you should keep your damned mouth shut, if you can't keep from biting off more than you can chew." It seemed worth saying, if only for the sake of seniority on the job.

"Hey, I'm just doing my job, Ray," Nina said defensively. "*Our* job. Sorry if I ruffled a few feathers. Remember, we leave no stones unturned. If these murders are connected in any way to the judge's courtroom, that means that *no one* can be ruled out as a suspect, including the honorable judge herself."

Deep down Ray knew she was right—at least where it concerned keeping an open mind about suspects. But that didn't mean they had to go overboard with their suspicions. Especially when they had absolutely nothing at this point to even be sure the killer was a female, much less a very attractive, sexy judge.

As for his serious interest in Carole Cranston, that was up for debate. He couldn't dismiss being attracted to her. What sane, straight brother wouldn't be, given her looks, presence, and position? But that didn't necessarily mean he wanted to get into her pants, or under her designer skirt. Did it?

"You're going down the wrong road, Nina, if you think Judge Cranston is our vigilante," Ray said flatly. "There are too many nuts out there capable of doing this to investigate before we start pointing fingers at people whose job it is to uphold the laws of this state. Not break them down."

Nina averted his stare. "You're right," she gave in. "Maybe I am a hound-dog sister sniffing up the wrong tree. Wouldn't be the first time. Guess I can be overzealous sometimes in an investigation where a vicious serial killer is cutting down men left and right."

Ray recognized that it worked both ways. He made a teasing face. "How about overzealous *all* the time, Parker!"

She poked him hard in the side, causing Ray to wince. "Don't press your luck, Barkley. It can run out at any time."

He chuckled, rubbing his suddenly sore side. "I think it already has. Come on; let's get out of here."

Ray couldn't help but think about Carole Cranston, the woman behind the judge. He imagined it wouldn't take much to get to like her in a big way, if he were given the chance.

8

The cab pulled away from the courthouse and cruised down the boulevard toward its new destination. Carole sat in back, pondering her day. Fresh on her mind was the encounter with the two homicide detectives. Part of her was unnerved by the gist of their investigation. The other part was somewhat piqued—mostly by Detective Barkley. She sensed that he also felt drawn to her. She wondered if they would have the opportunity to meet again under more favorable circumstances. *I think I'd like that,* she thought.

The cab pulled up to a Jamaican restaurant on Broadway. She had suggested the place for her meeting with Vivian Wolfe. Surprisingly, Stuart's wife had enthusiastically agreed to it, whereas Carole had remained dubious at best about becoming involved in her ex-lover's marital troubles. What right did she have to tell Vivian, or any woman for that matter, that she should bring a child into this world if her desire was to terminate her pregnancy?

What if things failed to work out between Vivian and Stuart? Carole pondered. Would Stuart be able to properly care for his child if called upon to do so? She could well imagine the child becoming lost in the shuffle. Dysfunctional in his or her own life and times. Like so many others in situations beyond their control.

By the time the cab zoomed off, Carole had decided not to decide what to say. She would play it by ear, and what happened, happened. Either way, she considered this the very last marker Stuart could call in.

Vivian was already seated at the table when the maître d' led Carole to it. Immediately she thought that Vivian Wolfe was younger than she had imagined, perhaps in her mid-twenties. This made Carole feel positively ancient at thirty-five. Vivian rose, and was nearly Carole's own height, and every bit as shapely. She wore a silky tan charmeuse-and-chiffon cap-sleeve dress with a fuchsia tie and sandals.

Vivian Wolfe had a curly, sandy-colored shag and brilliant café-au-lait eyes, matching her smooth complexion. High cheekbones rivaled Carole's, and pouty lips were opened just slightly in a sensual way. Carole felt almost envious in that moment of appraisal.

"Nice meeting you," said Vivian sweetly, as though she meant it.

"You too." Carole forced a bright smile.

The two shook hands. Carole couldn't help but notice that Vivian's small hands were cold as ice, in spite of the fact that the room itself was warm. She wondered if Stuart's wife had a chilly disposition, in more ways than one?

Seated, they both ordered coffee.

"Stuart's told me so much about you," Vivian remarked.

Carole raised her brows. "Really?" *I know almost nothing about you*, she mused.

"Yes. He says that you're one of the criminal justice system's bright lights when it comes to dispensing justice."

Carole took a breath. "I don't know how bright my light is." She downplayed it, admitting, "I try to do my job to the best of my ability. Sometimes that isn't always enough."

"Tell me about it," muttered Vivian. "There must be people who manage to slip through the cracks all the time, no matter what."

"Not as many as you might think," Carole said thoughtfully. "Most of the bad people have a way of getting their just rewards one way or the other."

Vivian licked her lips, staring across the table. "You're probably right. Anyway, it's cool to know that you're a judge. I'm not sure I have what it takes to put the fate of people, good or bad, in my hands."

"It certainly isn't for everyone," Carole said in an understatement. "Being a judge wasn't my life's goal. I just kind of evolved into it. A long story, really."

"I'd like to hear it sometime."

They were interrupted when the coffee arrived. This suited Carole just fine, as she felt uneasy talking about herself. Especially since she had gone there specifically to discuss Vivian's pregnancy. She had wanted to dislike the sister for some reason, but found herself feeling just the opposite.

After ordering brown fish stew and spicy squash, Carole approached the subject gingerly. "Stuart mentioned that you two were thinking about maybe having a child—"

Vivian reacted as though she had been slapped. "Is that what he said?"

Carole hesitated, knowing it wasn't quite what he told her. "Ever since I've known Stuart, he's talked about having a family someday."

"We agreed when we got married that there would be *no* children," Vivian said gruffly. "Don't get me wrong. I love kids and believe they're the hope for the future. But—" She checked herself, as if having run into a brick wall.

"You're not ready to bring a child into the world?" deduced Carole intuitively.

"Something like that," Vivian said noncommittally. "I guess I'm afraid I just won't be a good mother. Or maybe that he won't be a good father."

Carole couldn't imagine Stuart not being a good father. But then again, how could she really know what type of father he would make? *Let's be honest here*, she thought. Many men presented themselves to be good potential family men on the surface. Only they turned out to be lousy fathers and husbands when the facade was peeled away like old wallpaper.

Could Stuart be one of those types?

She certainly couldn't knock Vivian for fearing becoming a mother. After all, wasn't that one of the reasons she herself was reluctant to have children? Not knowing if she had the patience and understanding to make a good mother? Or even enough love to give to her child?

"I'm pregnant," announced Vivian unceremoniously. "I guess Stuart didn't mention that to you."

Carole sighed, not sure how to respond. "Are you thinking about terminating the pregnancy?"

Vivian sipped her coffee. "I'm not really sure what I want to do." She paused. "All I know is I just don't want to be pressured into doing something we'll both end up regretting. Does that make sense to you?" she asked nervously.

"Yes, it does," said Carole, comprehending more than she realized. "Maybe you and Stuart should consider some counseling in weighing all your options?"

"This has to be a *personal* decision," snapped Vivian, as if under attack. "I wouldn't want to put it in the hands of some damned shrink whose only real interest is in the bottom line or how much advice we can afford—"

"Well, I was thinking more of a family counselor," Carole said defensively, "rather than a psychiatrist. They have experience with child and family issues and could assist you in better understanding your options. Many offer reasonable rates for their service. If you like," she added reluctantly, "I would be happy to recommend someone I know who's very professional and truly believes in what she does."

Vivian tilted her head. "I suppose it couldn't hurt to give it a try," she said unenthusiastically.

Carole gave her a hopeful smile. For some reason the conversation made her want to reassess her own feelings about marriage and children. Not necessarily in that order.

Only right now there seemed little time for either.

Would there ever be time in her life for the things she truly wanted? she wondered. Or truly needed?

9

The bar was dimly lit and two blocks away from where Roberto Martinez's shattered remains were found. Ray entered, suspecting that Martinez had paid a call there last night to celebrate his unexpected freedom. Martinez's blood alcohol level had been high enough to make him legally intoxicated.

It wasn't much of a place, thought Ray. But then, by all indications Roberto Martinez wasn't much of a man. That still didn't give someone the right to be his executioner. Though that hadn't stopped someone from taking on that role.

Ray approached the bartender, a wide-bodied, balding, dark-skinned brother in his late thirties. "Do you remember seeing this man in here last night?" he asked him, handing over a mug shot.

The bartender studied the picture. He scratched his pate and lifted bulging eyes. "Yeah, maybe," he said in a coarse voice. "You a cop or something?"

Ray flashed his identification. "Homicide. Portland Police Bureau."

The bartender looked again at the mug shot. "Yeah, he was here. What'd he do?"

"It's what was done to him," responded Ray cryptically. "Name's Roberto Martinez. He was found beaten to death in an alley a couple of blocks from here."

The bartender's nostrils flared. "Damn," he muttered thoughtfully. "Too bad."

"Did he have any trouble with anyone in here?"

"Not that I recall. Had a few drinks and left."

"By himself?" Ray asked.

"Yeah. I think so."

"Could he have left with a woman?"

The bartender considered this. "Not many women hang out here, man. Know what I'm saying?"

"So that would make it easier to remember any who had, wouldn't it?" Ray pressed.

The bartender grinned, sporting a shiny gold tooth. "Now that you mention it, there was a lady here last night. But she wasn't with him."

"Tell me about her." Ray gazed at him intently.

"Tall, fine-looking sister," he recalled. "Stacked from head to toe. Wore blond braided extensions on her head, the way sisters like to these days. Had on shades like she had eye problems, 'cause it sure as hell ain't ever too bright in here. Sat right over there." He pointed to the end of the bar.

"Was she alone?" Ray asked, his curiosity piqued.

"Near as I could tell, though there were plenty of men who wouldn't mind keeping her company."

"Did that include Roberto Martinez?"

The bartender shook his head. "Nah. I think the dude was too busy getting plastered to notice much else. Or anyone else, including her."

Ray regarded him. "Do you know when she left?"

The bartender rubbed his nose, which looked as if it had been broken once or twice. "Come to think of it," he said, "I think she left right after he did."

The Cool Breeze restaurant was in southwest Portland, specializing in ethnic cuisine. Cops and lawyers, along with artists and writers, frequented it. This night saw most tables occupied.

Ray and Nina sat in a booth opposite the window, platters before them filled with grilled chicken, collard greens, sweet potatoes, and buttered biscuits.

"I think we may have something," Ray said, having already discussed his visit to the bar. And, in particular, the hot-to-trot black woman who could be labeled at this point a person of interest. "I want a sketch artist out there right away. Maybe we can find out who this sister is—and where we can find her."

"Will do," Nina noted dutifully, as the junior partner of the two. "Of course, since she was almost certainly wearing a blond wig and dark glasses, a positive ID is practically out of the question."

"I know," he moaned, in between stuffing his face. "But at least it'll give us more than we've got now, which is zilch. If this lady is our killer, someone, somewhere, just might recognize her."

Nina wiped her mouth with a cloth napkin. "That someone might just be at the Rose City Women's Shelter," she said. "I did some digging around today and it seems that all the battered-women victims of the murdered men sought refuge there at some point before going back to their batterers for more of what they ran away from."

"So you think the killer could be someone who stayed there?" Ray asked.

Nina eyed him narrowly. "Or is even there now . . ." she responded dramatically.

It made sense, he thought. A battered sister who got to see firsthand other battered women and took it upon herself to exact payback for all of them—making sure the batterer did not come back for more ever again.

He nibbled on his lower lip. "What do you say we pay this shelter a little visit?"

Nina smiled wryly. "That's the best suggestion you've had all day, Barkley." She tossed money down on the table and was on her feet. "Let's hit the road while you're on a roll."

Ray grinned, standing. "Yeah, let's." He put more money on the table. "We need to get serious and see who's spending time at the shelter and why. Maybe someone has more than one reason to seek refuge there."

At this point he wasn't prepared to rule out anything.

10

The Rose City Women's Shelter sat atop a hill in northeast Portland. It was the largest shelter for battered women in the city. Once home to a philanthropist, the Victorian property had been donated to the Portland Domestic Violence Foundation to be used as a battered-women's shelter. Its three stories and refurbished architectural elegance belied its intent as a temporary home for women escaping domestic violence.

Esther Reynolds had been the director of the Rose City Women's Shelter for the past ten years. The thirty-eight-year-old widow had dedicated her life to helping battered women, as she had once been helped to break the cycle of violence, helplessness, and hopelessness.

She extended a thin hand with long, carmine-polished nails at the detectives—who had just been invited in by one of her assistants—greeting each warmly. "How can I help to you?" she asked, though she already knew full well why they were there. Indeed, she had expected them long before now.

"We're investigating a series of murders," Ray told her, sizing up the tall, shapely, attractive sister clad in an eggplant African double dress with embroidery. She wore silver-rimmed glasses in front of sloe-colored eyes, and had a burgundy cornrow draped over her shoulders.

He took a sweeping glance of the premises with its high ceiling, hickory hardwood molding, rounded archways, angled bay windows, and cinnabar parquet hardwood flooring. The first floor furnishings, though sparse, were wicker and looked as though they belonged.

The place was impressive, no matter the purpose these days, mused Ray. He noted several women moving about like zombies, as if on drugs, alcohol, or maybe both. Some looked as if they had been worked over one time too many. Could one of them also be a murderess? Maybe it was time for payback in a big way, he thought.

Favoring the director again, Ray said, "Three men charged with domestic abuse have been beaten to death with a bat over the last five months."

"Oh, dear," mumbled Esther, for effect, putting her hand to her mouth.

"We have reason to believe that the women they allegedly battered all stayed here at some point."

"And what if they did?" she asked abruptly. "We're not responsible for what goes on outside the walls of this shelter."

Was this an admission of knowledge of the murders? wondered Ray. Or a plain disregard for what some vindictive abused women may have been capable of?

"You may be responsible," said Nina unkindly, "if it's proven that you or anyone who works here conspired or participated in any of these so-called vigilante killings."

Esther flung a wicked gaze at her. "I can assure you, *Detective*, that no one on my staff would be a party to murder."

Nina looked at the woman skeptically. "I wouldn't be too sure about that," she said boldly. "And I certainly am not prepared to rule out that one of your guests may be doubling as a serial killer."

Esther felt her chest heave. She had to steady herself to keep from losing her balance.

"Follow me," she uttered in a barely audible voice.

She led them through the downstairs to an office that Esther had decorated herself with textured wallpaper, Roman shades to let the sunshine in, hanging baskets with ferns, and country furnishings. She had hoped to make it appear as open and comfortable to outsiders, such as these detectives, and for the women who came there seeking protection.

"Can I offer you some coffee?" Esther felt her confidence returning. "Tea? Or maybe a Coke?"

Both detectives declined, but did sit in wine-colored leather chairs opposite Esther's rustic cedar log desk. She joined them in another chair, resisting the urge to sit at her desk, so as not to make this visit seem too official.

After gathering her thoughts, Esther informed them, "Our purpose here is to do all that we can to try to protect women from abuse at the hands of the men in their lives. You may not be aware of this, but two million women are battered in the United States every year. More than one in four women murdered in this country died at the hands of a husband or boyfriend. Some believe that as many as eighty percent of all domestic violence goes unreported." She took a deep breath, pleased with her lecture to the detectives. "I guess what I'm trying to say is that these women are the *real* victims of battering. I only wish you showed as much diligence in going after their abusers as you seem to in going after them."

Ray and Nina met each other's eyes thoughtfully.

"Let me assure you, Ms. Reynolds, we don't take lightly women or children being beaten, or otherwise mistreated in any way," stated Ray compellingly. "But we also don't condone murder or *anyone* taking the law into her or his own hands. You know what I'm saying?"

Esther pushed her glasses up. "Neither do I," she insisted. "Unless it's justified."

"By whose standard?" Nina challenged her, nearly rising from the chair. "Yours? Or some other lady in here with an ax to grind against all the accused batterers in Portland?"

"By a *higher* authority than either one of us," she responded tartly. "Men who hit women to make themselves feel big and powerful don't deserve to live."

"Is that what you preach to the women who come here for shelter and security?" Ray questioned. "That they should get rid of the men who beat them and suffer the consequences later?"

Esther felt hot under the collar but refused to be broken. That was what they hoped would happen. She was stronger than that. More than they knew.

"This is not a church, Detective!" came the sarcastic retort. "I don't preach anything in here. My job is merely to offer a safe retreat for women escaping domestic violence, and advice that I believe can help these women to better themselves and their children afterward."

"Would that advice include getting a damned wooden bat and beating to death their abusers?" Nina looked at her narrowly.

Esther stiffened. "I'd be less than honest if I didn't say I'll shed no tears over the deaths of these men, coming as they did. It sounds as if they only received what they gave. But I played no part whatsoever in their deaths."

"If you didn't, then someone else in here probably did," Ray told her brusquely.

"Proving that might be quite a task," Esther said brashly. "You see, we're *all* victims here—the staff and occupants alike. You'll get no help inside these walls in trying to nail someone who would be viewed by us as a hero."

Ray glanced at Nina. The look on her face told him that she reluctantly agreed with Esther's assessment.

"Maybe we will be stonewalled," he conceded, "for now. But that won't stop us from eventually bringing the killer to justice, wherever she might be holed up—along with anyone who helped her."

"If you're trying to scare me, Detective," said Esther courageously, "save it for someone who is easily intimidated by police tactics . . . or perhaps brutality. I understand enough about the law to know that search warrants and court orders are necessary to get information that otherwise won't be volunteered to you. On that note, I think I must now ask you both to leave."

"We were kind of hoping to have a chat with some of the residents and staff," Nina uttered sanguinely.

"You're welcome to," Esther stated flatly. "Just not inside the premises. I won't have anyone here being made victims again—not by you!"

Nina's nostrils grew. "Listen, we're not the problem, and I think we both know that! If you're sheltering a psychopathic killer, she's making every woman here a victim all over again. And each time she takes out a batterer, it will be on your head. I just hope you're prepared to deal with that!"

Esther saw the detectives out the front door. Inside she was left alone with her thoughts. She sensed trouble ahead. They weren't going to let up until they found the truth behind the murders.

She was determined that they would not find it there.

11

"What do you make of her?" Ray turned to his partner as they made their way from the shelter.

Nina wrinkled her nose. "I'm not really sure. Other than the fact that the sister has an obvious chip on her shoulder and is in sore need of a major attitude adjustment."

He nodded. "Amen on both counts!"

She squinted at him. "The lady definitely has no sympathy for dead batterers. Not that I can blame her any on that score. Alive, the assholes wouldn't be very welcome at my house either. Dead, they more or less dug their own graves."

"But the fact is that none of those men were actually convicted in a court of law of anything, much less the crimes for which they may have been executed," he muttered.

Nina took her keys from her purse. "Come on, Barkley," she scoffed. "We both know they were probably as guilty as hell."

"Since when have people in this country been put

to death based on probable cause," Ray asked, "rather than solid evidence of guilt? Forget the fact that domestic violence, for all its brutality, isn't a death-penalty crime in and of itself. Not in this state."

"You're missing the point," Nina said.

He flashed her a hard look across the hood of the car. "No, you are! Those men no more deserved to die than the women they allegedly abused. Someone forgot to tell that to their executioner."

Nina was suddenly at a loss for words.

During the drive each clung to their own thoughts before Nina said in a sorrowful tone, "Okay, those men didn't really deserve what they got, even if they gave nearly as much."

"Obviously there's a killer out there who would beg to differ," Ray said sourly. "My guess is that she's somehow affiliated, past or present, with that shelter. If it's not Esther Reynolds herself, then it's somebody else there—"

"I can't argue with you on that," Nina said reflectively. "The sister definitely knows something that she's not saying."

"If Reynolds wants to play games, she'll lose," he declared. "I want to find out everything there is to know about her and everyone who's been in that shelter for the last six months."

"That could be a tall order," Nina said. "Especially since many of the women are there only for a few hours, quickly replaced by others. Even the staff, mostly volunteers, probably show up only irregularly, or when there's nothing better to do."

"True," Ray conceded, "but I'll just bet that Esther Reynolds keeps detailed records of everyone who comes and goes—residents and staff alike. I'm sure with the right persuasion, like a court order, we can separate the maybes from the maybe-nots."

Nina looked at him studiously. "In the meantime, we have a very unstable killer out there who's likely to strike again at any time with deadly precision."

Ray acknowledged this in his own mind even as he wondered if they could be way off base in their sense of direction and possible suspects. He had seen more than his fair share of cases where the culprit was the last suspect on everyone's list. Were they on the right track on this one?

Julian Frommer was waiting in his office when Ray arrived. It was small and crowded with the tools of an assistant district attorney's office at his disposal. Frommer leaned back in his desk chair, a frown creasing his alabaster face.

"I was actually sorry to hear about Martinez," he said, running fingers through his greasy hair, then wiping them on the wool jacket of his suit.

"It sure made your job a hell of a lot easier," Ray said, studying the prosecutor's reaction.

"Not really. No one likes to see a suspect taken out like that. Nasty." Frommer narrowed apple-green eyes. "In fact, I was looking forward to hauling his ass back into court for a second round. I was convinced that, given time, I could have gotten Lucie Garcia to see him for the brutal monster he really was."

"Only someone beat you to the punch," said Ray humorlessly. "Or the bat."

"Yeah," the prosecutor muttered. "Something like that."

"It almost seems too coincidental when standing in my shoes." Ray used that moment to plant his hands solidly on the metal desk and stare across it. "Martinez meets Satan before he can do any more harm, much less face new charges and possibly walk again."

Frommer's brows knitted. "What the hell are you trying to say, Barkley? You don't actually think I had anything to do with that asshole's murder, do you?"

Ray leaned forward, holding his gaze. In fact, he didn't see Frommer as a murderer, particularly since he had not been the prosecutor in the other two vigilante-related murders. But that didn't mean he wasn't familiar with the killer, even if he didn't realize it.

"Relax, man," he told him nicely. "No one's accusing you of Roberto Martinez's death. But you may be able to help us nail the real perpetrator."

"How so?" the prosecutor asked guardedly.

I'm so glad you asked, thought Ray, and responded, "By providing me with the names of everyone you talked to in your investigation who might have had a beef with Martinez or his actions. There's a chance that someone may have decided to go after him once the case was dismissed."

Frommer scratched the back of his hand as if bitten by a mosquito. "Yeah, I can do that. Only it will be a very short list. Martinez had a history of domestic violence and other assault crimes. But the only ones willing to come out on the record against him were a known drug dealer with his own agenda and his alleged victim, Lucie Garcia, who ran scared when it came to crunch time."

"What about people who hung around the courtroom and seemed to take a keen interest in the case?"

Frommer shrugged. "The actual trial lasted less than a day," he said. "Hardly enough time to develop a profile of spectators or nuts posing as such."

Ray showed him a composite of the woman seen at the bar where Martinez was last seen on the night of his death. "Does she look familiar?" Even as he asked, he knew the picture was based on a suspect memory of a tall black woman wearing dark glasses and probably a blond wig of some sort in a dim atmosphere. He wasn't sure he would be able to recognize his own mother, if he were looking at such an image.

Frommer studied it with something less than intense scrutiny. "Not really." He looked up. "You think she offed Martinez?"

Ray was careful not to put the cart ahead of the horse. "Let's just say I'd like to talk to the lady about it."

"Can't help you, buddy," insisted Frommer. "Sorry." He extended his arm to pass back the composite.

"Keep it," Ray told him. "Just in case your memory is jogged later or you happen to run into her."

"Yeah, sure thing." Frommer met Ray's eyes head-on. "For the record, Barkley, I hope you get the one you're after. Justice belongs in the courtroom, not on the street."

Ray felt a knot in his stomach, and said musingly, "Someone who feels that the courts do a lousy job in dispensing justice would disagree with you."

After he left Julian Frommer's office, Ray drove around town collecting his thoughts. He believed the killer was someone within reach. *I can feel it in my bones,* he told himself. They needed only to put a name and face to her. Yes, he was convinced it was a woman, possibly African-American, whom they were after. But he didn't rule out that a man could be the killer—perhaps dressed as a woman—singling out other men for his own reasons.

Overall, though, Ray's gut instincts told him that this was the work of someone who had been the victim of battering by a male, either directly or indirectly.

Someone who had no intention of stopping her lethal vengeance on batterers.

Not till there were no more left to kill.

12

Carole read the verdict and then quietly passed it back to the bailiff. She fixed her eyes on the defendant, Blake Wallace. He stared back at her with eyes that were sinister in their darkness. The forty-nine-year-old real estate tycoon was just under six feet tall and solid as a rock in a tailored double-breasted charcoal suit. He had thinning gray-black hair, slicked backward as if to hide the balding. It surrounded a jowly face that was red like a pepper.

He had been charged with assaulting his wife, who had run from the house naked, badly bruised, and bleeding. Victoria Wallace now sat supportively behind her husband. She wore sunglasses, shielding the scars left from the vicious attack that left her partially blind in one eye.

Next to Blake Wallace sat his high-priced and confident attorney, George von Dorman. He whispered something in his client's ear, causing him to smile. That quickly vanished when the defendant's gaze centered sternly on Carole's face.

She turned away, showing no emotion to the verdict. After asking that the defendant rise, Carole directed the jury foreman to read the verdict.

The yellow-haired, thirty-something woman glanced in the direction of Blake Wallace before nervously looking down and saying, " 'We, the jury, find the defendant not guilty on the charge of first-degree assault. . . .' "

Carole closed her eyes for a moment, not wishing to see the jubilation at the defense table or the begrudging acceptance of the verdict by the prosecutor. The defense had gambled and won on an all-or-nothing verdict, opting for the one serious charge rather than lesser charges that might have made it easier on the jury to convict.

Blake Wallace would get to go home, probably to beat his wife again when the victory dance had long died down and the urge to inflict damage on her grew in him again like a tumor. For her part, in testifying on his behalf, Victoria Wallace had sacrificed her personal safety and that of her three children to keep the family intact, as well as her stake in her husband's considerable business interests and their estate.

Carole opened her eyes in time to see Blake Wallace with his arm wrapped around his wife's thin waist as they headed out of the courtroom. She could not help but think that justice had once again been denied the people—particularly those who believed that spousal abuse should be neither tolerated nor rewarded.

She left the bench feeling empty, as if she had run out of fuel—or the will to carry on for another day. Another case of domestic violence fallen short of desired results.

* * *

Victoria Wallace had lived in terror of her husband since the first day he hit her. It was on their wedding night, when he had accused her of not being a virgin. He had broken her nose and then raped her. He had told her that if anyone found out the truth he would kill her and himself.

Now, some twenty-five years later, she had learned never to take his threats idly. The beatings were less frequent now that he had his mistress and other interests to keep him occupied, but were more intense and seemingly came with more pleasure on the part of her husband. This last time had come without warning. He had flown off the handle because of a deal gone sour and decided to take it out on her. She had suffered a detached retina and a bruised kidney, lost three teeth, and received other injuries.

Neighbors had called the police, and she had raced to them in fear of her life, not caring that she was naked or about any sick kicks the two male officers might have received. She wished only to survive the night for her children and live to see another day.

Blake had been arrested.

He had hired the best lawyer money could buy. There was even talk of bribing a juror or two, if need be. Victoria had seen the writing on the wall. Were she to go against Blake she could lose everything. Including her life. Maybe even the precious lives of her children.

She had decided that for the sake of her children and the life they were accustomed to living, she had to support her husband through the trial while continuing to live under the veil of secrecy, shame, and apprehension.

13

Blake Wallace drove his white-on-white Mercedes to the town house he kept for when he needed to get away. More specifically, when he needed to be with his mistress, Rebecca. The bitch couldn't figure out left from right if he didn't point her in the proper direction. But she knew which buttons to push in bed better than most—something Victoria hadn't accomplished in twenty-five years of marriage.

It was her damned fault that he had lost his temper so many times, Blake thought. Right from the very start she had deceived him. Made a fool out of him. Only because she had gotten herself knocked up almost right away did he even bother to stay. Later, with more kids and a prospering career in real estate acquisitions, it was no longer good business sense to divorce her. He would be damned if he let that bitch wind up with the better part of his earnings and assets.

Right now he was just happy that prick of a lawyer he had paid a fortune and a half to had succeeded in getting him acquitted of assault, mused Blake. The moment he'd made eye contact with the woman on the jury whose kid he would put through college, with some spending money on the side, he knew he was free of the threat of a unanimous verdict against him.

But not until he heard the words "not guilty" did Blake Wallace feel confident that he had beaten this rap.

Now it was time to celebrate.

He pulled into the underground parking lot, unaware that another car had come in shortly after, keeping a safe distance.

Within moments Blake had parked right alongside the Subaru Legacy belonging to Rebecca. It was a birthday present from him.

And he fully intended to be reimbursed in the way she best paid her debts—under the sheets.

He got out of the car and headed toward the elevator in the low-lit garage. When he heard footsteps that weren't his own, he stopped instinctively, turning around.

Approaching was a tall, curvaceous, blond-haired black woman. Wearing dark gloves and a trench coat, she was carrying a long bag and a killer smile. He smiled back, feeling somewhat aroused.

"Aren't you *the* Blake Wallace?" she asked politely.

He regarded her more carefully. Who the hell was asking? Was she a friend of Rebecca's?

Someone Victoria knew?

Maybe a damned reporter looking for a cheap story at his expense? he decided.

"Yeah," he said cautiously. "Who the hell are you?"

He watched as her pretty face suddenly became ugly with fury. "Your worst nightmare, asshole!"

Before he could even digest what this was all about, she had removed something from the bag. It looked like a bat. With a swiftness that further took him by surprise, she had swung the bat backward and brought it forward at lightning speed. It slammed against the side of his head, dropping him as if he'd been hit by a heavyweight champion's right hook or run headfirst into a brick wall.

"Did you really think for one minute you were going to get away with what you did, you filthy bastard?" she cursed.

Dazed and in a state of shock, Blake tried to get up. But he was unable to ward off the next blow that crashed into the top of his head with such force that it shattered his skull like an eggshell. Thick, dark blood spurted out.

"Your wife may have been too afraid to stand up to your violence," the woman shouted. "But I'm not. You should have quit while you were ahead. Or *had* a head!"

Another blow exploded into his cheekbone, fracturing it in multiple places. A second or two later came yet another. This one landed squarely on his throat, crushing his windpipe.

One more pounded into his head, what was left of it, brain tissue spurting forth like an eruption from a volcano.

Though Blake Wallace had ceased to be among the living, she continued to inflict punishment on his battered remains as if to beat his soul into submission as well. Only after she had exhausted herself from clubbing him with the bat did the woman stop.

Her breathing had become erratic, and she felt perspiration pouring from her armpits down her sides and chest.

Again, as with the others, she felt a tremendous amount of relief. The satisfaction was akin to an orgasm, only much more powerful—and lasting. At least till the next time, when the urge to kill a brutal abuser would overcome her once more.

She tossed the bloodied bat on the corpse and walked to her car. Opening the trunk, she yanked off the wig, tossing it into a duffel bag. Then she took off the gloves, trench coat, and clothes beneath it. She quickly slipped into jeans, a jersey, and tennis shoes.

Within moments she had gotten into the car. She applied lipstick to her dry lips. She then put on some earrings, studying herself in the rearview mirror.

The woman drove out of the parking lot and calmly made plans for dinner. She was starving.

14

The detectives were glum as they viewed the crushed and battered body of Blake Wallace. Ray tried to imagine what it would be like to be the target of someone so full of hatred and rage. He supposed many battered women knew the answer firsthand.

And at least four men now knew too.

"Wallace had just today been acquitted on charges that he assaulted his wife," said Nina, taking an anguished look at the victim's ghastly remains. "I imagine he thought he was on top of the world."

"Think again," said Ray disgustedly. "Looks like it wasn't his lucky day after all."

"Maybe in some ways he was lucky." Nina twisted her lips. "My guess is that Blake Wallace was put out of his misery long before someone finished with his body in the batting cage."

"But not before he saw his attacker and felt the sting of this bat." Ray looked at the blood-drenched murder weapon lying harmlessly on the torso of the victim as if drained of its own raw power.

"Wallace was apparently here to meet his mistress," said Nina. "She's over there giving her statement."

Ray turned toward a young, auburn-haired woman talking to an officer. "Why don't you find out if there were any witnesses?" he told Nina. "I'll see what she can tell us, if anything."

"Maybe we'll both come up with something," Nina said, though she rolled her eyes doubtfully as she walked away.

Ray went over to the deceased's mistress, who looked as if she were still in high school, aside from her well-developed chest and heavily made-up face. She had a mole on the right cheek and wore a small nose ring. Tears flowed freely from her lake-blue eyes, which she wiped with the back of her hand. She was wearing a full-length, wide-ribbed lilac chenille robe and matching slippers, as if still waiting for her lover.

Ray identified himself, taking over for the officer, and learned that the woman's name was Rebecca Ferguson.

"Ms. Ferguson," he began, "I know this is difficult, but we need to try to find out what happened here tonight. Do you understand?"

She sniffled and said in a high-pitched voice, "Yes."

"You knew the victim?" he asked routinely.

"Yes. He was my . . . I was his . . . girlfriend."

Ray met her eyes, understanding her awkward position, considering Blake Wallace had a wife and three kids. "So you were expecting him?"

"Yeah," she said vacantly. "Blake called and said he was on his way."

Ray hesitated. "And when did you find out he was dead?"

Rebecca wiped at her tearstained cheeks. "I came down here to meet him. That's when I saw—" She choked back the words and started to sob.

"Did you see anyone else?"

"No."

"Did you hear anything?"

She sighed. "I think I heard a car pull out of the garage."

Ray touched his nose. "Did you see it?"

"No," she said apologetically. "It was gone when I looked up."

Damn, he thought, frustrated. *It was probably the killer. Or someone who may have seen the perpetrator.* Then he realized that if she had come down a minute earlier, she might have caught the person in the act, and in the process have become a victim herself.

Ray glanced over at Nina and saw that she was talking to a tall and slender, well-dressed African-American woman. Several other people were nearby, as if waiting for their turn.

Though the crime scene had been sealed off from spectators, the most dogged, along with the press, had found a way in to gawk and snoop.

"Why?" Rebecca cried. "Why would someone do this? Blake wasn't a bad man, despite the problems between him and—"

"His wife?" Ray finished tersely. The man was an asshole, pure and simple, he thought.

Rebecca fluttered curly lashes. "She just didn't understand him."

"And you did?"

75

"Yes," she insisted. "We loved each other."

There was only one thing he loved about you, mused Ray silently, regarding the chesty young woman.

But none of it mattered now, he thought. Let the lady think whatever made her feel better about her lover's untimely demise.

"We've got a possible witness. Her name's Jacqueline Monique Davis," Nina said to Ray en route to the victim's residence to notify his wife. "According to Ms. Davis, a dark-colored late-model BMW pulled out of the garage just as she was about to turn in."

"Did she see who was driving it?"

"She thought it might have been a woman, but admitted that the car shot out of there so fast that she never really got a chance to focus on the driver."

Ray stared over the steering wheel. "Maybe the car will be enough to point us in the right direction," he said. "Let's see if the witness can tell us anything more specific about the car—like the exact color, any marks, et cetera. Also, if she can remember any part of the license plate number, we might really be onto something."

Nina took notes. Shifting her gaze to his face, she asked, "What about the girlfriend? She any help?"

"Not really. Just another starry-eyed kid full of dreams and fantasies who hooked up with the wrong man."

"Some of us can relate to that," muttered Nina thoughtfully.

When Ray met her eyes, he wondered if she was referring to her ex-husband—or their brief affair?

Admittedly they were wrong for each other, he

thought, even if it had seemed right at the time. But then, he'd had little luck in the relationship department. Except maybe bad luck. His own ex had turned out to be *very* wrong for him. The only thing they'd had in common was that they had nothing in common. Combine that with her lack of focus on anything but herself and how much she could bleed him dry and it was the perfect recipe for a marriage doomed to failure.

When Victoria Wallace was informed of her husband's death, she appeared expressionless. Her face showed both old and fresh signs of the abuse inflicted by her husband, particularly around the eyes, with one nearly swollen shut. Although in her mid-forties, she looked much older. Her graying flaxen hair was thin and listless, her body so frail it looked as if it might snap like a twig beneath the rose-print jacket dress she wore.

At first Nina wondered if Mrs. Wallace even grasped what she'd just been told. The woman had obviously been drinking, she thought, observing her unsteadiness on her feet.

"It was only a matter of time," Victoria said resignedly.

"Meaning?" asked Ray, as they stood on thick moss-green carpeting in the cypress wood–paneled study of what was an expensive trilevel home in the upscale neighborhood of Winston Heights.

She fixed her hazel eyes on the detective. "My husband had enemies," she said without preface. "He didn't get where he got without them."

"Does that include you?" Ray narrowed his focus.

77

Victoria sighed. "I loved Blake. But I hated his temper and willingness to turn it on me whenever he saw fit."

"Did you hate your husband enough to kill him?" Nina asked point-blank. "Or hire someone else to do the job for you?"

Victoria's head jerked as if she'd been slapped. "How dare you!"

Nina was undeterred. "With all due respect, Mrs. Wallace, your husband was beaten to death with a bat less than an hour after being acquitted of charges that he beat the hell out of you." She met the woman's hardened gaze head-on. "No suspects can be ruled out at this stage—not even you."

Victoria seemed to gather her composure. "The last time I saw Blake, he was leaving this house to go to his mistress," she said levelly, looking from one detective to the other. "Yes, I knew all about his affair. It wasn't the first one. And wouldn't have been the last. I stayed with my husband for the sake of the children. If I had wanted to kill him I would have done so years ago, when I still had the strength—and maybe the desire—to take away Blake's life, the way he did mine."

Nina made eye contact with Ray before saying to the newly widowed woman, "Can you tell us if you've ever been to the Rose City Women's Shelter?"

Victoria's face flushed, as if ashamed to admit such. "Why do you ask?"

"Because we believe that whoever killed your husband may be affiliated with the shelter in some way."

After a moment or two Victoria said shakily, "Yes, I stayed there one night about six months ago when I needed somewhere to hide from Blake's fists. Just until things cooled off."

The detectives again exchanged glances.

"We'll need a list of some of these enemies you said your husband had," Ray told Victoria. "One of them may have decided to settle a score once and for all." He wasn't sure he believed that, not in this case, but would pursue all leads. "In the meantime, we'll need you to come and identify the body."

Rebecca Ferguson already had, Ray thought. And had probably seen more of it recently than the man's own wife. But in addition to standard and official procedure of positive identification by the next of kin, in some strange way he believed this just might put closure to this chapter of Victoria Wallace's dark life with Blake Wallace.

Their investigation still appeared to have a long way to go, the detective contemplated, admittedly more than a little disturbed that this was going on under their noses and they seemed almost powerless to do anything about it. With four men dead and countless others at risk, they sure as hell had their work cut out for them. And the clock kept ticking.

A madwoman was out there somewhere, waiting for the next opportunity to strike. Almost daring anyone to try to stop her before she put the bat and her rage to victim number five in continuing to draw deadly attention to the plight of battered women— and now battered men—in the Rose City.

15

The jogging trail provided breathtaking views of the Willamette River, with the Cascade Mountains peeking out of mounds of thick, white clouds. The morning itself was sunny, and birds could be heard singing, as if for an audience.

This was hardly noticed by Carole, her mind preoccupied with work as she did her daily run. She had been jogging for ten years now and loved pushing herself as hard as she could, as if to slow down would make it that much harder to catch up.

The results had been a sculpted and taut body that was the envy of women half her age. It also gave her a sense of personal achievement and satisfaction that could not be matched even in the courtroom.

She was so focused that she had not heard the runner come up behind her until he was right at her heels.

"What's up, Judge Cranston?"

Over her shoulder Carole flashed her eyes at Stuart Wolfe. He smiled at her, looking athletic in a sun-colored Reebok T-shirt, China-blue shorts, and well-worn black running shoes. She smiled back, and saw that he was taking in her less coordinated but comfortable attire of a short-sleeved jewel-toned running top, indigo leggings, and white New Balance running shoes.

"Hi, Stuart," she said on a breath. "What's up with you?" She was almost afraid to ask, given the recent troubles with his wife.

"Thought I might find you here." He pulled alongside her. "Have some good news. First, I wanted to thank you for talking to Vivian."

"It was not a problem," Carole told him, and mused, *At least not one yet*. She hadn't honestly known what might come from her chat with Vivian. Other than that it had made her reassess her own thoughts about having a family someday.

"She's decided she wants to have the baby after all."

"I'm happy to hear that, Stuart." Carole flashed him a smile in a genuine display of joy for them both. "I'm sure you'll make a great father, and Vivian will make a great mother."

"So would you," Stuart said warmly.

Carole felt a slight chill at the notion. "I wouldn't be too sure about that," she said. "I bite back when I'm bitten."

He laughed uneasily. "Well, as far as I know, it takes a while before babies can put some snap into their bite."

"I wasn't referring to babies," she said cynically. "I was talking about brothers who take it upon themselves to back sisters into a corner they can't get out of."

Stuart's face darkened. "Is that what I was doing?"

Carole gave him a weak grin, deciding she didn't like where this was going. "Forget it. Maybe I'm just living in the past too much, thinking about things that might have been and never will be."

"Listen, Carole," he said sympathetically, "beating yourself up over things over which you have little to no control is wasting energy that could and should be put to better use."

"Beating myself up," she groaned, as if given a low blow. "There's enough of that going around these days without being self-inflicted."

He wrinkled his nose. "Yeah, I hear you. Definitely the wrong choice of words. Sorry."

She playfully poked him in a rock-hard shoulder. "You should be, Mr. Criminal Defense Attorney. If you keep putting yourself into deep holes, Stuart, pretty soon you'll never find a ladder long enough to climb out."

Stuart chuckled warily, and said, "Hate to stay on this same track, but it appears as if we have a bona fide vigilante on our hands." His brow dripped with sweat as he frowned. "A man whom a partner in the firm represented on an assault charge was found beaten to death last night. Blake Wallace."

Carole lifted her eyes with surprise. "Really? I presided over his trial. I expected a conviction. But the jury felt otherwise."

Stuart said thoughtfully, "This is the fourth such local murder, I believe, of an accused batterer this year. The press is calling it 'justice served' to protect the innocent and vulnerable from these bastards."

"Maybe they're right," she said gingerly. "Our justice system does seem to be failing abused women."

His gaze fell on her. "But is cold-blooded murder the answer to helping them? Or is this 'angel in disguise' really doing more harm than good?"

Carole increased her speed as Stuart struggled to keep up. "Officially, no, murdering the bastards is not the answer." She drew in a breath. "Unofficially, this country needs a wake up call that can draw attention to the plight of battered and broken women."

Stuart's eyes widened. "I can't believe I'm hearing this from your lips, *Judge* Cranston. Don't tell me that you really think executing these men is somehow justifiable homicide?"

Carole could feel her heart racing, and it wasn't from jogging. She responded caustically, "All I'm saying is, do you really think we'd even be talking about battering, abuse, and domestic violence if someone out there hadn't chosen to make examples out of abusers on a dramatic stage?"

Stuart pondered this for a long moment. "Probably not," he granted. "That still doesn't give someone—anyone—the right to go after these men like a hunter killing deer."

"Agreed," Carole said, knowing it was what he wanted to hear. The jury was still out on exactly where she stood on the issue from top to bottom.

"The cops are all over this."

"I know," she mused. "They've already been to see me. At least two of them."

Carole immediately thought about Detective Barkley and got a tingly feeling. She wondered just how dangerous it was even to imagine being with him intimately.

"And . . . ?" Stuart seemed keenly interested.

"And I couldn't really help them in their investigation," she said evasively.

"They're not going to stop until they find the person," he told her.

Was he warning her? she wondered. Or was she being overly sensitive?

With a defiant look, Carole said flatly, "Who says they ever will? If she's smart—assuming it's a female we're talking about here—she'll know when enough is enough and disappear into the woodwork, having made her statement loud and clear."

Carole immediately shifted course, crossing the track onto jade-green grass fresh with dew. She turned and saw Stuart still on the track, running in place, mind buzzing, no doubt.

"Duty calls," she called to him. "I'm due back in court in less than an hour. I'll see you."

Even as she ran across the grass and onto the sidewalk, Carole could feel Stuart watching her every move till she'd disappeared from sight.

16

"Got something I think you might find interesting," Nina said, making her way into Ray's office.

He looked up from some paperwork and detected the glow in her eyes, as if she had just won the lottery.

"Don't tell me that my retirement with full benefits has come in?" he joked wistfully, sitting back in his leather desk chair.

"Only in your dreams, baby." She laughed. "Did some checking up on Esther Reynolds. Seems like the sister killed her husband, Sam Reynolds, fifteen years ago. Cracked his skull wide-open with a hammer, citing years of physical and mental abuse."

"Well, I'll be damned." Ray sat up and took the file she had in hand.

"She was charged with murder and went to trial," Nina said. "Some hotshot lawyer got her off using a battered-woman's-syndrome defense."

He raised a brow. "Guess the jury bought it hook, line, and sinker."

"Probably with good cause. Esther had a restraining order against Reynolds, which he apparently violated one time too many. And paid the ultimate price."

"Definitely shows Esther Reynolds is more than capable of killing," remarked Ray, "if she sets her mind and hands to it. But the pattern somehow still doesn't fit."

Nina frowned. "So maybe she decided that a bat inflicted even more pain and damage than a hammer."

"That's debatable. But it does give us an opening to get inside her head, as well as the legal means to find out who else in that shelter may be hiding more than themselves."

Nina plopped onto a chair. "Another thing to think about," she said, a catch to her voice. "Guess whose courtroom Blake Wallace was acquitted in?"

Ray needed only to look at the satisfied set of her mouth to put two and two together. "Judge Carole Cranston?"

"You got it."

"Just a coincidence," he said casually. Wasn't it?

"I don't think so," Nina said matter-of-factly. "There may be such a thing as a coincidence in two cases, even three—but definitely not four!" The last words flew from her mouth like sputum. "We're still waiting for that list the honorable judge promised to provide us. If you ask me, I'd say she's involved in this somehow."

It was a thought Ray was less than comfortable with. A sitting criminal-court judge, a serial murderess? A vicious vigilante underneath that black robe and hot body?

No way, he mused. He would not and could not believe it until proven otherwise.

"Why don't I go talk to the judge?" he volunteered, admittedly welcoming the opportunity to see the attractive sister again. Even if the circumstances were less than desirable.

"Sure you can handle it, Barkley?" questioned Nina, brow half cocked. "Wouldn't want you way over your head on this one." She gave a lascivious laugh.

"You've got your mind in the wrong place as usual, Parker," Ray countered defensively. "I think I can handle the judge just fine."

"That's what I'm afraid of," she quipped.

The rain was coming down in buckets by the time Ray arrived at the Criminal Courts Plaza parking lot. He grabbed his umbrella, opened it, and jogged across the wet concrete till he was inside the building. There he got himself together, including hand-pressing the creases out of his blue suit and smoothing the bristles of his mustache, before taking the elevator up to the second-floor judges' chambers.

Ray entered the outer office, where Carole's assistant sat, seemingly looking for something to do.

"I'm here to see Judge Cranston," he told the forty-something heavyset sister with a brunette twist. A nameplate on her desk read, SHEEBA ZAMBOTHA.

She batted fake eyelashes at him. "Do you have an appointment?"

He suspected she already knew the answer, but responded, "It's official police business."

"Who shall I say is here?"

"Detective Ray Barkley."

After muttering a few words over the phone, Sheeba said civilly, "Judge Cranston said to send you in."

He nodded with a slight smile, then was directed to go through two doors before entering the judge's chambers.

"Detective Barkley," she said. "Nice to see you again." She extended a hand, which he shook. The softness of her hand against his calloused skin felt like satin.

Ray felt as though he could hold that hand forever.

"Same here," he told her, as more elegant words seemed to have disappeared from his vocabulary. He forced his hand away from hers.

It took Ray only a moment to size Carole up, as if for the first time. Her stylish individual pixie braids curved nicely beneath her chin and seemed tailor-made for a heart-shaped face that had high cheeks and a sugar-maple glow to it. Umber eyes appraised him even as he regarded her. She had a dainty nose and full lips, while wearing little to no makeup. Without the oversize robe, she revealed a vibrant woman's body that looked to be in tip-top physical condition in an expensive ash-colored satin suit and ornamented sandals.

She was *hotter* than hot, he thought; no two ways about it. He was sure Judge Carole Cranston was well aware of the effect she had on brothers outside the courtroom. Inside it was another question altogether.

"Looks like you got caught in our little rainstorm," she said, her gaze falling on his clothing, which had managed to get and remain wet in spite of his best efforts to the contrary.

"Yeah, you could say that," he responded weakly.

Carole flashed him an amused smile. "So what can I do for you, Detective Barkley?"

Ray collected his thoughts, admittedly discombobulated in this fine sister's presence. Even her perfume—Animal Instinct, he recognized—was intoxicating.

"Actually I came to see if you had a chance to gather the names of regulars in your court?" he told her equably.

Carole put her hands to her mouth, disconcerted. "Oh, I'm sorry. It completely slipped my mind." She looked at her watch. "Why don't I bring it by your office this afternoon?"

"That sounds fine," Ray responded, hiding his disappointment that she hadn't seemed to grasp the gravity of the request, considering that people were dying sometime after leaving her courtroom.

"Look . . ." she said, "I was just about to go for lunch. If you're hungry, you're welcome to come." She paused. "It would give you the chance to ask whatever else may be on your mind."

Ray felt his armpits grow sweaty. He knew this was an offer he could not refuse.

Had the judge decided to stay one step ahead of him? Or was she playing catch-up here?

What was clear to Ray was that he was definitely attracted to the sister, and on that basis alone he'd be a damned fool not to at least see if the feeling was mutual.

"As a matter of fact, I haven't had lunch yet," he

told her, a crooked grin playing on his lips. "And I do have an appetite."

Carole smiled. "I'm sure you do, Detective." She wet her lips. "I hope you like Chinese food?"

I do now, baby, Ray mused.

17

Lee's Chinese Cuisine was located, appropriately, in the heart of Portland's Chinatown. It had been a favorite of Carole's for the past two years. But this was the first time that she had invited someone there. She wasn't sure why she had, Carole thought as she gazed across the table at the detective. Perhaps it was his laid-back, devilishly good looks. Or the fact that it seemed as if she somehow knew him on a deeper, more soulful level than their limited acquaintance would suggest. Or at least she felt in touch with the brother's character, thought Carole, interpreting it as naturally cynical, cautious, fiery, cerebral, and unsettled.

Very much like her own.

But above all else, she found Ray Barkley to be charming in a masculine, living-on-the-edge way; seeming to exude confidence, a trait many men she'd known were decidedly lacking.

The fact that he had come to see her alone suggested to Carole that the detective was his own man, and not a puppet to his partner's whims, whatever they might be. Already she found herself intrigued by him and suspected he felt the same about her.

So let the games begin, she thought.

His molten gray eyes assessed her over a glass of cabernet franc. It was as if Mr. Barkley had conflicting emotions over what he wanted from her.

Or what she may have wanted from him.

Carole found she could relate, as the same thoughts went through her head.

"So I understand that there was another murder?" Carole decided to break the ice carefully. "Blake Wallace . . ."

Ray nodded. "Yeah," he said. "Same as the others. Beaten to death with a baseball bat."

Carole furrowed her brow. "I'm sorry to hear it, Detective Barkley."

He leaned forward, giving her the benefit of an intense gaze. "Are you really . . . ?"

"Why wouldn't I be?" she responded calmly. *Don't let him rattle you. He's just doing his job. Whatever that may be.* "Just because a scumbag like Blake Wallace can hire a good lawyer to get him off for beating his wife to a pulp does not mean I believe in vigilante justice."

Ray paused, as if unsure where to go from here. "With all due respect, Judge, don't you find it just a bit peculiar that each of the victims spent time in your court before getting off?"

"Not really," Carole answered with a slight twist of her lips. "I handle hundreds of cases involving domestic violence each year. Many of them result in convictions. The fact that four defendants with a history of abusing women happened to 'get off' and then get murdered hardly suggests a pattern that couldn't easily be related to other factors well beyond my control."

"Such as?"

"Such as being male, living in Portland, being arrested by Portland police officers, being discussed on local TV news and in newspapers." She jutted her chin. "In other words, these men had common factors that a killer could have easily come upon outside of my courtroom."

"You have a point there," conceded Ray, tasting more wine. "All the same, you have to admit that it's not too far-fetched that some disturbed person with an ax to grind against batterers has somehow latched onto *your* courtroom, hoping to see justice served. And when it isn't, decides to do something about it."

Carole drank her wine, considering his words. Finally she responded in the only way she could. "You're more than welcome to any information I have on people who work in my courtroom, Detective," she told him. "Or, for that matter, any member of my staff, all of whom I can vouch for insofar as their integrity and dedication to the job. Personally, I think you are barking up the wrong tree. My guess is that whoever is killing these men is far less obvious than to make his or her presence known so easily."

"In my business, I've learned that killers often think everyone else is stupid," Ray told her with a catch to his words. "That means they tend to overlook the gaps in their actions until they get caught."

"Unless, of course, they want to be caught," Carole countered, aware that he was playing a sort of cat-and-mouse game with her. *It takes two to tango,* she thought. "Isn't that what most serial killers want at the end of the day? After they've made their point, if only to themselves?"

The dark-haired waitress interrupted the conversation in bringing them sweet-and-sour pork, egg rolls, and steamed vegetables with oyster sauce. It gave Ray the chance to ponder the poise with which the judge handled herself. She seemed to have all the answers, though not necessarily all the right ones. This impressed him, but not half as much as did the sister herself. There was something about Carole Cranston that captured his fancy. He hadn't felt so taken with a woman in longer than he cared to remember. He was not quite certain if that was good or bad in this instance.

"Hope you like it, Detective Barkley," Carole told him with amusement, watching as the sweet-and-sour sauce melted on his tongue.

"It's damned good," Ray admitted, cracking a smile. "Look, why don't you call me Ray," he suggested, wanting very much to change the formal tone they had established in communicating.

She wet her lips sensually. "All right, Ray. But only if you'll call me Carole—at least outside the courtroom."

"Sounds like a plan to me, Carole." He lifted his glass, as in a toast. She followed.

"Well, tell me, Ray, you have any suspects in these killings?"

Ray loaded his fork with the steamed veggies, wondering how forthcoming he should be. He decided there was little harm in sharing some information with the lady. After all, he thought, as far as he knew, they were both on the same page with regard to the law and justice. And just maybe in other areas as well.

"We're looking to speak to an African-American woman who was seen at a bar Roberto Martinez was at the night he was killed. She may have also been seen driving away from the parking garage Blake Wallace was murdered in," Ray added to see her reaction, though there was no proof to back that up.

He removed the sketch of the woman from his jacket. Studying it for a moment, Ray had to admit that at a glance there were some physical similarities between her and Carole Cranston. If you took away the blond wig, weave, or whatever the hell you wanted to call it, and sunglasses, it didn't take much of a stretch to believe the woman in the drawing could have been the judge. But then, he imagined, it was just as likely, if not more, that any tall, built-like-a-sexy-brick-house female in the city who happened to be African-American could fit the bill.

He passed the sketch across the table, intrigued by seeing her take on the depiction. Carole lifted it up and examined it as one might an artifact from the Ming dynasty.

"Look like anyone you know?" Ray asked evenly.

Carole shook her head. "I'm afraid not," she said tonelessly. "But it isn't a very good picture, is it?"

"Only the best we've been able to manage thus far," he muttered.

"I'll keep this, if you like, and show it around," she offered. "If she has any association with the court, someone may be able to identify her."

"Good idea." Ray found his thoughts drifting. He wondered if the judge was seeing anyone. He didn't see a ring on her finger, suggesting she was not married. But that didn't mean there was not someone in her life. Why wouldn't there be? he thought enviously. She was certainly the complete package.

He turned his thoughts back to the subject at hand, asking impulsively, "Are you familiar with the Rose City Women's Shelter?"

"Yes," declared Carole without prelude. "It's partly my business to be aware of the city's shelters for battered women. I have recommended more than my fair share of women to that and other shelters, knowing that it could well mean the difference between life and death to some."

Again Ray was impressed by Carole's coolness and sincerity under fire. He wondered how he could have even considered that she might have somehow been the Vigilante Killer, as the press had dubbed the murderer. This lady had too much on the ball to be moonlighting as a serial killer.

Carole almost seemed to be reading his mind. After presenting him with a soft smile, she glanced at her watch, and said, "Well, I have to get back to court. I've got a full schedule this afternoon."

"Yeah, I have my hands full as well with this case," Ray muttered, hating to see the lunch end. He waved for the waitress to bring the check.

Carole frowned. "Listen, I probably won't be able to get those names to you till tomorrow. I hope that's all right?"

"No problem," he told her, maybe a bit too agreeably, as Ray's mind was already conjuring up ways in which to see her again in a less formal setting than his office, the courthouse, or even a restaurant.

"Great," she said, finishing off her wine.

The waitress came, and Carole removed her platinum American Express credit card.

"I can take care of this," said Ray, reaching quickly for his wallet.

"I don't doubt it—but it's mine to take care of," insisted Carole, handing the card to the waitress. "I invited you, remember?"

Ray wasn't used to someone else footing his bills. But then, he wasn't used to a woman like Carole Cranston.

"I remember," he conceded. When the waitress had disappeared, Ray took a bold leap, suggesting, "Maybe I can return the favor, Carole. Why don't you let me make you dinner tomorrow, if that's all right?" He knew he was going out on a limb—considering that they'd barely gotten to know each other—but went for it anyway and hoped he didn't fall flat on his face.

Carole seemed surprised by the invitation, and was slow in responding.

Feeling as if he were squarely on the spot, and hoping to make the best of an awkward moment, Ray added, "I make a pretty damned good steak with all the trimmings. You can bring the list of names with you then. Save us both a trip to your office or mine."

A bright smile lifted Carole's high cheeks. "Sounds like an offer that's hard to refuse," she said. "You've got yourself a date, Ray. But I get to bring the wine."

"You drive a hard bargain, *Your Honor*," he joked. "It's a deal."

18

"What did the good judge have to say?" Nina cornered Ray in the coffee room at the station that afternoon. "Anything interesting?"

He thought about it. Casually he told her, "Not really."

Nina sneered. "So what *exactly* does that mean? Did she or didn't she?"

Ray looked her directly in the face. "She's clean, Nina," he said positively. "If there is any courthouse connection to these killings, Carole's not the source of it."

Nina looked skeptical. "Oh, it's *Carole* now, is it? What happened to *Judge* Cranston?"

He sighed. "Lay off, Parker! I'm not in the mood."

"And you think I am?" She slammed her coffee mug so hard on the counter that half the coffee spilled. "This isn't about your damned libido, Barkley, and how many conquests you can add to your list. It's about catching a serial killer."

"You think I don't know that?" Ray spat defensively. *Cool it, man*, he told himself. *Don't say anything you'll regret.*

Nina narrowed her eyes. "I'm seriously beginning to wonder."

"Well, don't," he told her firmly. "I know how to do my job, thank you very much. I've been at this just a little longer than you, Nina." He stirred cream in his coffee. "Carole—or *Judge* Cranston, if it makes you feel better—is no longer a suspect, as far as I'm concerned. The lady is no more the Vigilante Killer than you are!"

Nina gritted her teeth. "If you're wrong about this one, it'll be your black ass on the line, Ray, not mine!"

You're really pushing it, he thought, trying hard to keep his temper in check. But Ray needed to get to the bottom of what he considered an unwarranted attack from his partner. "What the hell is this all about, Nina?" he asked bluntly. "You jealous or what?"

She rolled her eyes and snickered. "Don't flatter yourself, Barkley. *Nothing* to be jealous over, that I can see. What we had ended a long time ago. Who you choose to play house with is your business."

"Then why the pit-bull act?"

"You have to ask?" Her jaw hung down in disbelief. "We're searching for a psycho killer who handpicks her victims right out of the judge's courtroom! I just don't want to see you screw things up by losing sight of that."

"That's not going to happen," Ray told her, seeking to convince himself as well. "I want this killer as much as you do."

* * *

Nina drove in utter silence while her partner, quiet as well, seemed as if he were in deep space. Why had she jumped all over him—coming across as a bitch? she asked herself. Could she really be jealous of Carole Cranston, who had the type of body she could only dream of? And, as a prominent judge, made being a detective, first grade, seem like second-rate stuff?

Nina wondered if she would be naturally jealous of anyone Ray Barkley was interested in, even when not conscious of it.

Was that what this was all about? She wanted Ray back for herself?

No damned way! a loud voice shouted inside Nina's head. Yes, she and Ray had been good together for a short while. Maybe in another life, another time and place, they could have given it a go and run with it.

But in this life, time, and place, there was simply no room for romance between them. *I have to be honest about that, if only to myself,* she thought. She was not about to wish for something that could only come between her and what she had worked so hard for professionally.

Nina decided that it was the pressure they were feeling from the top brass that had her acting so crazy. They in turn were feeling it from the press and public. It was her and Ray's case to solve. She didn't want that undermined by distractions neither of them could afford—including an ill-advised romance between him and Carole Cranston.

They had a search warrant for the Rose City Women's Shelter. Specifically, they wanted to see if Esther Reynolds had found that killing one abuser was not enough for her.

"My money's on Reynolds or someone else who's involved with the shelter as our killer," Ray had flatly told Nina earlier.

She was in general agreement but decided to keep her options open.

"Are we still on speaking terms or what?" Ray asked, cutting through the dreary quiet.

"Yeah," Nina said in a friendly tone, realizing that was his way of trying to get back on her good side. She glanced his way with something resembling a smile that quickly evaporated like water on a hot sidewalk. "I was just thinking that our vigilante broad could also be tuned in to the police band. That would automatically give her the jump on domestic-violence situations, which she could see through to their conclusion. Making up her own justice whenever she felt the outcome of the case was unjust."

"You may have something there." Ray looked at her. "Meaning she could even be hanging around the station when the suspect is brought in."

Possibly, Nina thought. But she still saw the courtroom as the more likely hangout of the killer—if not the Rose City Women's Shelter.

19

Ray served the search warrant as four uniformed officers accompanied him and Nina into the shelter. Esther Reynolds offered no resistance, aside from an arctic glare. Ray was not sure exactly what they expected to find. He doubted that Esther or anyone else would keep a closetful of bats or brain matter to be confiscated and used as evidence in a series of brutal bat-attack murders.

But if there were any other clues as to the identity of the killer, they hoped to discover them.

"You're wasting your time, you know," Esther said defiantly, standing menacingly in her office as files were being carted off. "There's nothing there but basic information on employees and battered women who need a place to stay."

"You could be right," Ray conceded, going through her desk. "But we believe it's a step in the right direction in preventing any more men from becoming victims of homicide."

Esther threw her arms up in the air. "You just don't get it, do you, Detective?" she growled. "Men are *not* the victims of domestic violence! They are the perpetrators! If they didn't do what they did to women, they wouldn't find themselves being targeted."

Ray looked up at her, his gaze sharp. "You don't happen to have any hammers lying around anywhere, do you, *Miss* Reynolds?"

She turned as dark as the night. "What the hell is that supposed to mean?"

"It means we know that you hammered your husband to death," he told her straightforwardly. "Do you get turned on by bats these days?"

"You son of a bitch!" Esther's face contorted. "You don't know the first thing about the hell that man put me through."

Ray sighed. "Why don't you tell me about it?"

Esther put her weight on one foot, her focus hard and unyielding. "He beat me till I damned near couldn't even eat or walk almost every day we were together. The police did nothing but give him a slap on the wrist, if that, and only after I had to beg them to help me. The restraining orders were a joke!" She snorted derisively. "All they did was make him angrier, more determined, more violent. I just couldn't take it anymore. I knew it was either him or me."

"So you chose him?" Ray was thoughtful.

"You're damned right I did," she retorted peevishly. "Haven't lost a night's sleep over it since."

"Maybe you decided killing your husband wasn't enough." Ray went after her with full force, hoping she might crack like an eggshell when too much pressure was applied. "Maybe this seemed like the right time to take some of that rage and use it against other battering men. How good are you at swinging a bat, Esther?"

"Go to hell!" she cursed.

Ray got in her face. "I'm already there, so long as this nut is on the loose in the city," he retorted. "Why don't you do us all a favor and confess to murdering four men in the image of your husband?"

Esther sneered. "You really think you can just come in here and accuse me of murder without proof?"

He kept tightening the screws, hoping she either was their culprit or knew who was. "Where are they? Where the hell do you keep the bats that are left behind as a calling card by the killer?"

One of the officers came in—a burly Hispanic female in her late twenties. "We're all finished in here, Detective Barkley. No bats anywhere. Not even so much as a stick."

Ray nodded disappointedly. "Thanks."

After the officer left, Ray turned to Esther, who had not backed up an inch. He realized the hard-assed approach had done little to shake the suspect. In fact, it had done more of a number on him. If he had hoped to intimidate her into a confession or some information, it wasn't working.

He took a breath and said to her quietly, "Are you sure there isn't something you want to tell me, Ms. Reynolds, while you have the chance?"

Esther glared and said in a strong voice, "Yes, I have something to say. How dare you come in here, accuse me of murder, and scare my residents and staff half to death with these gestapo tactics? I plan to file an official complaint with your superiors, Detective Barkley!"

"You're entitled to," he said, unaffected. "Don't think it'll do you much good, though. We had a search warrant and probable cause to believe that this shelter may be connected to a vigilante run amok."

"That's rubbish!" she assailed him. "You're grasping at straws, Detective. We both know you have nothing but vague and misguided suspicions."

Ray backed away, realizing she would not buckle. Not yet. "I wouldn't be too sure about that," he stated. "Sooner or later the truth will come out. For your sake, I hope you or this damned shelter aren't caught in the middle of it. In this state, female serial killers don't get a free ride from death row."

"I talked to some of the women," Nina told Ray after they had left the shelter. "Or let's just say that I did most of the talking and they did most of the listening. Seems as if there's a gag order in place. If anyone knows something—or someone—they're not saying."

"Same thing with Esther Reynolds." Ray groaned behind the wheel. "Couldn't get her to budge from her hard-as-granite stance. If she's not our killer, she sure as hell knows something. I can feel it!"

"You don't think they're carrying out these murders by committee, do you?" Nina widened her eyes. "All for one, one for all?"

"At this point, I'm not prepared to rule out anything," he said. "Who knows, they may well have decided collectively to pay back all the men who have done them and others like them wrong, taking turns swinging the death bat."

Nina turned in her seat. "I suppose if caught, they would all claim temporary insanity or use the battered-women's-syndrome defense."

"Or maybe the battered-women's-shelter syndrome," said Ray dryly. "We'll see if we can shake some of them up when we get them to the station one on one. In the meantime, maybe the files we took on the people who passed in and out of there in the last six months or so can yield some interesting results."

Long after the detectives had gone, taking away everything they could, Esther Reynolds sat in her barren office. There were two glasses on the table. She filled both with scotch, passing one to the woman sitting on the other side of the desk.

"They're not going to stop digging until they find who they're looking for," Esther warned.

The woman tasted the scotch, seemingly relishing its bitter tingle on her tongue. "Let them dig all the way to hell," she said confidently. "They won't find anything. I covered my tracks too well."

"Maybe you should lie low for a while," Esther suggested.

"Why should I?" The woman rolled her eyes. "Did they lie low for a while? Hell, no! They beat the crap out of us whenever it suited them, which was daily for most of us. I'll be damned if I take pity on them when their time comes to meet their Maker in a most appropriate way."

Esther brought her arched brows together. "I'm not talking about for their sake; I'm talking about for *yours!* Those detectives are clever. Sooner or later they're going to put two and two together—and they won't come up empty-handed. Don't give them a straight path right to your door."

The woman's mouth tightened, tiny lines deepening all around. "I'm on top of the situation," she insisted. "Barkley and Parker don't frighten me one bit. But *you* do, Esther. Don't let them get to you. It could ruin everything. Do you understand? For all of us."

Esther downed the rest of her drink as if it were water. As far as she was concerned her life had already been ruined those long years ago when she did the only thing she could to get away from a monster. And she had paid dearly for it. She would have to spend the rest of her life wondering if there had been a better way. Wondering if she could have seen the signs from the very beginning that set her up for a violent relationship. Wondering if she truly deserved to live after taking another's life, no matter how despicable.

All that was left for her was to help other women who had experienced the same horrible treatment that she had at the hands of a man.

That meant she could not turn her back on her sisters, Esther thought. Not even one hell-bent on ridding the streets of as many women abusers as the courts saw fit to return to those they had battered, beaten, and broken in spirit, soul, and body.

20

Carole went on her early-morning run, taking the time to enjoy the fresh air and spectacular, though distant, views of the Cascades. She thought about her dinner date tonight with Ray Barkley. Indeed, she had done little but think about it since their luncheon yesterday. Why had she agreed to go to his house, for heaven's sake? She was attracted to him, yes, but she hardly knew him.

What Carole did know of Ray concerned her somewhat. He was investigating crimes that seemed to lead right to her front door, at least in theory. She wondered if she was still the apparent target of his investigation. Or had she sufficiently quelled such suspicions?

That aside, she did find the detective to be very manly and appealing. And extremely sexy.

Though Carole hadn't figured she would ever get involved with a cop, there was no denying that Ray's chiseled, bald, arresting features worked for her. Even his personality was very intriguing.

Was there more?

What did he see in her? She knew that he saw something that struck his fancy. She had known that from day one.

It would have been easy to suggest it was merely her good looks that captivated him, which Carole saw no reason to deny. After all, if she had a quarter for every man who came on to her, she would probably be halfway toward fulfilling that dream of living in retirement in the Bahamas or Jamaica.

No, she sensed that his interest in her went beyond the superficial, per se, into something deeper, of greater appreciation and perception.

The entire notion of this meeting excited Carole more than she cared to admit. But she knew she still had to tread carefully with Ray Barkley. *I can't let my guard down too much,* she thought. Otherwise she just might find herself knee-deep in something she couldn't get out of.

When Carole returned to her condo, she was surprised to find Vivian Wolfe waiting by the entrance. Vivian flashed a nervous but wide smile when she saw her.

"Vivian!" Carole did not hide her surprise. "What are you doing here?"

Vivian ran her tongue across lips that were covered with bright red lipstick. "I was just in the area doing some shopping," she explained. "And thought I would drop by and say hello. Stuart told me where you lived. He didn't think you'd mind my coming over. I know I should have called first, since you're probably all worn out from running."

Was it that obvious? wondered Carole, even then

trying to catch her breath. What else had Stuart told Vivian about her? More important, why?

"No, it's fine," she told Vivian, even if Carole would have preferred to take a long shower and a nap. And be alone.

She unlocked the door, and the two of them went inside.

"Make yourself at home," Carole told her guest, but didn't mean it too literally. "I'm just going to go and freshen up."

Ten minutes later Carole returned to the living room, wearing some clean Old Navy jeans and a sea-foam rib-knit tank, along with suede summer clogs. She had applied a hint of makeup, though her naturally radiant skin tone made such unnecessary for the most part. She saw that Vivian was admiring one of her ivy plants hanging from the ceiling in a wicker basket. Vivian was wearing white French-terry pants and a light-green short-sleeved mock turtleneck, her nipples protruding. There was no sign of her pregnancy as yet, thought Carole, noting the flatness of Vivian's stomach.

Just how far along was she? Carole wondered. She had actually heard of some women being as far as seven or eight months along and still being virtually undetectable to the naked eye.

"Nice," cooed Vivian. "You obviously have a green thumb."

"More like a brown one." Carole laughed.

"I would love to have some lush plants like these," Vivian said. "Only I doubt I'd have the patience to properly care for them like I should."

Carole gave a modest smile. "Well, they can be a

handful," she admitted. "At the same time, they give back far more than they take from you."

"Right now I just have some silk plants." Vivian touched the ivy plant. "Maybe I'll give one of these a try and see how it goes."

"Would you like something to drink?" offered Carole. She didn't really want to encourage a pregnant woman to drink alcohol. "Coffee, tea, juice, Pepsi . . ."

"Pepsi."

"Pepsi it is."

Carole filled two glasses with ice and their beverages. They sat on the sofa. She felt somewhat awkward becoming friends, if she could call it that, with Stuart's wife. Yet somehow she felt drawn to her like a younger sister, and it was obvious that Vivian liked her as well.

"So what are you shopping for?" Carole asked, trying to strike up a conversation.

"Shopping?" Vivian seemed at a loss for a moment, and then broke into a bright smile. "Oh, some toys for the baby. I wanted to buy some clothes too, but since we don't know yet if it will be a boy or a girl . . ."

"I'm glad that the family therapist was able to help you," Carole told her thoughtfully.

"Oh, she didn't," said Vivian over the rim of her glass. "We never went to see her."

"No . . . ?" Carole arched a brow.

"Actually, after my talk with you, Stuart and I had a long conversation. And . . . well . . . the more I thought about it, the more I felt that maybe this was a good time to start a family after all."

Carole was amazed that Vivian had changed her mind so quickly. Had it actually come on the strength of her words of wisdom alone?

Or had Stuart managed to impose his will and wishes on his wife? And, as a result, their unborn child?

"Well," said Carole, "I hope everything works out fine."

Vivian crossed her fingers. "So far, so good. My doctor says that I shouldn't have any problems, that she can see."

For an instant Carole tried to imagine herself with child. She knew that at thirty-five her biological clock still had some charge to it for a few years yet. Her mental disposition was not nearly as flexible. Had her past pretty much doomed her future insofar as having a family? Or even a loving spouse?

Maybe there is still hope for me yet, she mused.

"Are you from Oregon, Vivian?" Carole asked, realizing she hardly knew anything about this woman who had seemed to just drop into her lap. Vivian may have known too much about her for comfort.

"No, California," she answered. "Grew up near Sacramento."

"How long have you lived in Portland?" Carole assumed that Stuart had met his bride in the Rose City.

"Two years. My job relocated me here. I was a legal secretary before I hooked up with Stuart." Vivian seemed to reflect on the notion. "Of course, after we got married he insisted that I not work. I kind of miss the job, but not that much. It wasn't exactly as challenging as, say, being a judge."

Carole felt she almost detected sarcasm in her tone, then realized it was merely her own overactive imagination. She had earned her way to the bench through damned hard work and couldn't conceive of giving it up—at least not to be a stay-at-home wife.

"You must come across some interesting people in your job," Vivian broke into her thoughts.

Carole nodded. "Some," she said. "And some not-so-interesting ones as well."

"What about those men who were found beaten to death recently?" inquired Vivian casually. "Were any of them interesting?"

Carole looked at her in shock. "Excuse me?"

Vivian twisted her lips awkwardly. "Stuart told me that all those men killed by the person the newspapers are calling the Vigilante Killer were actually on trial in your courtroom and released, just before they were wasted."

Her pulse racing, Carole felt her palms grow sweaty. She was none too pleased that Stuart had taken it upon himself to discuss these murders in relation to her courtroom with his wife, as though there were a clear connection. What was the point? Had he put Vivian up to this little visit?

Seeming to detect her uneasiness, Vivian said, "Did I say something wrong? Oh, I'm sorry, Carole. I didn't mean to upset you. I was just curious about them, that's all. I mean, since it seems to be the talk of the town these days . . ."

"It's all right," Carole said, in what sounded almost like an apology. *I blame your husband for this.* "It's just . . ." She checked herself, not wishing to open a can of worms better left sealed. "I'm afraid none of the men were very interesting, as far as I'm concerned. They were all being tried for spousal abuse of some type. Each got off for different reasons."

Vivian cringed. "Does it scare you, the thought that a killer is out there murdering these men you set free?"

Carole sighed. "I didn't set them free, per se," she pointed out. "It's the way the system works, Vivian. People are released if their case runs afoul due to technicalities or plea bargains. Not to mention jury verdicts of acquittal. Many times the judge acts merely as little more than a referee."

Carole wondered why she felt the need to go into detail with Vivian, who had brought it up in her face. Did she really owe anyone an explanation of why defendants—some of whom had not been proven to be guilty of committing a crime—avoided doing jail time?

"I think it scares everybody that such a thing is happening—how could it not?"

"It sure as hell gives me the chills," Vivian said, wringing her hands. "Especially if what they're saying is true."

"Saying . . . ?" Carole widened her eyes.

"You know, that it's a woman beating those men to death with a bat." Vivian shook her head. "I just can't see it. We can take a lot—but dishing it out like that . . ."

"Don't believe everything you hear or read," Carole said. "Until they capture the person, it could be anyone of any race or ethnicity or gender."

Vivian sipped her Pepsi. "Actually, I always thought it was only men who committed these types of crimes."

"It usually is," Carole made clear.

"But this is different . . . ?"

"Maybe," she allowed unsteadily.

"Not that I can really blame abused women for fighting back," Vivian remarked. "Only I personally wouldn't want to carry it that far!"

The two women shared an uneasy moment of silence.

Carole sighed softly. "I agree," she said levelly. "There are other ways to deal with batterers that won't eventually come back to haunt the person rather than killing abusers."

Vivian chuckled. "Yeah, like castrating them and leaving the scumbags for the wolves to finish off?"

"Not exactly what I had in mind," Carole said with a nervous laugh. "But that certainly doesn't sound like a bad idea, if all else fails."

Both chuckled again.

"Well, I guess I'd better be going." Vivian finished off her drink and stood. "Here I was only dropping by to say hello, and I end up talking your ear off. Sorry about that."

"Don't be," insisted Carole politely. "I'm glad you came."

Carole rose, taking a breath along the way.

"So," Vivian said, "you think it would be all right if we got together again sometime, maybe for lunch?"

Carole pasted a placating smile on her lips. "Yes, that would be nice." *But not before I have a good talk with your husband.*

"Or Stuart and I can have you over to dinner— maybe next week. I know he'd love that!"

Would he now? Carole mused, not sure she liked the sound of that. In her limited experience, old and current lovers being in the same room with the object of that intimacy did not work very well. She was in no hurry to test the theory anytime soon.

115

Besides, she was starting to have some doubts about Stuart's trustworthiness. Though she had agreed to remain friends with him, Carole wondered if he had abused the privilege.

Just how much had he confided in Vivian about her past?

Looking at Vivian, Carole responded elusively, "I'm usually pretty busy much of the time, with court work and all. So we'd better just leave that one up in the air for now."

Vivian smiled. "Of course. I understand. Consider it an open invitation."

Carole showed her out the door, waved good-bye, and was left to contemplate her life and the strange twists and turns it had taken. Would the future prove to be more promising?

Or was she doomed to be forever haunted by past demons?

And present uncertainties?

21

The sixty-foot houseboat was docked on the Columbia River, with a magnificent view of the Cascade Mountains. Ray had lived there for the last eight years, which was precisely how long he'd been divorced. His ex had taken the house they'd lived in and most everything else she could get her hands on. It suited him fine, as they were memories he'd just as soon forget.

In the kitchen, Ray stood on vinyl flooring as he checked the steak and rice pilaf before tossing a salad. It had been a long time since he'd cooked for anyone, and it both excited and scared him. *I have to do this right,* he thought. He wanted to make a good impression on Carole Cranston. Or at least show her a side of him that wasn't on duty.

Could they actually get something going? he asked himself. *I could see myself with a classy sister like Carole.* Then the doubts came. Was he too old and his goods too damaged to be thinking about starting up with someone else? He had seen more than his share of failures when it came to romance—including his short-lived relationship with Nina that he was still trying to get completely out of his system.

What was Carole's story in the romance department? He sensed that she too had run into some obstacles along the way to happiness and fulfillment. Was she looking to get past that and try again? Or had he totally misread her?

When the doorbell rang, Ray felt a thump in his chest that seemed to reverberate throughout his body. It was the kind of first-date nervousness he had last felt when he took a girl to the senior prom.

Only in this case, he wasn't in high school.

And now he was dealing with a woman. One who was out of this world.

Ray dashed into the master bedroom and slipped on an oak-brown silk-and-wool sport coat over a paprika-striped shirt and dark herringbone twill trousers with tan oxford shoes. He had freshly shaved his head for the occasion, wanting to look his best, and sprayed on a bit of Paco Rabanne.

Ray went up three steps to the upper-deck door. Before he even opened it, he could see Carole through the corner glass window. She had a bottle of wine in her hand and a look of thoughtfulness on her face.

"Hi," he said, awed by the terrific sight of her.

"Hi." She showed him teeth that were as white as the powder dusting the top of Mount Hood.

"Come on in." He stepped to the side as she did so, following her down the stairs. "Hope you had no trouble finding the place?"

"None whatsoever," claimed Carole. "Your directions were right on the money."

In the cabin living area, Ray regarded the lady judge. She wore a figure-flattering floral sundress and low-heeled sling-backs, with long, shapely bare legs in between. Her brownish individual pixies rested on tawny shoulders. He noted now the rose-tone cultured-pearl necklace and matching earrings.

"The necklace and earrings are beautiful," Ray felt moved to say. *Especially on you,* he thought.

"Thank you." Carole touched the necklace, ruminating. "They belonged to my mother," she said. "And before that, my grandmother."

He smiled out of the corner of his mouth. "Good taste definitely runs in the family."

Carole reacted, blushing. She handed him the wine. "I hope you're into sauvignon blanc. A friend of mine has a winery. She always sends me a bottle of her latest wines to hit the market."

"Sauvignon blanc sounds great," Ray told her, impressed. He hardly considered himself a connoisseur of fine wines. In fact, he was more up to speed with malt liquor and cheap wine. But then, he thought, it was definitely time to move up.

Carole removed a folder from her bag. "Here's that list of names I promised you." She handed it to him. "Most are career government employees who, as far as I know, have never been in any trouble. I also included the names of several reporters who revolve in and out of my courtroom, covering trials for local media."

"Thanks for going through the trouble," Ray said guiltily, almost wishing he hadn't insisted on what in all likelihood would turn up nothing relevant to the investigation.

"It was no trouble," she said sincerely. "I'm only sorry I didn't get the information to you sooner."

Ray set the folder on top of a hardwood cabinet near the door, not wanting to even think about it for the rest of the evening.

"I've always thought it would be really romantic to live on a boat," Carole said as Ray gave her the grand tour, inside and out. It was not as large as some of the houseboats on the dock, but was still more than enough room to allow for freedom of movement and fair-sized decks and cabin quarters. He'd recently had new carpet installed, a beryl blue, and put in hemlock paneling and cabinets himself. Log furniture was accentuated with a few pictures on the walls, and central air kept the living space comfortable.

"Oh, it can be romantic, Carole," Ray told her, having come full circle to where they began the tour. "Especially when the sun is setting, or in the dark of night when the moon is overhead. But there are other times when the high winds and rising waters make you want to be anywhere but on a houseboat. You know what I'm saying? On balance, though, I can't think of anyplace better to live, in Portland anyway, than on the water."

Carole was thoughtful. "Maybe someday when I retire from the bench I'll get the nerve to buy myself a condo right off the ocean in the Bahamas or Hawaii. Or maybe the Cayman Islands. That's probably the closest I'll get to being on the water."

Ray grinned, happy just to watch her sensual lips move. "That's cool," he said, and imagined himself retiring with her anywhere she wanted to go.

After a moment or two, Carole said, "Tell me what I can do to help with the food, Ray."

"There are plates and glasses in the cabinet in the kitchen," he said. "And silverware in the dinette, if you want to set the table."

"One set table coming right up," she said cheerfully.

Ten minutes later they were eating and chatting like old friends— or lovers.

"So what made you decide to become a cop?" asked Carole, sipping wine.

"I often ask myself that very question," Ray mused, "and have come up with more than one answer. I guess at the time it seemed a better bet than joining the service, like my old man, who made a career of it. And later, just maybe, I thought I could make a difference in someone's life as an officer of the law," he added. "Not really sure that I have, though."

"I think we all make a difference in someone's life," she stated. "It only takes one person to make it all worthwhile."

Ray peered at her. "Is that why you became a judge?"

Carole stuck a fork in her salad. "In a manner of speaking," she said. "I suppose I wanted to make something of myself beyond what was expected of me. I also wanted to put myself in a position where I could do some good in getting criminals off the street." She paused. "Sometimes, though, they have a way of slipping through the cracks, no matter what."

Ray knew she was referring to recent defendants, who had walked, only to wind up dead.

"Don't blame yourself for a system that doesn't always work, even with the best of intensions," he told her sincerely, cutting off a slice of well-done steak.

"You can't put all the bad guys away, any more than I can catch them all."

Carole lifted her wine. "Maybe if I had put a few more away they'd still be alive today. . . ."

"Or maybe they would have ended up killing their girlfriends and wives—or making them wish they were dead," Ray said. "How the hell do we know, really? In any event, my guess is that this so-called Vigilante Killer was prepared to carry out these executions whether the victims were on trial or not. It wouldn't have taken much for the person to find some assholes who fit the bill. The truth is, none of us can predict when a serial killer will decide to go after someone, or where, or why. All we can do is try to catch the son of a bitch before he—or she—kills again."

"You really think you'll catch this one?"

"Count on it." His jaw tightened. "Serial murderers, regardless of the reasons behind their crimes, can never simply walk away. They keep upping the ante, playing with fire, pressing their luck till they shoot themselves in the foot, so to speak."

"You make it sound almost like a game, Ray," Carole said with a chuckle.

"It is in a way," he told her. "Only the stakes are high for all sides." Ray drew a breath, exhaling slowly. "At the end of the day we can only hope that there are more winners on the side of real justice than losers."

"I'll drink to that," she seconded, raising her glass.

Ray held his own up in toast, spying the inviting glint in her eyes.

22

They went out to the upper deck, bringing the wine with them. The lights of boats taking advantage of the calm, warm night could be seen out on the river.

Carole felt comfortable with Ray Barkley, unusually so with someone she'd barely known. He was charming, caring, tough, and could stand on his own two feet. He wasn't pushy, obnoxious, arrogant, or otherwise a bastard, like so many men she had gone out with.

She wondered if their connection had more to do with their professional lives. Or their personal desires?

"Is there anyone special in your life, Ray?" Carole asked nonchalantly, though she sensed the answer. He didn't seem to be the type of man who would be with her now if there were. Aside from that, she thought, there were no signs that the houseboat, neat as it was, had a woman's touch to it.

"Not at the moment," he said calmly. "I was married once but it ended in disaster. Took a long time to get over her, but I did, and have moved on with my life. What about you?"

Carole had expected the quid pro quo here, and was prepared to respond. That didn't make it any less difficult. *I hate talking about myself—especially the past, which I'd rather leave alone,* she thought.

"I'm not seeing anyone right now," she told him candidly. "I too was married once. I met what I thought was the perfect man when I was in college. Only he turned out to be not so perfect." A knot formed in her stomach, but she wanted to finish. "He ended up a drug addict and eventually committed suicide."

Carole could see that this took Ray by surprise.

"I'm sorry," Ray said in a low, melancholy tone of voice. "It must've been pretty hard on you."

"It was," Carole admitted, thinking back. "I never saw it coming till it was too late." She sipped her wine. "On the bright side, it propelled me to go on and finish law school, pass the bar, and work for the DA's office for a while, before becoming a judge."

"Something good definitely came out of it then." Ray ran a hand across his head. "I hear that you're one hell of a judge, Your Honor." He smiled at her.

She smiled back. "I'm sure you're one hell of a detective, Mr. Barkley."

He laughed. "I try to hold my own out there on the mean streets of the Rose City."

"You mean when you're not holding your partner," she inquired jokingly, adding quickly, "I meant in the line of duty."

That was what she meant—wasn't it? Carole asked herself. There was no reason to believe any hanky-panky was going on between Ray and Detective Parker. But then, anything was possible. And either way, it wasn't any of her business what he did on or off the job. Or who he did it with.

Ray leaned toward her and said smoothly, "If anything it's Nina who holds me up—in the line of duty. We may not see eye-to-eye on every tiny thing, but the sister's got my back when the going gets tough."

"Nice to know." Carole wished she had someone who would watch her back, be there when the chips were down or the sun wasn't shining. Someone, she thought, like Ray Barkley.

Carole gazed into his amazingly compelling gray eyes. She felt a bit light-headed from the wine, but in a nice, mellow way. He was becoming more desirable to her in ways she hadn't felt in some time.

"Looks like we've both had it rough when it comes to relationships," she commented.

"I try to think of it as simply learning experiences in life *and* love," Ray uttered, "that can maybe prove useful in the long run."

Carole found herself drifting toward him, their fingers touching, caressing one another. "How about the short run?" she said sotto voce.

Ray put his hand to her cheek, sending electrical charges into Carole's face and then her body. "That too."

Their eyes met, and both knew what was about to happen, encouraging it.

Carole did not try to fight her growing feelings for this man that went beyond merely wanting his body. She knew there were implications down the line that would have to be dealt with. But for now she saw only an inner need they both shared.

"Do you want go back inside?" Ray asked her eagerly.

"Yes," she answered softly.

She felt herself slowly sinking onto the bed while in Ray's arms. Her head rose upward so that her mouth was perfectly aligned with his. They kissed. It was a light brushing of the lips that ignited embers within.

Carole pressed for more, prying Ray's mouth open for a deeper, more intimate kiss. He responded by putting his tongue in her mouth and holding her tightly against his rigid body.

"I want you," he whispered huskily into her mouth, the words echoing in Carole's ears.

"You can have me," she gasped back, barely able to contain her own unbridled desire.

Ray put a hand on Carole's full breast, fingers grazing her nipple, sending a torrent of fire burning within; he moved to her other breast and nipple, having the same effect. The other hand went under her dress. Roaming, deliberate fingers moved effortlessly inside her panties and into her. It was all she could do not to have an orgasm on the spot.

She hadn't realized until now just how much she had needed someone. How long it had been since there was anyone to interest her. Or anyone she wanted to be interested in her.

Caught up in a dreamlike state, Carole was barely cognizant when Ray buried his head between her open legs. She came instantly.

Then it happened again as he seemingly knew exactly what it took to bring her to this state of euphoria with his mouth and tongue.

She went with it, enjoying every moment, and then some. Her mind tried to keep up with the pleasures of the body this man feasted upon.

When her turn came, Carole unfastened Ray's trousers and took all of his erection in her mouth. His breathing quickened, and a low groan erupted as she brought him to climax in a matter of minutes.

Without a word between them, they removed their clothes and began to make love, as if totally in tune with each other. Carole started on the bottom and ended up on top. Her thighs clenched and her body gyrated as another wave of orgasm hit her like a bolt of lightning. Every cell in her body seemed to come to life. It was as if she had been awakened from a deep slumber to find herself in the firm grasp of a man bent on satisfying her every whim and doing so masterfully.

Ray held on to Carole like a lifeboat while they kissed, fondled, and caressed. Her every move led to a countermove on his part, as if they were engaged in a game of chess. Only there would be no losers. Just winners.

At last a powerful mutual release gave way to an easing back to earth. A calming of the river. A softness of breath. A time for reflection. Contentment.

Carole lay in Ray's powerful arms for a long time afterward, savoring the moment and the man. She felt a little embarrassed about what had happened, as if it had been her very first time. Or perhaps because of how long it had been since the last time.

But the better part of her knew it was something she did not regret. Ray had been everything she had hoped, and much more. She wondered he if thought the same about her. Or if it really mattered.

I'll just be happy that we enjoyed this wonderful night together, without looking too far ahead, she thought.

When Carole left early the next morning there were no promises or expectations. No declarations of love and commitment. No talk of further rendezvous. Each agreed to let the dust settle and see what happened.

Deep down inside Carole knew she wanted to see Ray Barkley again and again, each time soaring to new heights and new possibilities with this fine and sexual man. But the little girl in her knew that when you played with matches you could easily get burned.

In spite of any other feelings she might have for the detective—no matter how strong, thought Carole—she might do well to remember that.

23

"You look positively glowing this morning, Barkley," Nina said with amusement, blocking his path as he headed for his office. "Or should I say, like a man too long without sleep?"

Ray yawned as if to support the last suggestion. "Rough night," he told her, "you could say."

"Oh, really . . . ?" She flashed him a curious look.

"Yeah. Worked on some stuff around the houseboat." He somehow managed to keep a straight face as he went into the office. She stayed hot on his heels as if his shadow.

"Right," Nina said wryly. "And I'm the president's mistress—you know, old Thomas Jefferson with his fine lover—come back to life."

Ray couldn't help but chuckle. "You can really be a trip sometimes, Parker." He rounded on her, feeling a bit guilty in doing so. The last thing he wanted was to cause a rift between them. But now was not the time to tell her about his escapades into the wee hours of the morning with Carole Cranston. He was still trying to come off the high himself and not even wanting to think about any future lows that might come out of it.

Nina backed off, as if she had been pushed. "Hey, lighten up, man, will you? I'm just playing with you. There's nothing in the manual that says you can't get laid if you get lucky."

Ray thought about the night he and Carole had just spent together. He wouldn't exactly call it luck—though he sure as hell felt like he was living a charmed life in her company. She was everything he could possibly have hoped for in a dinner date, lover, and a lady.

Had he had his way, they would already be well on the road to a full-blown relationship. But sensing Carole that was not ready to declare this as anything more than a one-night stand or, at the very least, wanting to take a wait-and-see approach, he had exercised restraint in going along with it—for now anyway.

He didn't want to screw this one up if he could help it, Ray thought, and he was determined to give it everything he had to make it last.

This feeling ruled Ray, in spite of the fact that something told him Carole was holding back on him, as if being weighed down by something dark and ponderous. Did it have anything to do with the fact that she was not in a relationship? Had she recently come out of a bad one? Or was it more professional in nature?

He sat at his desk, eyeing Nina still standing there with her mouth half-open as if unsure what to say.

"Is there something else on your mind?" he asked brusquely.

"Yeah, Barkley, there is," she responded, an edge to her voice. "In case you've forgotten, there is the little matter of a serial killer that we're investigating."

A tiny smile brushed his lips. "I haven't forgotten. What have you got?"

Nina sighed, pressing her palms into the desk. "What we don't have is Esther Reynolds," she said disappointedly. "Seems she has a fairly solid alibi for the time frame when each of the men was killed. Not to mention that there's no physical evidence thus far to link her to the crimes. The search of her home turned up nothing"

Ray wasn't surprised. Reynolds seemed too obvious a choice, as far as he was concerned. Too hardened. Too bitter. Too visible. He still didn't rule out that she knew more than she was willing to tell about the murders. But proving it was another story altogether.

"What about the other women connected to the shelter?" he asked.

Nina leaned forward, her Bantu knots getting in her face. "There're a few interesting ones to look into," she replied. "Some have records for assault or attempted murder, usually of their abusive significant others. A couple of them were in mental institutions for a while, related to physical or emotional abuse. One was only six years old when she saw her daddy strangle her mother after inflicting a serious beating."

Ray considered the possibilities. "Well, I suppose any of these woman could be our serial killer. Or none of them."

Nina looked at him hesitantly. "There's something else I think you should know. I ran a check on contributors to the shelter's financial coffers."

"And . . . ?"

"Looks like one of the largest donations in the last year came from none other than Judge Carole Cranston herself!"

Damn. Ray swallowed hard, though he tried his best not to waver under the scrutiny of Nina's gaze.

"Please tell me you're not sleeping with her?" she asked bluntly.

Without responding directly, he lied, "I already knew about Judge Cranston's financial contributions to the shelter."

Nina's eyes ballooned. "You knew, and you never said anything?"

"What was there to say?" Ray tried to sound nonchalant. "She told me when she delivered the list of names of people from her courtroom. She also admitted that she often suggests the shelter to battered women as an alternative to being beaten. That hardly makes the judge a serial killer."

"It points to another possible link between her and the crimes," Nina contended. "That makes her a suspect in my book! If you can't see that, Ray—or are blinded by her long pixie braids and big breasts— then maybe you don't belong on this investigation!"

Their eyes locked for a long moment. It was Ray who averted his gaze, realizing that his objectivity may well have been compromised where it concerned Carole Cranston. Even then he refused to believe that Carole had had anything to do with the bat murders, other than being the judge who was forced to release the defendants-turned-victims. But he doubted he could get Nina to see things from his point of view.

Ray regarded his partner again. "I'm with you on

this one, Parker," he declared unsteadily. "Judge Carole Cranston can't be ruled out as a suspect."

"Good," Nina said. "Because I'd really hate to see
you go down with her—if it turns out that the good
judge is really a cold-blooded murderer!"

24

Father John Leary sat in the confessional without judgment as the woman sat on the other side of the window. He could not make out much of her through the narrow and low-lit opening. She was a coffee-with-cream-skinned, voluptuous African-American, wearing dark shades and what looked to be a blondish hairpiece of sorts.

"Father," she said in a clear, yet shaky voice, "I have sinned."

"How have you sinned, my child?" he asked routinely.

She paused, wondering if he could understand and be confided in.

As if reading her thoughts, he said, "You can tell me. I am here to listen and not to judge."

She took those words to heart, knowing she had to tell someone. After a moment or two, she said, "I have killed, Father."

He paused, unsettled. "Killed?"

"Yes."

"Who have you killed?"

She felt herself trembling. "Batterers. Abusers. Bastards. Assholes," she responded tartly. "Men who beat the heaven and hell out of their women and think they can get away with it. I have stopped them when others could or would do nothing."

Father Leary sighed, more than a little alarmed. He had heard of this purported Vigilante Killer in their midst. It had been speculated that the perpetrator was a female. Possibly African-American. Was this truly her? He strained to get a better look at the woman through the obstructed view, but regrettably was unable to.

"Why do you feel the need to take the law into your own hands?" he asked, unsure whether he believed her. Or how to handle this if he did.

She could feel her heart racing like a locomotive. "Because they are monsters!" she spat. "Each and every one of them. I couldn't allow them to go free after committing the most heinous of crimes—abusing and debasing women."

"You have been abused by such men?" he asked.

She hesitated. "Yeah, such a man."

He looked through the window. "Does killing these men make you feel better about yourself?" he asked. "Or the man who hurt you?"

She considered this. "No," she admitted, "not really."

"Then why do it?"

"For justice, Father," she answered tersely. "My own brand of justice."

Father Leary did not know what to say at this point. Was she telling the truth or a distorted form of truth? Even a gross exaggeration was not out of the question, he considered. Perhaps she identified with the real killer. Someone who in her head answered her prayers of vengeance against those who physically and perhaps psychologically violated women.

"Would you like my help?" he asked her.

"No!" The woman's voice was resolute. "I don't need any help, Father. Not the type you're offering. I only came to confess to you my sins . . . to someone who I thought might be understanding."

"It was good of you to come to me," he told her. "I can understand what you must be going through for you to be driven to take such actions. But this isn't something you should deal with alone." Was she killing people all by herself? he wondered. Or were there others involved? "There is a legal system in place—"

"Are you listening to me, *Father?*" She felt her temperature rise. "The legal system *is* the problem. They can do nothing to stop these bastards—at least not the ones with smart lawyers or dumb-ass prosecutors. Don't you see, if I don't make them pay for their crimes, no one will!"

He gulped. "Are you saying you plan to kill again?"

She didn't hesitate, knowing this was her calling. "I have no other choice," she responded, her confidence returning. "These men, if you can call them that, don't deserve to live—not in my neighborhood. Or yours, Father. They must be punished in a way that fits their crimes against women."

Shifting his body, Father Leary again tried to get a better look at the woman who had just confessed to being a serial killer, but to no avail. In truth, what could he do even if he could see her clearly? he wondered. Was it up to him to try to save her victims? Or even to save her from herself?

His role here was one of a listener, no matter the nature of confession or the instability of the confessor. He was bound by his own vows as a priest.

She sensed his uneasiness, which in turn made her begin to question coming to him.

"When?" he asked her directly. "When do you plan to kill again?"

Her temples pulsed. "I can't tell you that, Father," she replied with a catch to her voice. "How do I know you won't rat me out to the cops? How do I know you won't betray my trust, as men have done to me and other women?"

He wiped the sweat from his brow. "I would never betray your trust," he avowed. "Or rat on you to the authorities. I just want to try to—"

When he looked again she was gone.

25

Ray chose a coffee shop as a neutral site to meet with Carole. He didn't want the temptation of his place or the austere and intimidating judge's chambers to talk. He was certain that she could explain any concerns he had. Or concerns Nina had, for that matter. As much as he wanted them to go away, he knew they wouldn't. Not so long as a ruthless killer remained on the loose with no suspects in custody.

The place was crowded at the noon hour, but Ray still managed to find a little corner table with a window view. He had already finished half a café latte when he saw Carole. She gave a little wave and weaved through other bodies like traffic.

He stood to greet her. "Hello, Carole."

She was huffing and puffing. "Hi, Ray," she offered with a smile. "Sorry, I'm late. Court ran over a bit when the prosecutor and defense attorney locked horns like bulls. Pit bulls are probably more like it."

She chuckled. "I let them go at it perhaps longer than I should have."

Ray gave a little smile, while noting that Carole was as lovely as ever. She wore a tailored amethyst suit and matching ankle-strap pumps. Her pixie braids were gathered together and tied in a bun behind her head. He couldn't help but feel himself aroused in her presence, remembering their night together. The mere thought that she could be a killer made his stomach turn and his skin crawl.

After they were both seated with their coffee, Carole remarked, "You sounded tense on the phone."

"I was," he admitted reluctantly.

She raised a thin brow. "What is it, Ray?"

He paused, looking her in the eye. "Why didn't you tell me you gave money to the Rose City Women's Shelter?"

She blinked. "Was I supposed to? I give money to several local organizations whose purposes I care about. So what?"

"So it doesn't look too damned good that you're financially supporting a shelter that's connected to all the victims of men who have appeared in your court—only to wind up beaten to death themselves."

Carole grimaced. "I'm not quite sure what to say, Ray," she muttered. "If you really think I'm this Vigilante Killer, you have a strange way of showing it. Or do you make a habit of sleeping with *all* your suspects . . . ?"

Ray bit his lip, knowing he had that one coming. "You're not a suspect, Carole," he said weakly. "This is just routine follow-up that I have to do as a detective investigating these murders. I'm sorry."

"No, you're not. But I sure as hell am! You're not turning out to be the man I thought you were, *Detective* Barkley. And as for my charitable gifts to the shelter, they are strictly tax-deductible contributions for a worthy cause. If you check your records carefully I'm sure you will find that several other donations come from some of my colleagues in the court system." She ran one hand steadily across the other. "If this somehow makes me guilty of multiple murders, then arrest me right here and now."

"Look, baby—" he tried to say on a personal level.

Carole cut him off with the sharpness of a knife. "I don't have any control over the women who go to the shelter. I have recommended shelters to hundreds, if not thousands of battered women, but I don't keep track of who goes and who doesn't. I have no role whatsoever in how the Rose City Women's Shelter is run, nor do I profit from it in any way." She took a quick breath. "I certainly can't be blamed as somehow engineering the release of defendants brought to my court for abusing their wives and girlfriends. You should know as well as I do that these kinds of trials can be dismissed for a variety of reasons, most of which are up to the lawyers and jurors. Not the judge."

Ray knew there was truth in everything she said. He had attacked the woman he was really beginning to care about and may have lost her in the process. *Damn, sometimes this job really sucks*, he mused.

"I had to ask," he said. "It's my job, Carole. If not me, it would have been another cop." He wondered if Nina would have handled things any better.

"Then maybe it should have been," Carole hissed.

"I don't like being interrogated by a man I just spent the night with! Makes me think it was merely a police tactic to soften me up for the shark attack!"

With that Carole stood, glaring at Ray as though he were suddenly her sworn enemy.

"Good-bye, Ray. Next time you want to interview me, we'll do so at my attorney's office!"

She stormed away and he was left thunderstruck, unable to say a word in his own defense—were she still there to listen. At least not one that could change the outcome in his favor.

In the meantime, his troubles with Carole aside, there was still the hard truth that a killer was out there, unknown and very dangerous.

Carole took the rest of the afternoon off. Her meeting with Ray had unnerved her. And that was putting it mildly. Had he truly believed her to be a killer? Or was he only grasping at straws for lack of more concrete evidence? Or suspects? She wondered if he actually expected her to somehow break down and confess to the crimes.

She, Judge Carole Cranston, had lost her cool. Her poise. Something she almost never did in public. Would that cause Ray to dig deeper? Was she bound to have secrets unearthed that were better left buried forever?

Carole's mind turned to the man she had made love to last night, rather than the cop she had left this afternoon. Was it all a charade? Could the way he made her feel have been part of a calculated setup and nothing more?

Carole knew she needed time to sort out her feelings. To think of what needed to be done next. *I have to keep a level head, even under fire,* she thought. *And, yes, desire.*

She could not allow her life to become unraveled. She had been there, done that. This time she would not lose it. Not even for a handsome man she had thought was on her side in more ways than one, like Ray Barkley.

26

Ray had driven around for an hour that night, his mind absorbed with both the case and Carole. It had driven a wedge between them—one that he was not sure he could remove. But he had to try. Though knowing full well he was breaking all the rules concerning becoming involved with someone who was still technically a suspect in a murder investigation, he had to go with his instincts on this one. Carole was no more a serial killer than he was, in spite of some unanswered questions.

Ray still wasn't ruling out that someone might have been using her courtroom to play judge and jury to the accused. If that were true, Carole was merely an innocent pawn.

He drove to her downtown condominium, having gotten the address from a friend in the department's administration office. He had no idea if she would even talk to him, much less allow him to try to make amends. But it was driving him crazy thinking about her. *The lady's gotten under my skin*, he thought.

Carole had reached something in Ray that had him believing in the future again. A future that could include her, if it wasn't too late.

Ray buzzed the intercom. A moment or two later Carole answered. "Yes?"

"It's Ray," he said tentatively.

She paused. "What do you want?"

"Can we talk?"

"Not sure we have anything left to talk about," she told him frankly.

I can think of a few things, Ray thought. He sucked in a deep breath before saying, "How about us?"

It was a while before Carole said anything. "I'll buzz you in," she finally acquiesced.

A couple of minutes later Ray stood at her doorway. The door opened before he could knock. Carole, dressed in a short-sleeved crewneck sweater, striped capris, and moccasins, regarded him with caution. He felt the heat beneath his polo shirt and chino pants.

"Come in."

He followed her into a spacious apartment filled with an assortment of plants, both hanging from the stucco ceiling and on the floor, as if it were her own private botanical gardens. Pastel paintings graced the walls, and floor lamps complemented recessed lighting. The French provincial furnishings in the living area fit perfectly with the surroundings. He noted a large bay window behind open faux-wood blinds that seemed almost to overlook the entire city.

Ray homed in on the lady of the house. Carole had a hand resting on her rounded hip, her gaze centered on his face. For once he was at a loss for words. He didn't want to say the wrong thing that would only make things worse between them. Or the right thing that she might somehow misinterpret.

"Look," he said in a level tone, "I don't want things to end between us."

Carole took an involuntary step backward as they stood on a Persian area rug. "So what exactly do you want, Ray?" she challenged him.

He stepped closer. "I want you." He made no pretense, cupping her face in his hands.

She fluttered her lashes but did not back away. "Are you sure about that?"

"Yeah," Ray said positively, "I'm sure."

Her voice shook when Carole uttered, "I'm sure I want you too."

Ray took her into his arms, feeling the weight of their mutual need. Their mouths touched. They kissed. The kiss was deep, powerful, long lasting, as though with a mind of its own.

It was Carole who broke away. She took Ray's hand and wordlessly led him to her bedroom. Ray allowed himself only a glance at the darkened room, making out the antique furnishings and French doors that led to a balcony, before returning his gaze to Carole.

They slowly began to undress each other, taking in every inch of each other's body as though their lives depended on it. Both fell atop the bed's cream-and-taupe matelasse coverlet, where they resumed kissing passionately, their tongues tasting and titillating each other from top to bottom and everything in between.

Ray caressed Carole's taut nipples, his body pressed up tight in between her splayed long legs. As Carole urged him on with her cries and fingers running across his back, he responded, wanting only to please her in every way. He took in her invigorating scent and body movements, which were driving him mad with desire.

They made tempestuous love, bodies molded together and moving symmetrically and spontaneously, as if this were the last day on earth and they intended to make the most of it, of each other.

An hour later they lay still, soaking in the air-conditioning as their sweat-drenched bodies cooled off from the fiery passion that had consumed them like lovers in a romance novel.

Carole raised her head from Ray's chest, meeting his gaze. She hesitated, then said, "Baby, there's something about me I think you should know—"

Ray put a finger to her lips. "Don't," he said, not wishing to spoil for even a moment what they had shared. *I like you just as you are, whatever I don't know,* he mused. Besides, he could not truly imagine anything about Carole that would change the way he was rapidly starting to feel about her. "There will be plenty of time later for us to talk about our lives and pasts . . . and the future—"

Carole began to object in typical courtroom fashion, but seemed to have second thoughts. Lying back on his chest, she murmured, "I'm enjoying your company, Ray. I haven't been able to say that to anyone in a long time."

"I'm enjoying spending time with you too, baby," he told her sincerely. "And I haven't had anyone to tell that to in longer than I care to remember."

She reached up and kissed him. He returned it with the same amount of energy.

"You taste so good," Ray murmured, his erection

building again, his need for this beautiful, sensual sister insatiable.

"So do you, baby." Carole licked his upper lip and mustache.

They made love again.

And again.

And once more.

By the time Ray left, he no longer considered Carole a viable suspect in the murders that rocked the city of Portland like an earthquake.

27

Nina awoke with a start, straining her tired eyes. It was six A.M. She dragged herself out of bed, slipped on a terry kimono robe over her nude body, and padded into the kitchen, where she turned the kettle on.

During a hot shower Nina wondered if she had been too hard on Ray. Just because there was no man in her life at the moment didn't mean he had to live like a monk. Even if he was seeing Carole Cranston, it was his choice, she thought, though ill-advised under the circumstances. As far as she was concerned the judge was not off the hook yet, even if she seemed to have wormed her way on to Barkley's good side, and probably into his bed.

But for now, Nina was prepared to keep an open mind as they pursued all possible suspects. Her only hope was that they could get to the killer before the crazy lady got to another abusive man.

Ray picked Nina up at eight on the nose, looking

weary but ready for another day on the trail of a psychopath.

"Good morning, beautiful," he told her with his usual flare for the dramatic.

Or perhaps it was a carryover from their brief stint under the sheets, thought Nina mischievously, when he got to see just how beautiful she really was.

"Morning, Barkley," she said, keeping her voice unemotional as she got into the car.

"Got some news." Ray flashed Nina a hopeful look. "Based on the witness's recollection of part of the license plate number of the BMW that drove off from the garage where Blake Wallace was murdered, we've been able to narrow it down to ten possible vehicles. Meaning that we could be closing in on our killer."

Nina refused to get her hopes up, knowing that an eyewitness's memories were often unreliable and dubious at best, especially when trying to remember license plate numbers that they had no reason to remember at the time. But at this point she would take any lead they could get. No matter how small.

"What do we have on the owners of the cars?" she asked.

Ray frowned. "Not much," he admitted. "None of the owners have criminal records. Nor have we been able to match any of them to police reports of domestic violence or the names taken from the Rose City Women's Shelter."

"Sounds like we're definitely on the right track," Nina scoffed sardonically.

He chuckled. "Yeah, well, we both know that most

crimes are solved not because of hard evidence, but a series of lucky breaks."

"Yeah, tell me about it," she muttered. "So why is it I don't feel so lucky today?"

And it had absolutely nothing to do with her love life, or lack thereof, Nina told herself, but rather the exasperation with this case and their difficulty in pinning down the killer.

"Could be it's your natural pessimism kicking in," Ray quipped. "Must be a sister thing."

Nina rolled her eyes. "Yeah, right . . . probably because of the grief we sisters have to put up with from you brothers."

Ray laughed. "Guess I deserved that one."

"I guess you did."

Nina's thoughts turned elsewhere—or more to someone in particular. She glanced Ray's way and ventured boldly, "You wouldn't happen to know what type of car Judge Cranston drives, would you, Barkley?"

He shook his head and glared. "You just won't let it go, will you, Parker?"

"Is there any reason why I should?" Nina countered, though wishing she hadn't.

A vein bulged in Ray's temple. "Yes, dammit! Because she's the *last* person in Portland we should be looking at as a murder suspect."

"Oh, really? Do you know something that I don't?"

"I know that Carole—Judge Cranston—doesn't even own a vehicle. She walks, jogs, and cabs her way around the city. Beats looking for places to park when there never seem to be any. Not to mention saving on those damned car repairs."

Nina wanted to ask how he knew these little details about the judge's private life, but decided otherwise. She was not sure she really wanted to know, though one didn't have to be Einstein to put two and two together.

Instead she said dryly, "Well, looks like you're way ahead of me on this one, Ray."

"So what else is new." He grinned crookedly at her.

"Don't press it, mister," she warned, poking him in the side, causing him to groan.

"I won't." Ray shrugged, peering out over the steering wheel. "Consider it a dead issue, no pun intended."

"Who's first on the list?" Nina looked at her partner.

"An attorney by the name of Stuart Wolfe," replied Ray. "The first three letters the witness made out on the license plate are a match for those on his black BMW. It's probably a long shot here, but you never know. We could hit the jackpot on this lawyer dude, or someone who uses his car."

"Maybe he's a cross-dresser?" Nina half joked.

"Don't laugh," Ray shot back. "Why the hell not a cross-dressing serial killer? We've seen just about everything else in this business. There isn't much left to shock me—except maybe a cunning female killer who preys on men and isn't afraid to really sock it to them."

The black-on-black BMW with the license plate number SLW 402 sat in plain view in the circular drive of a large, redwood Victorian house. It was in the West Hills, a section of the city known for its exclusive homes and breathtaking mountain views. Large bay windows occupied much of the two-story residence with a gabled roof and Corinthian columned porch. Tall, manicured bushes and very old magnolia trees bordered a wide, olive-green lawn.

"Whatever else you can say about the man," chirped Nina, "he sure has good taste in a home, and obviously the money to back it up."

"Not too surprising," Ray said, parking on the street outside the house, "considering he's starting to come into his own as one of the top African-American criminal defense attorneys in the Rose City. Yeah, I'm familiar with him. Think I read that Wolfe got married a little while back."

"Well, whoop-de-do," Nina said, trying to sound unimpressed, though she was anything but. "Let's just see if Mr. Married Black Attorney has any skeletons in his closet, shall we?"

As they drove up the driveway they studied the car that could have possibly been driven by a killer. It had recently been washed and showed no signs of damage or indication of where there might have been. Inside, there was an overcoat thrown haphazardly over the front seat and a newspaper folded neatly on the backseat, alongside a briefcase.

"What do you think?" Nina asked.

Ray shrugged. "I think if this is the BMW that fled from the scene of the crime, we may have our work cut out for us proving it."

The ring of the doorbell brought an immediate response, almost as if they were expected. Nina saw in the entrance a tall, fit, dark-skinned man with a short, gleaming Afro. He was perhaps in his late thirties, she guessed. He stood mute in a gray designer suit and wing-tipped leather shoes, his coal eyes wide with anticipation.

"Can I help you?" he asked in a deep voice.

"Are you Stuart Wolfe?" Nina asked.

"Yes, that's me."

"I'm Detective Parker," she said. "And this is Detective Barkley. We're with the Portland Police Bureau, homicide division. I wonder if we might ask you a few questions?"

A thick brow cocked. "What's this about?"

Nina looked up at him. "We're investigating a homicide in which a BMW fitting your car's description was seen leaving the scene."

Stuart grimaced. "What? You're joking, right?"

Ray stepped forward with pursed lips. "This is no joke, sir."

"There are probably any number of black BMWs in Portland," Stuart noted disbelievingly.

"Yeah," allowed Ray, "but not many that have SLW in the license plate."

Stuart showed no signs of nervousness. "I see," he said equably. "Come on in."

They went to his study, bypassing several impressively furnished, architecturally fascinating, spacious rooms along the way. Stuart offered the detectives a seat on a country-style couch, sitting himself on a matching love seat.

"I would offer you a beer or something," Stuart told his guests curtly, "but I'm sure you don't drink on duty."

"Right on that one," Nina said tersely. "Thanks anyway."

Ray watched the attorney thoughtfully.

Stuart furrowed his brow. "I actually thought customizing my license plate numbers to reflect my initials would make it distinctive—though certainly not like this. You know what I'm saying?"

"Oh, your initials are not all that common," she pointed out. "That's the problem we're having here. . . ."

"So what murder are we talking about?" asked Stuart straightforwardly, casting his gaze directly at Ray.

"The victim is a man named Blake Wallace," he told him, sure the brother was already on top of it.

Stuart reacted. "The businessman who was beaten to death with a bat?"

The detectives exchanged glances before Ray replied, "Yeah, that's him."

Stuart sighed. "Since you obviously did your homework before coming here, I'm sure you know I'm a criminal attorney. Blake Wallace was being represented by one of the partners in my law firm during his trial for domestic assault."

Nina and Ray again looked at each other with surprise, not anticipating this angle.

"Actually that little tidbit had escaped our attention," Ray admitted.

Stuart seemed unfazed by this. "Well, it's pretty irrelevant, as far as I'm concerned. I had nothing to do with Wallace's case. And as for my car being at the murder scene, you obviously picked the *wrong* BMW with the partial license number SLW. I wasn't anywhere near that location that night." He set his jaw. "I gave a lecture at Portland State University, which I do on occasion, from seven to ten. I believe Wallace was killed within that time frame. There were about one hundred and fifty–odd students who can vouch for my presence."

"You drove your car that night?" Nina peered at him.

"Yes," Stuart said confidently.

Ray allowed his eyes to wander thoughtfully, settling on a walnut bookcase filled with law books before returning to the man on the hot seat.

"Any other drivers in the house?"

"My wife, Vivian," he responded effortlessly.

Ray regarded Nina and back again. "Could she have driven your car that night?"

"Not a chance," explained Stuart coolly. "Vivian *never* drives my car. Besides, she has her own car."

"And what type of car would that be?" asked Nina.

"A white Lexus."

The detectives seemed reasonably satisfied for now.

"I think we've taken up enough of your time, Mr. Wolfe," Ray said half apologetically. The other half would come once the attorney had been completely exonerated.

"No problem, man," Stuart said in a friendly, calm voice. "I understand that you have a job to do. I think we'll all feel a lot better when you catch whoever it is that's targeting these men."

Nina fixed the attorney with soulful, inquisitive eyes as he led them to the front door. "Your wife—Vivian—wouldn't happen to be around, would she?"

Stuart met her gaze head on and said excitedly, "Actually she's at the doctor. We're expecting our first child early next year!"

Nina smiled slightly and made herself say, "Congratulations."

Outside, the detectives considered the suspect.

"His alibi for that night should be easy enough to

verify," said Ray. "Personally, I don't think Wolfe had anything to do with Blake Wallace's murder—aside from the law-firm connection. Which seems to be pretty weak at best."

"What about his wife?" wondered Nina out loud. "Show me a man who says his wife never drives his car and I'll show you a woman who drives it all the time."

Ray rolled his eyes. "C'mon, Nina. You don't seriously believe our serial murderess is a *pregnant* woman . . . ?"

Nina thought about it, unwilling to rule anything out, no matter how unlikely. But common sense kicked in. This did not seem likely, she mused. The rage with which the victims were savagely attacked suggested a killer with only one main focus, leaving little room for the pursuit of motherhood.

"No, I don't," she told Ray candidly. "I guess that lets these two off the hook . . . for now."

One by one they went down the line on the list of suspects. In each case the potential perpetrators either had solid alibis, or were otherwise eliminated from contention.

The hot trail had once again grown cold and old, and the detectives found themselves practically back to square one in their search for a killing machine.

28

"You've been avoiding me," Stuart told Carole, an irregular crease lining his brow.

He had literally cornered her on the side of the building as Carole left the Criminal Court Plaza during a recess of the trial she presided over.

"That's not true," she lied. "I've just been really busy, Stuart."

He sighed. "I wasn't born yesterday, Carole. You don't return my calls. You don't call me. What's up?"

She thought about Ray Barkley. He had entered her life unexpectedly and seemed to occupy her thoughts more than she cared to admit. They had managed to dodge a rough patch of road and seemed well on their way to something wonderful.

Her fears about their being together had subsided for now, and she was content to let this thing play out and see what happened.

As for Stuart, Carole no longer saw the point in giving him her time. After all, now that she had Ray in her life there was simply no need to hang on to someone who had already moved on to another woman. A pregnant one at that. They would only end up interfering in each other's private affairs, something she didn't want to see stand in the way of her potential relationship with Ray.

Besides that, thought Carole, she was still somewhat pissed that Stuart had decided to let his wife in on the particulars of her life, as if it were his right. She feared that he had divulged far more than he should have. Or still could.

She gazed at him. "I think we should just cool this friendship thing for a while, Stuart," she tried to say gently.

His eyes darted from side to side, as if watching a tennis match. "You want to tell me why?"

She sighed. Why was he making this so hard for her? "I'm seeing someone."

Stuart nodded understandingly. "I see. So that's what this is all about."

Carole's eyes narrowed at him. "Actually, if you want the truth, it's about you opening your big mouth too much with your wife."

Stuart looked shocked. "What the hell are you talking about?"

"Vivian seems to know more about me and my courtroom than I'm comfortable with," she said bluntly. "My life is not an open book for you to share with your wife without my permission, Stuart."

He colored. "I'm sorry, baby. It only seemed natural to talk about us after what we had."

"I'm not talking about *us*," Carole pointed out. "I'm talking about *me*, dammit." She could feel her heart pounding as if trying to escape from her chest.

Stuart put his hands on Carole's shoulders and stared into her eyes. "Listen to me, Carole," he said with a sense of urgency, "I may have mentioned some peculiarities regarding your courtroom and the recent crime wave hitting this city, but that's about it, and it's certainly not an indictment of you. I would never tell Vivian or anyone else anything about you that is strictly between us."

Carole read the sincerity in his eyes. She felt her breathing return to normal and her blood pressure lower.

Maybe she had overreacted, presumed the worst without sufficient proof to back it up. Wasn't that the first thing she had been taught in law school: innocent until proven guilty? Not that she felt for one minute that Stuart was totally without fault. After all, she suspected he had still shared more with Vivian about her than she would have liked. But apparently not those secrets that she had most entrusted him with.

"I believe you, Stuart," Carole said emotionally. She put a hand on his, squeezing it gently. "Sorry for jumping on you like that. Thank you for everything you've done for me. And I mean that."

Stuart's face brightened. "No need to thank me, Carole. That's what friends are for, right?"

"Yes." She yielded, forcing a smile. "That's what friends are for."

"Besides, Vivian is just starting to like you," he remarked. "She thinks you are one *cool* judge. How would it look if you suddenly made yourself scarce?"

"Probably not too good." Carole recognized that

Vivian would likely need a friend even more at this delicate time in her life, with a baby on the way. It looked as if she had been elected to fill the role. *Now, whether I can live up to it may be another matter altogether*, she thought.

"Exactly." Stuart brushed his nose with the tip of his thumb. "So can I buy you lunch? You can tell me all about your new boyfriend."

Carole felt a twinge of uncertainly course through her veins. *Boyfriend?* Had her relationship with Ray, if that was what this really was, reached that level where he could be called her boyfriend? And she his girlfriend?

She contemplated whether or not dating Ray could withstand the pressures of their—at times—conflicting and tumultuous careers. Her past and deep regrets. His life and times before her . . .

Carole moistened her lips as Stuart waited for an answer. She would have preferred to eat alone, if the truth be known. She was not particularly in the mood for company. At least not his company. But she decided to go for it, if only for old times' sake. And because she knew it was probably a good thing to keep him on her side.

"You're on for lunch," she told him. "So long as we stay away from my personal life."

He smiled disingenuously. "Whatever you say, Your Honor."

"Ray Barkley," voiced Stuart loudly over a mug of beer. "He wouldn't happen to be *Detective* Barkley, would he?"

Carole favored him with surprise across the table.

He had slyly brought her "boyfriend" into the conversation, compelling her to set the record straight.

"You know Ray?" she asked incredulously. Usually criminal defense attorneys and police homicide detectives didn't mix very well.

"In a manner of speaking." Stuart looked at her, frowning. "He showed up at my house this morning, with his partner."

"Oh . . . ?" Carole found her curiosity more than a little piqued. Why would Ray and Detective Parker pay Stuart a visit? she pondered.

"Apparently a car with a license plate that partially matched mine was seen leaving the crime scene the night Blake Wallace was murdered." Stuart stiffened. "They wanted to know the whereabouts of my BMW at the time. Can you believe that?"

Carole watched him shake his head in dismay. She kept her cool as she asked, "What did you tell them?"

"The truth. That I had the damned car at PSU while giving a lecture."

"And . . . ?" she coaxed.

"And that was that," Stuart said flatly. "They realized they had the wrong car and presumably went after the right one." He took a breath. "I have to tell you, Carole, the whole thing really irritated the hell out of me. I may defend criminals, but I'm not one of them. Certainly not this serial killer they're after."

Carole put a finger to her chin. "Did they ask about Vivian?" she wondered curiously, aware that the common perception was that the killer was an African-American female.

"Vivian does not drive my car!" he blared protectively. "There was nothing to ask. Besides, she's probably the last person they need to be talking to in Portland. Next to you."

Their eyes connected in a moment of edgy contemplation.

Carole sank back into her chair. "You don't think that I actually . . . ?" She could barely get the defensive words out.

"Not for one second," Stuart said quickly with a chuckle. "Just making a point that this femme fatale, if it is a woman, is not someone like Vivian or you. It's a person with no regard for the law and probably strung out on drugs or whatever the hell else they're into these days." He paused. "Whoever the killer is, she certainly hates men."

"Not all men," Carole felt she needed to point out.

Stuart shrugged, keeping his gaze fixed on her. "I suppose. Unfortunately, it isn't much comfort to men who don't beat up women, but could be mistaken as such assholes by a killer who doesn't seem to have a conscience."

"I don't disagree with you about the position it places innocent men in," said Carole carefully. "But I think this person has a clear conscience in what she does and how she chooses to do it. It may well be that she thinks it's the only option available to her and women like her to stop the abuse."

Stuart wrinkled his nose. "Clear conscience or not, this bitch is not doing battered women any favors by beating a few brutal men to death. If anything, she's making it worse for women who stand up to their batterers by putting them in an even more dangerous and vulnerable position against men freaked out by this vigilante."

Carole digested that for a moment or two, trying to offer a rebuttal that did not make her sound supportive of the killings or the killer.

She stirred her vegetable soup while saying evenly, "I think that maybe in her own way the killer's actually empowering women to strike back even harder at their abusers. Or at least give them second thoughts about hitting someone who could turn the tables on them in a deadly confrontation."

Talking mostly to himself, Stuart muttered, "Either way, this person needs help." He stared at Carole. "Let's hope that when all is said and done, she gets it before she takes out the whole damned city."

Carole felt that spoke for itself, and offered no further comment. Instead she turned her thoughts to Ray. She wondered where he and Nina were now on the investigation. Would the sketch point them to someone? Anyone?

Am I still considered a suspect, though Ray indicated otherwise? she asked herself, unsettled at the thought.

Could they possibly make a case against a sitting judge with nonexistent or insufficient evidence? Did the police have any real evidence?

They ate in contemplative silence.

Before long Stuart raised his eyes. "So how did you become involved with Detective Ray Barkley?" he asked studiously.

Carole wet her lips with white wine. "He and Detective Parker came to see me to talk about the case they were working on."

"The Vigilante Killer," deduced Stuart. "Yeah, of course. Did you give them anything they could use?"

"I don't know," she admitted. "I'm not sure they know themselves what they're after. Or who . . ."

"Well, apparently the brother's after *you*."

Carole blushed. "Maybe I'm after him," she suggested, the thought arousing her as she recalled their frenetic and nonstop lovemaking.

Stuart let out a sharp sigh. "Good luck," he said with an edge to his voice. "Just hope you know what you're getting yourself into. Cops don't always make for the best partners."

Carole mused over the advice, while thinking, *Neither do attorneys*. "I'm a big girl, Stuart," she told him solidly. "I can take care of myself."

Inside, Carole wondered if she truly could. Or would her fragile past catch up to her and jeopardize everything she held dear? Including Ray Barkley?

Stuart smoothed an eyebrow. "I'm not trying to get into your business," he said. "I just want you to be careful, Carole, that's all. Wouldn't want Barkley to have ulterior motives in mind for this romance— at your expense."

Carole pondered this. *Ulterior motives?* She hated to think that Ray could actually be using her for his own purposes other than romance. Not that the thought hadn't crossed her mind. If so, would she be able to spot such motives and deal with them? Before it was too late . . . ?

29

Ray drove to the house where Thelma Kennedy lived. The thirty-eight-year-old single mother of two had crippled her abusive ex-husband, shooting him with his own gun and severing his spine. She had beaten him with a bat afterward, claiming it was the result of years of abuse and pent-up anger. The court had gone along with this to a degree, convicting her on one count of aggravated assault rather than attempted murder, for which she served five years in state prison.

Her parole report suggested that she had been a model citizen since she was released from the Oregon Women's Correctional Center a year ago, thought Ray. She had since regained custody of her daughter, who had been placed in a foster home. Records indicated that before doing time Thelma had been a frequent guest at the Rose City Women's Shelter. More recently, she had been one of the volunteer staffers at the shelter.

Ray pulled up to the modest-sized redbrick home

in a subdivision. There was a mauve Pontiac Bonneville in the driveway. A spruce-colored bicycle lay against the side of the house as if holding it up.

Ray rang the bell twice before an African-American girl about ten years old opened the door. On the chubby side, she had long, black corkscrew braids that interlocked. She looked at Ray through thick glasses as though he were an alien.

"Is your mother here?" he asked.

"Yeah."

"Can I talk to her?"

"Who are you?" she asked suspiciously.

It was a good question, but he didn't want to scare her half to death, so Ray answered, "Mr. Barkley."

"Mama!" she screamed, running inside. "A man named Mr. Barkley is at the door to see you."

A few moments later a woman appeared in the doorway. She was around five-five and heavyset, with a wheat-bread complexion, blonde microbraids, and tar-colored eyes with heavy bags underneath. She wore a patchwork A-line dress and sandals.

"How can I help you?" she asked snappily.

Ray put on his detective face. "Are you Thelma Kennedy?"

"Yeah, that's me." Her eyes widened nervously.

"Detective Barkley," Ray introduced himself. "I'm with the Portland Police Bureau, homicide division." He flashed his identification. "I need to ask you a few questions."

"Questions about what?" she stammered.

Ray laid it on the line, telling her about the murder of Blake Wallace, in particular, and all the victims they knew of, in general. Thelma reacted as if she had been sucker punched, but quickly recovered.

"Come on in," she said.

Ray stepped into the house, the smell of cooking cabbage and fried chicken infiltrating his nostrils. The living room was small but neat with an old roll-arm sofa and chair, a cherry-veneer coffee table, and a television that was turned on.

After sending her daughter scurrying upstairs, Thelma offered Ray a seat, sitting directly across from him.

"Look," she began uncomfortably, "I'm real sorry about what happened to those men, but I don't know nothing about it."

Ray reserved judgment for now. "The victims were all beaten to death with wooden bats," he said equably.

"Yeah, I heard. So . . . ?"

"So you used a wooden bat when you attacked your husband," Ray said point-blank. "It doesn't look good, under the circumstances, if you know what I'm saying?"

She hit him with a look of indignation. "Yeah, I took a bat to my husband. That don't mean I went after those men!" Her nostrils flared. "I defended myself against a man who beat up on me because it made him feel superior. I don't have a beef against nobody else."

Ray leaned forward. "Not even some other batterers that were set free, perhaps prematurely, to hurt their victims again?"

Thelma's jaw hardened. "Hey, I done did my time for what happened between me and my ex. He'll never walk again or touch me again. I got a kid to raise. Why the hell am I gonna beat to death some abusive sons of bitches—even if they deserved it—

only to end up back in prison? Who would take care of my little girl then?"

Ray ignored for the moment the logic in her words, knowing that killers were rarely logical in their actions. "Even abusive bastards don't deserve to die the way these men did," he pointed out.

Thelma's eyes bulged. "And we don't deserve to get our asses whipped by men just for the hell of it. With nobody willing to lift a finger to help us. Till now . . ."

Ray found himself in the uncomfortable position of actually having to, in effect, stand behind men who battered their wives, girlfriends, and even children—though he didn't support their actions in any way, shape, or form. But as an officer of the law, he was duty-bound to uphold it.

Ray fixed the suspect with hard eyes. "I'll need to verify your whereabouts during the times these men were killed."

"No problem," she said confidently. "I ain't got nothin' to hide."

"Do you keep bats in the house?"

Thelma clearly resented the question. "No. It was *his* bat I used. He used it on me more than once. But nobody wanted to hear 'bout that."

Ray flinched. "I understand you've been volunteering your time at the Rose City Women's Shelter," he confirmed.

"I do what I can, when I can, to give something back," she said proudly. "They helped me out there when I needed it."

Ray narrowed his eyes. "Do you know of any other volunteers or people who stayed there who might have decided to take the law into their own hands?"

Thelma shifted unsteadily. "All the women I see there are decent people—not killers." She paused, adding, "If they wanted to kill anybody it would be their own abusers!"

"My theory," stated Ray matter-of-factly, "is that someone there decided other abusive men would be just as acceptable to target."

She shrugged. "That's your theory. Sorry. Can't help you there."

Or won't, he suspected.

Ray left the house doubting that Thelma Kennedy was the woman they were looking for. He saw no signs of a black BMW, which they still believed might have been driven by the killer. But he still didn't rule out that this sister, an embittered ex-con, or others associated with the shelter knew a hell of a lot more than they were willing to let on. Except maybe to each other.

And the victims of the Vigilante Killer.

30

Ray and Nina stepped into the KJM Studio in north-west Portland that afternoon. They came to talk to Laura Gleason. The twenty-eight-year-old legal reporter had been a regular in Judge Carole Cranston's courtroom during every domestic-violence trial that year. Her nightly reports had a de-cidedly hard edge on the victimization of women and the injustices of the legal system when it came to punishing batterers.

It made her a good suspect in the vigilante slay-ings of four men.

"She's visible," said Nina as they made their way through several corridors with various personnel in stages of production. "And she takes no prisoners when it comes to giving her views on the air."

"Makes you wonder what she does off the air," Ray remarked. "Maybe that's when she takes the prisoners *fatally*. Only the sentence of death is car-ried out swiftly and without mercy."

The door was slightly ajar, the nameplate on it reading, LAURA GLEASON, LEGAL REPORTER. Nina half knocked as she opened the door.

Laura was seated at an ergonomic pearwood laminate desk piled with papers, what appeared to be court transcripts, two coffee mugs, and a computer. She was tall and slender with a honey-brown skin tone, wearing a light-gray silk-twill suit and amber charmeuse camisole. Cinnamon-colored yarn braids bordered her square-shaped face. Green-brown eyes behind gold-rimmed glasses took in her visitors with curiosity.

Ray tried to imagine the attractive reporter wearing a blond wig, and armed with a wooden bat and a killer swing.

"How can I help you?" She spoke in a soft, friendly voice.

Ray showed his badge. "Detective Sergeant Barkley, Portland Police Bureau," he said. "And this is Detective Parker. We're investigating a recent rash of murders—"

"Ahh, the vigilante killings," said Laura, her wide eyes showing instant recognition. "Yes, I know all about them."

"We know," Nina said tersely. "We've seen your reports on the victims and their court appearances. You seem to have taken their releases very personally, Ms. Gleason."

Laura contorted her face. "I do take it *very* personally, Detective," she hissed. "Every woman in this city should, since we are all potential victims of abusive men like those bastards."

Ray moved up to the desk and peered down. "We

believe that someone has taken it upon herself to dispense her own brand of deadly justice on these men. Just how personal is this to you, Ms. Gleason?"

Laura remained unruffled, actually giving a mirthless chuckle. "If you're asking me if I killed those pricks, the answer is no. If you are asking if I shed any tears over their departure from this world, the answer is yes—tears of joy that they got a lethal dose of their own violent medicine!"

The detectives looked at each other.

"Those are tough words," snarled Ray, eyeing the suspect sharply. "Maybe too tough."

"I'm a tough reporter, Detective Barkley," Laura responded unflappably. "It's how I make my living and what my viewers expect. I won't apologize for that."

"No one's asking you to," Nina told her. "But I think you should know that your being at the trial of all the victims and doing volunteer work at the Rose City Women's Shelter makes you a viable suspect in their murders. For your sake, I hope you can account for your whereabouts in each instance?"

Laura yanked her glasses from her nose and glared. "Oh, I can," she spoke tartly. "You see, I was one of the first reporters on the scene when the news of the murders came in. But before that I was right here in the station preparing for the day's show. And there were plenty of witnesses around to vouch for me." She took a deep breath. "As for my volunteer work at the shelter, it's something I choose to do with my free time. You see, my daddy had a nasty habit of hitting my mother in the face with his fists till it was so swollen you couldn't even recognize her. Before she had even healed properly, he was back at it again. And again. Up until the day that son of a bitch died. Not by her hands, in case you're wondering. He got off easy with a heart attack. She wasn't so lucky. She died of cirrhosis of the liver after years of heavy drinking, often as an escape from the pain he'd inflicted upon her."

Some of these details had managed to elude them, thought Ray, in their investigation into her background—which included a number of failed abusive relationships, and time in a detox center for cocaine addiction.

All the more reason to consider Laura Gleason a serious candidate, he told himself, for brutally attacking and killing battering men.

"Nice try," Laura seemed to enjoy saying, "but you have the wrong sister. If the killer really is a woman, that is."

"Oh, we think it is," Ray said straightforwardly. "Someone who took her abuse *very* personally." *Maybe that someone is you*, he thought.

Their eyes locked.

Laura did not yield. "If you're trying to intimidate me into some sort of guilt-trip confession, Detective, you're wasting your time—and mine. I'm only doing my job. If I offend some abusive men in the process, they should take it up with my superiors."

"They might," said Nina sarcastically, "except they don't seem to live long enough to do so."

"Not my problem," Laura said coldly.

Ray found himself resenting having all men grouped into one dirty bag of laundry, as if male violence toward women were a given. He shot her a mean stare and said, "Maybe the woman killing these men should think the same way. She's only making things worse for herself . . . and all women." He paused deliberately. "I'm quite sure we'll be seeing you around, Ms. Gleason."

She glared at him defiantly. "I'm sure you will, Detective Barkley. You know where to find me!"

The detectives saw themselves out, the reporter not bothering to look up from her desk until they had left. A thoughtful expression appeared on Laura Gleason's face.

"Is she for real, or what?" Nina asked, shaking her head as they walked down the corridor.

"Scary, isn't she?" Ray said pensively. "Even scarier is the fact that she may not be our killer. If she is, she sure is daring us to prove it. And I'll be damned if we can even come close at this point."

Nina's mouth dropped. "Makes you wonder just how many Laura Gleasons there are out there— male haters with a passion."

"I wouldn't even want to venture a guess." Ray scratched his head glumly.

"Well, I'd guess there might be as many as the Blake Wallaces and Roberto Martinezes in the country," Nina ascertained with a hint of wryness in her voice. "And they're probably every bit as dangerous in their own way."

"Yeah, certainly one is," Ray said. "In her own unique way."

31

The defendant, Eddie Jackson, was a tall, thickly built African-American man in his mid-forties. His receding hairline was a dull gray, and his hostile eyes were as dark as asphalt. He wore a snug-fitting navy suit. It was a shade darker than the one worn by his attorney, a woman named Stella Howard. She was petite next to Eddie, with a curly brownish bob, tea-colored skin, ruby lips, and a petulant pout.

Eddie Jackson, an auto mechanic, was on trial for assaulting and raping his girlfriend, Emilie Evans. He had stubbornly resisted a plea bargain, insisting he was merely defending himself from her attack and that there had been no rape. In the process he had broken her nose and knocked out most of her front teeth.

The prosecutor was a grim-faced attorney named Alex Wright. He was white haired, long nosed, red faced, and on the lean side in a craggy gray suit. He liked to look at his watch as if it contained the mysteries to the center of the universe.

Carole watched him from her vantage point, from which she could see the entire courtroom. She waited impatiently as the lawyers went back and forth, presenting their cases, almost toying with the jury, daring them to convict or acquit.

A tall, husky man wearing a cheap brown suit entered the courtroom and walked up to the prosecutor without missing a beat. He whispered something in his ear, causing Wright to wrinkle his nose as if he had just smelled a dead rat. Wright then got the attention of Stella Howard, who had seemed to be gaining points with the jury.

The two lawyers conferred, as if no one else were present. They finally split up, and Howard said something to her client. Jackson shook his head a couple of times, though he seemed to be miles away from understanding what was going on.

The attorneys met with Judge Cranston, and she listened with interest. She finally nodded with a look of disappointment on her face, and sent them back to their respective tables.

Favoring the defendant with a look, the judge said colorlessly, "Mr. Jackson, your attorney and the prosecutor have come to terms on a plea bargain. It will require that you pay a fine, undergo substance-abuse treatment and counseling for batterers, and complete two hundred and fifty hours of community service. Is that agreeable to you?"

Eddie Jackson scanned the court, as if he were looking for someone, faced his attorney, and then looked at the judge. "Yeah, Your Honor," he spoke huskily. "It's agreeable."

Judge Cranston looked at him with serious reservations, glared at both lawyers, and back at Jackson again. "The defendant is free to leave," she said sternly. "Court's adjourned."

There was a smattering of mild exclamations of surprise and murmurs in the courtroom as the defendant and his attorney left the room quickly, as if to escape a lynch mob.

The judge lowered her head as if in shame and took a deep breath to compose herself. She quietly escaped to her chambers amid the commotion that followed.

Stella Howard declined to answer any questions from a few overzealous members of the press who seemed to live for these types of domestic-violence cases. She also recommended to her client that he avoid drawing any further attention to himself. She, and anyone else who followed the local news, knew that a psychopath was on the prowl killing accused or convicted batterers who were set free. Or escaped justice, according to some. The last thing she wanted was for Eddie Jackson to become another victim.

As it was, he was lucky to have gotten off with a relatively weak sentence and no jail time, she knew full well. This was the result of DNA tests that were inconclusive on the rape charge, implying that Emilie Evans could have had sex with another man. The prosecutor had suggested that it might be best for all parties concerned if they accepted a plea bargain.

Stella believed she had a good chance to win this case. But, given the recent climate with respect to domestic violence, she had advised her client that this might be the best he could hope to come up with to avoid jail time.

Now she regarded Eddie Jackson as she pulled up

to the bungalow where he lived. He looked at her with a smug smile.

"Thanks," he said gratefully. "I owe you one."

Stella dismissed this, wanting no favors from the man. "You owe me nothing, Eddie. I only did what you paid me to do."

He grinned lasciviously. "And you were worth every penny, Counselor."

"I hope you take advantage of your freedom by staying away from Ms. Evans," Stella warned him, noting that she had been the prosecution's star witness against him.

"Don't worry about that," he said. "Far as I'm concerned that bitch and I are through! I just want to get on with my life and find someone who can appreciate me. Know what I mean?"

Stella felt the weight of his menacing eyes ogling her. For the first time a trickle of fear ran through her veins. Or maybe not the first time, if she were honest about it. She had believed all along that he had been guilty of beating up his girlfriend and had probably raped her as well. But as a criminal defense attorney, Stella also believed firmly that it was her duty to defend her clients to the best of her ability. Even if it meant getting them off—or him, in this case. Now she began to have second thoughts about that.

She glared at him. "Don't even think about it, Eddie," she told him with a sharp edge to her voice. "I'm definitely not your type."

He got the message, flipping her a cocky grin. "If you say so, Ms. Howard."

Stella watched for a moment as Eddie Jackson

sauntered away confidently. She drove off, hoping she had not made a tragic mistake in taking on this client. And in the process possibly putting some other woman at risk of bodily harm.

32

Eddie Jackson lumbered up his sidewalk, still watching as Stella drove away. He envisioned what it would be like to have a piece of that fine sister when she was without the lawyer clothes. Under other circumstances he might have taken what he wanted. But he wouldn't press his luck with that frigid bitch. It wasn't worth it.

Eddie unlocked the front door and went inside the bungalow. It was dark and smelled of mildew, as though uninhabited and closed off for years. He put on the light in the kitchen and got a forty-ounce bottle of malt liquor out of the refrigerator.

In the living room he flopped onto a well-worn recliner, opened the bottle, and guzzled down about half. He thought about Emilie. That bitch was a fighter. He gave her credit for that much, often giving as good as she got.

But that night he had been the one doing the taking. He'd had it with her mouthing off to him and coming up with one lame-ass excuse after another for not putting out. Finally he lost it and forced himself onto and into her after beating the bitch into submission.

Even with that he had never expected Emilie to turn him in. To testify against him. To humiliate him. To damned near send him to prison.

The stupid bitch had been seeing someone else all along, thought Eddie, swallowing more malt liquor. At least that was what the DNA tests of semen taken from her suggested. He wanted to hurt her badly for that. But his mama didn't raise an idiot. Beating the hell out of Emilie again would only give him some satisfaction, but not enough to make it worth serving time as a result.

And there was something else, he considered nervously. There was a killer on the loose, going after brothers like him. Taking batting practice on their heads like they were human baseballs. Right now wasn't a good time to be too visible. He had to be careful and keep his guard up. He would be damned if some bat-wielding bitch got the better of him!

Just then Eddie Jackson heard a sound, almost like the drop of a pen on the stained brown carpeting. In the shadows he thought he saw someone.

"Who the hell's there?" he asked, his heart suddenly racing. He jumped to his feet, straining his eyes in the direction of the darkened dining room. But he could see nothing and decided he had let paranoia get the best of him.

Get a grip, man, he told himself angrily. *Don't let this broad mess with your mind.*

There was another sound. This one was heavier, as

if something were being dragged. Eddie swiveled toward the kitchen. There was a tall, good-looking sister standing there with blond locks and a fierce look in her eyes. She was holding a wooden bat and wearing dark clothes and gloves.

For an instant Eddie felt as if he had seen her before. Where? Before he could digest this, much less decide how to deal with the threat; the bitch came at him with blinding speed, lifting the bat in the same motion. She swung at his head. He managed to get his arm up to catch the force of the bat. It shattered the bone in his elbow, and he let out a howl that could wake the dead.

"Did you really think you would get off that easily, Eddie, *brotha?*" she told him in a chilling voice.

"Who the hell are you?" he asked, trying to fight the pain and get away from this crazy woman.

"I'm the last *sistah* you will ever see, you sick bastard!" she shrieked. "At least in this world. See you in hell."

She swung the bat again. This time it went right through his limp arm and landed squarely on the side of his head. Eddie fell to his knees, his vision blurred, his head feeling as if it were about to explode.

He was right, as the next blow landed with such force that it fractured bone and spewed tissue from his head. Another blow to the head and it splattered like a watermelon.

"You knocked out practically all of poor Emilie's teeth, asshole!" the woman screamed. She then proceeded to knock out most of *his* teeth. "How does it feel to have the tables turned on you? Then you raped her, you black cocksucker!"

She dug the bat into his groin and then pounded away at it mercilessly.

"I hate men who beat and rape women to satisfy their depravities!" she blared.

Remarkably the victim was still semiconscious and cognizant that he was about to die. The intense pain that ripped through Eddie Jackson made him want the end to come sooner than later.

He got his wish.

She rammed the bat into his face, crushing it and Eddie's life with it.

The woman was outraged. "Don't you go out on me, asshole. I'm not through with you yet."

She proceeded to continue beating him to a pulp, until there was literally nothing left but blood, broken bones, and a distorted mass that had once been a human being.

Satisfied that her mission had been accomplished, the woman dumped the bat on the messy pile of flesh and bones. She then quietly walked to the batterer's bedroom. There she removed her gloves and clothing, putting them in the duffel bag. She slipped on a sweater, jeans, and running shoes.

She went out the back door and into the alley, where her car was waiting. After putting the duffel bag in the trunk, she climbed into the front seat and drove off.

For a millisecond she regretted what had happened—as she had with the other bastards whom she had delivered straight into hell. But this misgiving was overcome by a sense of purpose and duty. She considered herself the avenging angel for all women who suffered at the hands of men. She couldn't let them off the hook, even if the courts saw fit to, any more than the men showed mercy on the women they beat and brutalized.

She blended in with traffic and appeared to be merely another rush-hour driver simply looking to get to the safety and comfort of home.

33

Carole arrived home at five thirty sharp. She was tired after a long, exhausting day, and looked forward to having a nice, hot bath and a glass of wine. She kicked off her mules and began rummaging through the mail when the phone rang.

"Hello," she answered on the third ring.

There was a grunting, gasping noise.

"Hello?" she repeated.

"Carole," said the rushed voice, "this is Vivian Wolfe."

Carole sensed by her labored breathing that something was wrong. "What is it, Vivian?"

"I think I'm having a miscarriage," she slurred. "There's blood and—"

"Where's Stuart?" asked Carole frantically.

"I don't know," Vivian cried hysterically. "I tried to reach him at his office, but he wasn't there. I didn't know who else to call."

"It's all right." Carole tried to remain calm. "I'll call nine-one-one."

"Can you come over?" pleaded Vivian. "I don't want to go to the hospital alone."

"You won't have to," promised Carole. "I'll be right there." She paused. "What's your address?"

Without giving much thought to anything else, Carole quickly dialed 911 for an ambulance. She had no experience in dealing with pregnant women, but knew enough to recognize that time was of the essence. Maybe it was not a miscarriage, she prayed, and the baby would be unharmed.

Carole called a cab. With any luck she would arrive at the house at the same time as the ambulance.

She wondered where Stuart was at a time when his wife needed him most?

Carole felt a bit nervous as the cab pulled up to the residence. She had never been to Stuart's house, which he'd purchased shortly after getting married. Though he and Vivian had invited her over, it somehow didn't seem right, considering the nature of her previous relationship with Stuart.

Now none of that seemed to matter. All that was important was trying to save his unborn child's life.

Carole rode to the hospital with a frightened Vivian, holding her hand tightly along the way. "It'll be all right," she tried to console her.

"Will it?" asked Vivian skeptically, sobbing. "If I lose the baby, Stuart will blame me. I know it!"

"Don't be silly," Carole scoffed. "He can't hold you responsible for something that's not your fault any more than his." *Could he?* she wondered. *Not the man I thought I knew.*

Vivian's lips trembled as she said, "This can't be happening. Not now . . . not when things seemed like they were finally starting to come together in my life."

Carole wiped the perspiration from Vivian's brow and tried to remain positive. She could only hope that Stuart came home and got the message that they were at the hospital. She felt uncomfortable taking his place in this delicate situation.

In the emergency room, doctors and nurses attended to Vivian like the trained professionals they were, while Carole paced in the waiting area. The ordeal made her wonder how she would deal with a similar situation. Could she ever get over losing a child? Would she ever be in a long term, loving relationship where having a child was even possible? Or was there no hope for that at this stage?

Stuart came running into the corridor as if his pants were on fire. Carole met him halfway.

"I came as soon as I got the message," he told her, huffing heavily, as if he had just completed a marathon. "Where is she?"

Carole told him, watching the strain on his face deepen. "Vivian said she tried to reach you. . . ."

"I had to meet a client," Stuart explained defensively. "I left word at the office where they could—"

"It doesn't really matter now," Carole cut in, realizing he owed her no explanation. "What's important is that your wife needs you."

"I know," he lamented, running his hand across his face like a towel. "I have to go to her . . . them!"

Carole followed as Stuart raced down the corridor to the room where Vivian was being treated. A burly, dark-haired doctor stepped out, blocking Stuart's advance like a defensive lineman.

"Are you the husband?"

"Yes." Stuart's voice was gravelly. "How is she?"

The doctor averted his eyes, instead meeting Carole's. She could see by the sadness in his deeply tanned face that the news was not good.

"I'm Dr. Sheppard," he said, facing Stuart again bleakly. "Afraid I have bad news. Your wife lost the baby—"

"No, dammit!" Stuart cursed, as if his whole world had suddenly fallen apart.

"I'm truly sorry," the doctor said. "She's been sedated, but you can see her now."

Carole was at a loss for words. She knew Stuart was hurting, and she could not put herself in his shoes. All she could do was give him a hug in support. He hugged her back, as if not wanting to let go.

Then abruptly he did, and dashed into the room to be with his wife. Carole was left alone with the doctor.

"Will Vivian be all right?" she asked him hesitantly.

"Physically, yes." He frowned and his mouth hung open while waiting for the words to catch up. "Mentally, I don't really know. . . ."

Carole sensed there was something else on his mind. "What is it?"

He paused. "I probably shouldn't be saying this, but it's possible that she may have helped herself to lose the baby."

Carole thought she might not have heard him correctly. "What?"

Suddenly Dr. Sheppard looked as if he regretted mentioning it to her. "This is strictly off the record and likely can't even be proven," he stressed, "but I've seen cases like this before where a mother who didn't want a baby badly enough was able to virtually will it out of her."

This made no sense to Carole, and she doubted its credibility. Still, as she looked through the door at Stuart comforting his wife, she couldn't help but think about Vivian's earlier reluctance to bring a child into this world.

Was it even possible that she made this happen? she wondered.

Feeling it was best to leave Stuart and Vivian alone to share their grief, she left the hospital.

34

Eddie Jackson had been dead for approximately twelve hours, according to the medical examiner. His brother, who had a key to the house, found his badly beaten, bloodied, and disfigured body. Police technicians combed the place for possible evidence, with yellow crime-scene tape cordoning off the property.

"Someone sure worked this brother over!" groaned Ray as he observed the latest handiwork of the so-called Vigilante Killer. The bat—coated with blood and what looked like brain matter from practically top to bottom—was her calling card, leaving little doubt as to its use as the murder weapon. It lay near the head of the corpse, as a reminder of the damage the murderer had inflicted on it specifically, and the entire body of the victim in general.

"Looks like our killer is getting bolder," remarked Nina. "She's even willing to follow her victims home now and do them in."

"Maybe she already had the place staked out,"

Ray suggested, "and was waiting here when Jackson arrived."

It didn't take much digging to learn that the deceased had just copped a plea, ending his trial prematurely. Or, for that matter, that it all took place in Judge Carole Cranston's courtroom.

All of which disturbed Ray, but still did nothing to make him believe Carole was involved in any way. Though clearly someone wanted them to think in those terms.

"If our killer was at the trial," he said, "she would have had plenty of time to beat Jackson here, then take him by surprise."

"I agree." Nina nodded thoughtfully. "And I'll just bet this was the surprise of his life—or should I say *death*. . . ."

Ray sighed. "The dude probably never even had a chance." Which, he thought, was the advantage the killer had over her victims: catching them off guard and unable to react before it was too late.

They sidestepped the body as if it were a poisonous snake and made their way outside, where permission was given to remove the deceased.

Walking toward their car, Nina said, "We're definitely dealing with a woman who believes in making sure the deck is heavily stacked in her favor."

Ray's brows knitted. "All the more reason why we have to catch her while we still have a few cards up our sleeves."

Nina looked at him dubiously. "You aren't hoarding any cards you haven't told me about, are you, Barkley?"

"Now, would I hold out on you, Parker?" he said earnestly. "I think not."

She gave him the evil eye. "So what's up with these cards . . . ?"

He faced her. "Well, we know our killer's connected in some way to the shelter and the court, as well as indirectly to who she's targeting. And that she has more than likely been abused by one or more men. Probably badly enough that she has nightmares about it, which she turns into a private hell against others who fit the bill. That gives us something to work with, and maybe more than she realizes. Now all we have to do is try to get one step ahead."

"Try telling that to our superiors. I'd say they're probably sweating bullets about now, wondering if we have our heads stuck up our asses."

Ray tried to smile but couldn't. Not when he knew she was right. It wasn't just batterers whose lives were on the line. He and Nina too were on the spot with this case. The longer it took to catch this elusive killer, the tighter the noose would be around their necks.

He put his hands to his throat, as if feeling the increasing pressure.

Stella Howard had been the last-known person to see Eddie Jackson alive, aside from his killer. Ray and Nina sat in her office on the fifth floor of the Ticknor Building downtown, hoping she might be able to provide information that could be helpful.

Ray studied the small stature of the attorney. He tried to imagine her as a murderess, thinking, *What better cover than to represent scum like Jackson, only to kill them later?*

For some reason this very thought made him think of Carole. She too had the perfect cover for a killer, in theory, given her association with the court and her outside interest in domestic violence—right down to being a contributor to the Rose City Women's Shelter. But he knew that reality gave way to such far-fetched macabre scenarios. Neither Carole nor Stella fit the psychological profile of a serial killer or psychopath, Ray told himself doggedly. In Stella's case, even the body type was inconsistent. The tall, statuesque woman they were looking for was far less balanced and much more cunning and dangerous.

"I dropped Eddie off at his house at around seven thirty," Stella was saying, sitting behind the mahogany desk that was seemingly too large for her size. Her wide-eyed look betrayed the shock of his death.

"Did you see anyone else?" Ray asked.

She mused. "Not that I can remember."

"What about cars?" Nina looked at her. "Did you see any on the street that you can identify? Make? Model?"

Stella made an embarrassed face. "I'm sorry, but I can't help you there either," she said with obvious regret. "I'm usually pretty good at details, but I guess my mind was preoccupied."

"Did Jackson give you any indication that he was expecting company?" Ray tossed at her, though he doubted the man had any knowledge of his deadly visitor. Not unless the brother had a death wish.

"No," Stella said. "Eddie Jackson kept to himself for the most part."

"Maybe there was someone at the courthouse that he talked to?" questioned Nina. "Or seemed unusually attentive toward?"

Stella considered this. "Only Judge Cranston," she said nonchalantly. She added, "But, of course, that's not what you wanted to hear, is it?"

Nina and Ray exchanged glances, each thoughtful.

Ray said, "We believe that whoever killed Jackson probably attended his trial or stayed close to it. The killer probably either followed him home or got there before he did. Anything at all that you can remember or tell us might help us find whoever did this to your client."

Stella fidgeted. "I'm sorry, but this has really freaked me out. I actually thought about Eddie Jackson being a possible target of this Vigilante Killer, but the fact that it actually happened—"

"Unfortunately it may not be the last time it happens," warned Ray. "As long as the killer remains on the loose, no man in this town can afford to let his guard down."

"There's nothing else I can tell you," Stella told them, "that I haven't already said. Except—"

She hesitated, prompting Nina to urge her on. "What . . . ?"

Stella gazed away and back again. "Well, Eddie sort of came on to me just before I dropped him off. It was kind of eerie and uncomfortable. I remember thinking that he wasn't the type of man I could ever be interested in." She sighed. "I guess in a strange way, someone else was."

Ray made a wry sound. "Yeah, whoever put Jackson out of commission has an unnatural interest in abusive men."

"I hope you catch her—and soon!" Stella said vehemently. "It's reaching the point where many lawyers are beginning to question the wisdom of getting their clients off, only to see them killed by someone who couldn't—or wouldn't—accept the outcome of the case."

"Maybe you should try switching to the other side," suggested Nina dryly. "It seems these days prosecutors are in a no-lose position. They either win the case outright or do so by a self-appointed judge and jury."

Stella shook her head. "Thanks, but no thanks. I like to know I win or lose my cases fair and square."

35

Emilie Evans worked at a department store in southwest Portland. Ray and Nina found her stocking shelves. The thirty-three-year-old former girlfriend of Eddie Jackson was nearly six feet tall and slender, wearing the store uniform. She had jet-black hair pulled back severely into a short ponytail, and big brown eyes. Her soft brown skin had an ashen tint, and her nose was crooked from having been broken.

The detectives identified themselves, and Emilie flashed an awkward smile, revealing recently replaced teeth.

"I guess I was expecting you," she said, putting some cleaning products on the shelf. "Eddie's brother phoned me with the news."

"Is there someone where we can talk?" asked Ray.

"Sure," Emilie said, wiping her hands on her pants. "It's time for my break anyway."

They went outside the store, where Emilie lit a cigarette.

"So I guess you want to ask me about Eddie?" she asked, exhaling smoke through her nostrils.

Ray studied the victim's ex. "Had you seen or spoken to Jackson since his release?"

"No." Emilie sucked on the cigarette. "I had no reason to. We were through. After what he did to me, I never wanted to see him again." She sighed. "To be honest with you, I was afraid he'd come after me after I testified against him."

"Only someone came after him with a bat instead," noted Nina. "Do you know anything about that, Emilie?"

She blinked her curly lashes. "If you're asking me if I killed Eddie or had someone else do the job, the answer is no. I'm not stupid—not anymore, since I left that bastard. I know I'm the first one you'd suspect. But I could never have been involved in murder—no matter how much I hated the person."

"But you did hate Jackson enough to *want* him dead?" Nina asked straightforwardly, glancing at her partner.

Emilie wrung her hands. "No, I didn't hate Eddie enough to want him dead," she responded tersely. "I'm not even sure I hated him at all. I only wanted to be left alone to get on with my life."

"Can you account for your whereabouts last night between seven and eight o'clock?" Ray peered at her.

"Yeah," Emilie answered easily, taking a drag on the cigarette. "I was right here. Worked the cash register from five to nine. You can look at my time card, talk to my boss, or whatever."

Nina stepped forward. "Have you ever been to the Rose City Women's Shelter?"

Emilie drew a sharp breath. "A couple of times," she replied self-consciously. "For a while there I felt as if I had nowhere else to go. The people at the shelter were really supportive of my situation."

Someone may have been too damned supportive, thought Ray, before asking, "Was there anyone you can think of at the shelter who seemed particularly hostile toward batterers?"

"Yeah," Emilie said matter-of-factly. "How about *everyone* who's ever been hit by a man? When you're forced to live with strangers in a place that ain't hardly the Ritz because you're too afraid to go home, it makes you hostile toward all abusive men. You know what I'm saying?"

"Looks like someone did you a favor then," Nina said abruptly. "Eddie Jackson won't be around to hit you or anybody else ever again. His killer made damned certain of that with a bat and lots of hostility."

Emilie tossed the cigarette. "You'll probably find this hard to believe, but I really am sorry that Eddie is dead. We used to be good together—even great. Maybe after he'd had some counseling or something he could have gotten better with his temper . . . and drinking. I don't know." She looked down at her shoes. "I guess none of that matters now."

"It matters," Ray told her. He felt a certain degree of sympathy for women like her who couldn't seem to let go of the men who abused and conned them, even in death. He couldn't even begin to put himself in their shoes, any more than he could those of the killer who seemed hell-bent on ridding the streets of such men.

* * *

It was nearly nine o'clock that night when Ray rang the bell at Carole's building. He had missed her like crazy for a few days now, but work and long hours had kept them apart. Just as it was now bringing them back together, he thought uneasily.

She buzzed him in.

At her door Ray thought of just how fine Carole was—more attractive each time he saw her. But he also saw a vulnerable side to the lady, one that he had yet to tap into.

"Hello, there, stranger," Carole greeted him with a smile; practically modeling the slinky periwinkle dress she wore.

"Hello, yourself, baby."

Inside he kissed her hard on the mouth, and she gave it back to him just as hard. He could feel her trembling.

Or is it me shaking? Ray wondered.

He pulled back and gazed into her cocoa eyes, wishing to hell he didn't have to spoil the mood.

"There's been another murder," he said bleakly.

Carole blinked. "Eddie Jackson," she stated knowingly.

"Yeah," Ray muttered. "Looks as if the killer laid a trap for him in his own house. And he fell into it like a damned rat."

"Any leads on the killer?" Carole asked steadily.

Their eyes locked as Ray considered the question.

"Nothing that can lead to an arrest," he told her honestly. "This killer has been very good at covering her tracks and making us look bad." That was putting it mildly.

"I wish I could help you, Ray." Carole furrowed her brow. "Or is that why you're here? Do you need to know if I have an alibi for the time of Jackson's death?"

Ray felt knots forming in his stomach. "I'm not here to question you, Carole." *But since you brought it up . . .* he thought miserably.

Carole seemed to read his mind. "Just so happens I was at the hospital helping a friend try to save her pregnancy. . . ." Her voice trailed off. "Unfortunately, she lost her baby."

Ray could see how much this had affected her. And because of that it affected him too. He was glad, though, that she could account for her whereabouts to others who might try to railroad her.

"I'm sorry."

"So am I," she lamented. "Sometimes the world is just so unfair."

"I know," he told her sympathetically.

"Even worse is that I'm not sure she really wanted the child she lost," Carole reflected. "Certainly not as much as her husband did. Now they're both being punished for it."

"Losing a child isn't punishment, Carole." Ray put his hand on her soft elbow. "It happens. And in most cases there's not a damned thing you can do but deal with it." He sensed she felt some sort of guilt, as though this were her fault. He was seeing a whole new side to the lady. One that showed just how much she cared about life.

Carole seemed to take comfort in his words as Ray wrapped his virile arms around her.

They kissed again, this time for a longer duration and with a more profound sense of need. Ray could feel the stiffness of Carole's body give way to the tenderness of his touch. They ended up in the bedroom, where they made love.

The sex was more passionate than ever, their bodies in harmony with their minds. Each raised the height of their intimacy to a new level of lovemaking, focusing all their thoughts and attention from head to toe and everything in between.

Ray and Carole were pressed against each other on their sides, panting and grasping, limbs intertwined this way and that, desperate to achieve every ounce of satisfaction from each other, as if tomorrow would never come. When it was over, all that was left was the slow and pleasing recuperation, as though returning from a fantasy vacation, or perhaps a sixth dimension, where all was right with the world.

Ray wondered if this was something akin to heaven on earth. He had never known a woman like Carole Cranston. Never had feelings for a woman the way he was starting to feel for her. This frightened and exhilarated him at the same time. Was this the person he'd been waiting for all his life? Was he what she really wanted? Or were both biting off more than either of them could possibly chew?

"Have you ever thought about having a family, Ray?" Carole broke into his reverie.

Ray looked down at the top of her head resting on his shoulder. "Thought about it once," he admitted. "But not too deeply, since I had a wife who was too damned busy thinking about herself to notice. Hasn't been anyone serious enough in my life since to do much thinking along those lines. How about you?"

Carole absorbed the question for a moment. "I once thought I would never be ready for a family," she said. "My husband didn't seem to object much. And my career seemed to affirm my choice."

"And now . . . ?" he asked with interest.

She sighed. "Now I think a family might not be such a bad thing," she said. "But only if my man felt the same way, and if it it was practical within the scheme of our lives."

"Spoken like a true judge." Ray chuckled, surprised that he could talk about this so naturally, as if he had no qualms about the issue of a family. And maybe he didn't, with the right woman.

Carole blushed. "Well, let's face it, I don't have that many years left before the decision to have children will be taken out of my hands. I guess I'm hoping it doesn't reach that point."

Ray knew he had Carole at a decided disadvantage in that regard, and felt a trifle guilty because of it. Still, he hardly considered her over the childbearing hill just yet. He put a hand on her exposed right breast, caressing. "These days, baby, many women are having children well into their forties," he said comfortingly. "So I don't think you have too much to worry about, as far as having to make any snap decisions."

Carole moaned as Ray's finger circled her nipple. "Hold on now," she said. "I'm not going to be one of those forty-plus-year-olds giving birth for the first time, thank you. The idea of being in my sixties when my children are ready for college doesn't have a great deal of appeal."

"I heard that," Ray conceded. "Then they might accidentally call you Grandma."

"Not without a *grandpa* handy, honey," Carole countered, and laughed thoughtfully.

Soon both were laughing at the odd notion before settling down into touching and holding, in between some kisses.

Ray found himself wondering what it might be like to have children of his own—*their* children. As long as they had their mother's looks, everything would be perfect, he mused.

"So what are we taking about," he ventured curiously, "one, maybe two kids?"

Carole did not hesitate when she responded, "One or two kids." She favored him. "Why, are you ready to become a daddy, Mr. Police Detective?"

Ray licked his lips, feeling put on the spot. "Hey," he responded jovially, "I might be game. Of course, I'd want to practice the process a whole lot first—so we can make sure we've got it down pat."

Carole chuckled. "Come here, baby," she murmured, reaching for his mouth with hers. "Practice does indeed make perfect."

Ray lingered in tasting her lips. "Oh, you think so?" he teased.

"Why don't we just find out?"

"Why don't we?"

They made love again, taking it slowly, discovering all there was to learn about each other's body and erogenous zones, and then some.

When Ray left, there had been no more talk about family and children. There would be more time for that later, he hoped, when the time and circumstances were right.

For now, there were more immediate things to occupy his attention. Like a relationship that was beginning to grow on him like ivy.

And a vicious killer run amok.

36

Esther Reynolds made sure she wasn't being followed, doubling around three blocks before she went to the secret place. As expected, the woman was there waiting for her.

"You're late!" the woman said impatiently.

"Had to be careful," Esther told her. "The streets are crawling with cops. Any one of them would love to get their hands on you."

"Over my dead body, honey," she growled.

"Well, my dear," Esther spoke uneasily, "it may well come to that. You're scaring everyone nearly half to death. Chances are if they even come near you they'll shoot first and ask questions later."

The woman, who was standing in an intimidating posture, glared at Esther. "Let them try. I'm only doing what I was meant to do—for me, for you, and all the others like us. Those bastards can't be allowed to ruin our lives anymore."

"I agree." Esther felt herself perspiring. "But there

has to be a time when enough is enough. I think that time is now."

The woman walked up to Esther, her breathing quickening, and stated emphatically, "I'll decide when enough is enough—you hear me? I've come too damned far to stop now. There's still work to do. Scores to settle, once and for all."

Esther edged back a step or two. "But don't you see, you're jeopardizing our entire operation. The shelter could be shut down, and then where will those women go who need a safe place? They could be turned away from other overcrowded shelters and end up back with men who will abuse them, and worse." She took a ragged breath. "The price is simply too high to continue to support your actions."

The woman grabbed one of Esther's wrists with such force that she winced in pain.

"You listen to me, bitch! If I go down, you'll go down with me. And everyone else who supported this thing but ran scared when the going got tough."

"But the police are—" Esther's voice quavered as she tried to speak. She was cut off.

"Don't let those dumb-ass cops intimidate you!" the woman screeched. "They have nothing to go on but the dead bastards who deserved the ass whippings they got. By the time I was through with them, believe me, they were damned glad death had come. If this has opened some eyes, then so be it. Isn't that half the point—letting those sons of bitches and all who support them know that we won't tolerate the beatings anymore? It's them or us. They're the ones who are on the defensive now. We can't go back to the way it was. I won't do it. *And neither will you!*" She released her iron grip on Esther's wrist.

Esther bit her lip to fight back the searing pain. "But they have a list of names," she stammered. "Your name's on it. It's only a matter of time before the police question you."

"Maybe they already have," the woman said with wry amusement. "Do you think I can't handle myself when confronted with assholes who would try to lock me up in some damned prison? Or a nuthouse?"

"I-I didn't say that." Esther tried not to look at the rage in the woman's features.

"You didn't have to. I can see it in your face and hear it in your voice." The woman sucked in a deep breath, then forced a smile to her lips. "Don't worry about me, girl. I think I know a little bit about the legal system and how to deal with nosy, think-they-know-it-all police detectives. I'm not about to make it easy for them to put an end to the only justice some of us have ever known. All I need to know is if you can be counted on to keep your big mouth shut. Or are you willing to jeopardize everything so sisters like us have to crawl back into holes to try and escape the abuse through drugs, alcohol, self-abuse, suicide, and desperate prayers that never seem to be answered?"

Esther thought about it. She was caught between a damned rock and a hard place. To betray the woman would, in effect, be betraying herself and millions of other women who were not being adequately served by the justice system.

But to look the other way would be to reject her sense of decency and responsibility, and her feelings against taking the law into one's own hands. The killings, no matter how justified, simply could not continue.

Yet what choice did she have? Esther mused honestly. To hang the sister—no matter how far off the deep end she had gone—would, for all intents and purposes, be hanging herself as well, along with countless other women whose fates and fortunes may have rested on the fear and intimidation their batterers were feeling these days at the prospect that they might actually be hit back—only with deadly consequences.

"Well," the woman demanded coldly, "are you with me or against me?"

Esther gulped. When all was said and done, she knew that there was no turning back. Things had simply gone too far to retreat, even if she wanted to.

"I-I won't do anything to stand in your way, girl," she stammered.

The woman flashed a humorless smile, her eyes betraying the ire that motivated her actions. "Good to hear, girlfriend. We wouldn't want our persecutors to think it was open season again on all women, now, would we?"

Esther had no response, leaving well enough alone.

The two went their separate ways from there after agreeing that the safe house might not be so safe anymore. A new place would have to be established for future meetings.

The woman wondered as she drove away just how many more meetings there would be. She sensed that Esther was becoming a weak link in the chain of justice to be served. But she also knew that there was little chance the sister would mess things up for her. It would only endanger more women in the long run, something she doubted the shelter director wanted on her fragile conscience.

In the meantime, she knew what had to be done and was more than willing to carry it out as she had before.

Again and again.

She believed that no matter what happened to her there would always be someone to take her place in the battle to regain control over their lives from those who tried to dominate them with their fists. The genie was out of the proverbial bottle and could never be put back in.

The bastards had to pay for their sins, one way or the other. And she was going to collect in full force!

37

Nina was troubled by the connection between the courtroom and the shelter with regard to their vigilante. In her eyes there was only one real common denominator: Judge Carole Cranston.

But did that mean there was a serial killer beneath her judge's robe?

Or had her own objectivity been somehow compromised? Nina pondered uneasily, while sitting at her desk. It didn't take a rocket scientist, or even a damned good detective, to realize that brother Barkley was sleeping with the judge. She could see it in his eyes, his body language, and his disposition. Hell, she could even smell sex on the man.

But what was it to her what he did when off duty? And whom he did it with? Nina contemplated, drinking coffee that had turned cold.

Was she actually jealous of Carole Cranston, who seemed to have so much going for her? Or just envious of Ray's seeming happiness when her own personal life was in shambles?

Nina told herself it was neither. *I can deal with Ray having a life, even if I'm still trying to find one,* she thought. She was a detective first and foremost and took her job very seriously. This was no different. She had come too damned far to go back to shuffling pages at some corner desk while she watched others move up the ranks ahead of her, all because she and Ray had blown this case. That was the *only* reason why she had decided to go behind Barkley's back on this one. She was convinced she was onto something. Or someone.

But what?

Or who?

She enlisted the aid of a former cop turned private investigator to do a background check on Carole Cranston, with an emphasis on anything in her history that was unusual, such as domestic violence or any other violent activity. He'd left a message for her at the office to call him back, keeping it as innocuous as possible.

Nina had resisted running an official check on Carole Cranston, not wanting to make waves. *If you were going to accuse a prominent criminal court judge of murdering five men,* she thought, *you had damned well better have more to back you up than a bad feeling.*

Or concerns that a partner and ex-lover is doing the nasty with someone who may have been involved in a series of brutal murders in the Rose City.

Nina phoned the private eye that afternoon. Nelson Ross had been with the police bureau for fifteen years before retiring due to a bad back, bad attitude, and lack of motivation. Private snooping had given him a second career and a lot more time to engage in his favorite pastimes—women and fishing, not necessarily in that order.

"Ross Investigations," the deep voice answered.

"Hey, it's Nina."

"See you got my message."

"Loud and clear," she quipped.

"Got something for you," he said ambiguously. "How about you buy me lunch, and I'll tell you all about it?"

She had already eaten and knew he had a voracious appetite, but said with some misgivings, "This had better be good."

He gave a raspy chuckle. "Oh, I think it's enough to whet the appetite, baby."

Nina agreed to meet him at three. She took the afternoon off, claiming she wasn't feeling well. Even poor Ray had seemed overly concerned about her, making Nina feel even guiltier for pursuing this. But she could not ignore the fact that there were five people dead and one killer very much alive.

And Ray's girlfriend, for better or worse, was her prime suspect.

Johnnie & Aljean's Taste of Soul was one of the best restaurants in the city for Southern soul food.

Wearing a juniper pantsuit and mocs, Nina walked in and immediately saw the man she was looking for. Nelson Ross waved both hands at her from a table, as if he were doing jumping jacks. By the time she had glided through tables, he was standing—all six feet, six solid inches of him.

"Hey, girl," he said, grinning from ear to ear.

"What's up, Nelson?" she responded, a tiny smile playing on her lips.

Along with being tall, Nelson Ross was a mass of muscles and biceps inside a taupe houndstooth sport coat over a moss windowpane shirt, olive gabardine trousers, and tasseled loafers. He had a Hershey bar skin tone, was bald, and had bulging burnt-almond eyes. A tiny diamond stud earring was almost molded into one ear.

Nina had dated him briefly when she was a rookie. Nothing came out of it but a few laughs, a few tears, and a lasting friendship, along with an occasional favor both ways.

They sat.

"Caught the biggest bass you ever saw," Nelson bragged, spreading his massive arms in opposite directions, revealing an impressive wingspan.

"Hope *she* didn't bite," Nina couldn't resist.

Nelson's teeth gleamed. "Still got that quick wit about you, baby." He chuckled. "What is it they say about the bark being worse than the bite?"

"Touché," she tossed back at him.

"You want something to drink?" he asked, still smiling. He already had a pitcher of beer on the table, half-empty.

"Just coffee," Nina said, resisting the temptation of something stronger. She considered this still an official call.

Nelson nodded. "That's cool." He waved over a cute waitress with long groomed locks and a tight ass. She filled Nina's cup and left menus.

Nelson peered across the table. "So they've got you tied up in knots at the bureau with this vigilante thing, huh?"

"Let's just say it's been damned frustrating," Nina muttered, "to say the least."

"Yeah, I can imagine. It's definitely got me on my best behavior. You know what I'm saying?" He cracked an only slightly amused smile.

"Maybe that's a good thing, Nelson. You know that we've never taken any crap from brothers. Seems like someone wants to make sure you're reminded that if you get out of line, there's a heavy price to pay."

"I heard that," he moaned, drinking beer. "Problem is, the price seems to be *too* damned high these days. . . ."

"Can't argue with you there." She tasted the coffee thoughtfully. "So what have you got for me, brother man?"

Nelson licked his lips. "Well, I found out some real interesting things about the judge."

"Such as . . . ?" Nina could feel her stomach churning with anticipation.

He opened a folder on the table. "Looks like Judge Carole Cranston's had a hell of a tough go of it when it comes to domestic violence. At seven, she witnessed her old man beating her mother to death with his fists. After that she spent a few years in and out of mental hospitals trying to deal with it. . . ."

He put the mug to his mouth, and Nina waited with interest and contemplation.

"Then fifteen years ago her best friend from college went on trial for murdering her husband." Nelson glanced at the information. "Her defense was that he had abused her repeatedly over the years till she couldn't take it anymore and snapped. Carole Cranston testified on her behalf. A good lawyer got the friend off, but the whole thing must have seemed like déjà vu to Carole."

Nina sipped her coffee, her mind racing. Best friend? On trial for murdering her husband fifteen years ago? Got away with it as a battered woman? It all had an eerie familiarity to it.

She looked at Nelson. "You wouldn't happen to have a name for the best friend?"

"Sure do." He lifted a sheet of paper. "Let's see . . . name's Esther Reynolds."

Nina's eyes lit as though she had come face-to-face with an alien. Or perhaps the devil herself.

Nelson noticed. "Name ring a bell . . . ?"

"You could say that," Nina said, as some disturbing pieces of the puzzle began to fit into place. "Maybe a few bells."

Nelson scratched his pate. "In case you're interested, Reynolds's defense attorney was a dude by the name of Stuart Wolfe. I understand he's still practicing in the state."

Stuart Wolfe? The attorney with the black BMW whom they had visited.

Well, I'll be damned, thought Nina.

Could the killer have driven his car after all the night Blake Wallace was murdered? Perhaps someone who was Esther Reynolds's best friend and strong advocate against domestic violence—the honorable Judge Carole Cranston?

The plot thickens, Nina mused, feeling the rush of adrenaline. And Barkley, she feared, might be caught smack-dab in the middle of it.

"So what's going on in that pretty little head of yours, Nina?" asked Nelson.

"I don't think you want to know," she told him.

"Try me."

Nina reluctantly tossed some of her theories at Nelson regarding Carole Cranston as a possible serial killer, leaving out Barkley's unwitting involvement with her.

Nelson shook his head in amazement. "Man, if any of this turns out to be true, you could be sitting on a damned powder keg ready to explode."

"Tell me about it," she hissed. At the same time, she didn't want to have this thing blow up in her own face.

Nina grabbed the folder and rose to her feet. Looking down at Nelson she said, "I've got to go."

"Wait a minute." He frowned. "What about lunch?"

She pulled twenty-five dollars out of her purse and put it on a saucer. "It's on me, sweetheart, tip and all. You've earned it. See you around, Nelson. Thanks again!"

Nina left him sitting there while turning her attention to Carole Cranston and the Vigilante Killer.

Were they one and the same?

38

The law offices of Simmons, Wolfe, and Whitehead were located on the tenth floor of a downtown high-rise. Nina wasted no time flashing her identification at the startled receptionist and insisting on speaking to Stuart Wolfe. She buzzed him, and Nina was directed to his office.

Stuart met her at the door, looking dapper in a tailored dark suit and oxford shoes. "Detective Parker," he greeted her with a strained smile. "Didn't expect to see you again."

"Something's come up," Nina told him succinctly.

"Oh?" There was the slightest bit of alarm in his face. "Come in."

She stepped into a corner office with a large window overlooking the river. The mountains were also in view, presenting a lovely picture.

At what price was the brother's success? Nina wondered. Had he sold his soul to the devil? Been a party, willing or otherwise, to at least one murder? And quite possibly a string of others?

Stuart told his secretary over the speakerphone to hold all his calls. Directing his attention to Nina, he asked calmly, "So what's this all about? Surely you don't still suspect that I had anything to do with Blake Wallace's murder, or that my car was somehow involved?"

Nina regarded him shrewdly. "You tell me. . . ."

He gave her a befuddled look. "Excuse me?"

"Why don't you start by telling me about your defending Esther Reynolds fifteen years ago after she killed her husband?" Nina said straightforwardly. She watched him react. "Then you might tell me about *Judge* Carole Cranston's testimony during the trial and what your relationship is with these two women today. And last, I'd like to know if you think either or both might be capable of committing these vengeance murders that have sent shock waves throughout the city."

Stuart looked as if he had been frozen with his mouth half-open. He stared at Nina for a moment or two before saying languorously, "Please, sit down. . . ."

Nina sat in a plush maroon leather chair and watched as Stuart sat opposite her. She removed a small tape recorder from her purse and set it on a walnut table between them.

"Hope you don't mind?"

"Actually, I do," he said sternly. "I'll answer your questions, but *strictly* off the record."

"All right," Nina muttered, expecting as much from the clever attorney. She put the recorder back in her purse, turning it on at the same time.

"I defended Esther Reynolds because I believed she was justified in killing her husband," Stuart said evenly. "The man had beaten her senseless for years. She reached the breaking point that day, feeling it was either him or her."

"So like a black knight in shining armor, you came to the rescue and got her off on a charge of murder?"

"No, Detective—it wasn't quite like that," he responded tartly. "The *jury* got Ms. Reynolds off on self-defense."

"Thanks in large part, I assume, to Carole Cranston's testimony?" Nina peered at him as Ray crossed her mind.

"I'd be lying if I said otherwise. Carole's testimony was crucial to convincing the jury just what type of monster Esther Reynolds was married to." He sighed. "Since you're privy to this, I assume you also know that the two women have known each other since college?"

"Best friends, I heard," chirped Nina.

Without acknowledging this, Stuart said, "Well, Carole . . . Judge Cranston witnessed the abuse on more than one occasion and urged Esther to leave her husband. Unfortunately, by the time she did it was too late. He was too far gone in his addiction to beating the living daylights out of Esther at his whim."

Nina chewed her lower lip. "Are you still in touch with either Ms. Reynolds or Carole Cranston today?" *I think I pretty much know the answer to this one*, she thought.

Stuart hesitated. "Yes. I try to keep tabs on all my clients."

"But Carole Cranston was not your client." Nina gazed at him, one brow raised. "Was she?"

He crossed his legs nervously. "No, she wasn't.

But Ms. Cranston is a judge now," he pointed out. "And we run into each other from time to time in the courtroom."

Nina widened her eyes as she asked, "Were you aware that the judge witnessed her own mother being beaten to death at the hands of her father?"

Stuart's mouth tightened. "I'm not sure I should answer that, Detective."

"I think maybe you should, Counselor," she strongly urged. "This is not an attorney-client privilege thing. And it could be related to a murder investigation."

He clasped his fingers. "All right. So I did know. What the hell does that have to do with anything?"

"She told you?" Nina pressed.

"Yeah," he said reluctantly. "We became friends, and Carole thought I ought to know. There's no crime in that, Detective."

"Never said there was, sir. The crimes came years later—like now." Nina leaned toward him. "Were you and Carole Cranston ever lovers?" she asked bluntly.

Stuart's brow creased. "Now wait just a damned minute, *Detective* Parker," he blasted her. "My relationship with Carole Cranston is between her and me. I sure as hell am not going to allow you to trample over my personal life—or hers—for some sort of vicarious thrill! If you have anything else to ask me about the case you're working on, do it. If not, then this meeting is over!"

So they had been lovers, Nina told herself instinctively. Perhaps they still were. And possibly also in bed for a conspiracy to commit murder against abusive men who hadn't been held accountable for their sins.

She doubted that Barkley had any inkling about the long-term relationship between Carole Cranston and the very married Stuart Wolfe, with whom Ray could be competing for the judge's affections.

"I wasn't trying to get into your pants," Nina said, "or business. Or for that matter, the judge's sex life, per se. But I am trying to solve a number of brutal murders and need to work every angle. For instance, I'd like to know if you and Carole Cranston were still on friendly enough terms that she may have been able to borrow your car—since she doesn't have one of her own—to go to that garage and beat to death Blake Wallace?"

"That's totally absurd!" Stuart insisted, narrowing his eyes into slits. "Do you honestly think I'd allow my car to be used by Carole Cranston—or anyone else—to commit murder?"

Admittedly Nina found it hard to fathom the high-flying attorney risking it all under such circumstances. But then, people did all types of unfathomable things when it came to love, lust, or past fond memories.

She sucked in a deep breath. "In that case, Counselor, I'm sure you won't mind if we dust the car for prints and look for other evidence that it may have been a party to one or more murders?"

"You're welcome to," he said, regaining his cool demeanor. "You won't find anything. There's nothing there to find."

Was he that confident? Nina wondered. Or misguided?

"That notwithstanding," Stuart added, upon further reflection, "I think it's probably a good idea if you bring along a search warrant, Detective. I assume you and Detective Barkley have enough credible reasons and cause to convince a judge?"

Nina suspected that Stuart Wolfe knew this part would be an uphill battle. All she really had at this point were some rather loose circumstantial factors, at best, and gut instincts. But the fact that Wolfe was exercising this option made her even more suspicious.

"I think we have what we need to do just that," she said assertively. "If it's a search warrant you want, then you'll have it."

Stuart stood up, glaring at her. "Your case is headed in the wrong direction, Detective Parker!" His voice thickened. "If you seriously expect to be able to pin this Vigilante Killer rap on Carole Cranston or Esther Reynolds, then you're sadly mistaken. These women, for all their past grief and victimization, should be applauded for the contributions they've made to society, not vilified by people who are supposed to be on their side of the street!"

Nina knew from the look in his eyes that "those people" included sisters like her, who also happened to be an officer of the law. She felt the slightest guilt, as though she had turned her back on African-American women who were trying to do some real good. But in reality, she knew this wasn't about sisterhood or strides within the black community. It was about murder, plain and simple, and doing her job to see to it that a vindictive killer was brought to justice. Even if she had to step on a few tender toes along the way.

Nina got to her feet and met Stuart Wolfe's hardened gaze head on. "All I can say, Counselor, is that I honestly hope you're right about these upstanding women. I wouldn't want to see either end up behind bars as a serial murderess. But if you're wrong, then it's up to me to get a killer off the streets before she sets her sights on another target to murder."

Neither person gave any ground in their positions, staring each other down as if to blink might somehow lessen their resolve.

At the door Nina said as an afterthought, "By the way, Mr. Wolfe, I'd suggest you keep your own attorney handy. You just might need him."

In the corridor, she shut off the tape recorder and mused.

It was half past four when Nina arrived back at the station. Her journey had yielded some surprising and disturbing results. Now came the hard part.

Nina found Ray in his office doing paperwork, the one thing all cops dreaded most, next to counting dead bodies. She wondered how to tell him what she had dug up without his knowledge. And what the fallout might be.

I'll just have to take my lumps and hope that we can get beyond this, she thought.

"What the hell are you doing here, Parker?" Ray asked, surprised. "If I'm not mistaken, didn't you take the afternoon off after coming down with something?" He gave her a worried look. "Hope you didn't think I couldn't do without your bitching for even half a day?"

Nina made no attempt even to smile at his half-hearted effort at humor. "I do feel somewhat sick to my stomach," she told him. "But it has nothing to do with something I ate."

Ray cocked a brow. "So what does it have to do with?"

She breathed in deeply. "Carole Cranston."

"Carole—" His voice stopped on a dime.

Nina closed the door. She took the tape recorder from her purse and set it on his desk. Gazing at her partner, she said solemnly, "You need to listen to this. Then we need to talk. . . ."

39

Ray tried to come to grips with what Nina had just laid on him like cinder blocks.

Carole had seen her own mother murdered by her own father?

She was best friends with the director of the Rose City Women's Shelter, Esther Reynolds, and actually testified at her trial for killing her husband?

Carole had been involved with the married defense attorney Stuart Wolfe? As in, *lovers*?

Nina had said plaintively, "He didn't admit to it, but by the still-got-the-hots-for-her look in his eyes, he might as well have."

Damn, Ray cursed to himself, feeling like a jealous boyfriend—or even an indignant husband. *Why wasn't Carole up-front about her past—especially regarding Stuart Wolfe?*

This thought alone consumed Ray. When were they together? he found himself wondering. For how long? Was Carole still seeing Wolfe? Or wishing she could?

Even worse, Ray thought bleakly, was the prospect that Carole might really be the Vigilante Killer. Meaning he could have fallen in love with his worst nightmare, from a professional point of view. Hell, it wasn't exactly something he could stomach from the personal side of things either.

It made Ray ponder if he really knew at all this woman he'd let into his life. What other secrets was she harboring?

Did he truly want to know . . . ?

He answered in his mind: *Not necessarily, but I need to know.*

"Why the hell didn't you come to me with this from the start?" he demanded, though he knew what she would throw back at him.

Nina squirmed in the chair across his desk, but kept her gaze fixed on Ray's face. "Why the *hell* do you think?" She snorted. "To you the judge seemed to walk on water. Maybe I would've felt the same way, had I let my *personal* feelings get in the way of my *professional* judgment, as you obviously did."

Ray bit his lip. "Maybe you don't know me as well as you seem to think you do, Parker," he hissed, feeling as if he were about to explode on the inside. "Or maybe you don't really know *her*."

"Will you wake up and smell the coffee, Barkley, for crying out loud!" Nina nearly levitated out of the chair. "I'm trying to save your black ass here. Mine too. This isn't about your sex life. Or senior detective status and superior attitude. It's about solving a case and saving lives. This was a judgment call, okay? I went with my instincts and common sense, which told me Judge Cranston was the one person who seemed to tie all the disjointed pieces together. If that's wounded your male ego or taken a bite out of your romantic adventure, I'm sorry!"

Ray took a long breath, steadying himself in the process. Deep down he knew she had done the right thing. Just as he would have had the situation been reversed.

That still didn't convince him that Carole was their killer. Not the woman he believed her to be. The one who had reached a part of him few others had.

But, he conceded, the circumstantial evidence was hard to ignore in the face of the facts they did have.

His feelings for Carole would have to be put on hold until he saw where this went. He hoped it wasn't all the way to hell and back.

"You did good, Parker," he told his partner in a sober voice. "Even if you didn't trust me enough to let me know what you were up to." He sighed. "Why don't we follow up on this information and go from there?"

Nina nodded thoughtfully, resisting any notion of rubbing salt into his obviously deep wounds. "All right. Deal."

They rode in awkward silence as Ray pondered what he knew about Carole and what he didn't. She had tried to tell him something, but he wouldn't let her. Maybe it was about her parents, he thought. Her father killing her mother, and how it affected Carole.

She could have wanted to tell him about her past relationship with Stuart Wolfe . . . and where they stood today.

Or had Carole actually wanted to confess to being an avenging angel for battered women? Ray tried to imagine. A serial murderess living on the edge of sanity?

He wondered if any of what they had was real. Or had Carole only been using him as a means to stay one step ahead of the investigation?

The questions seemed to outnumber the answers about ten to one. Ray wasn't sure he was up to having the pieces of the puzzle filled in where it concerned Carole the judge, lady, and lover. But he also knew he couldn't run away from the facts any more than he could the woman herself.

They had secured a warrant to search Stuart Wolfe's vehicle, in case he decided not to cooperate after all. Another warrant would be easier to get for other property searches, if this yielded anything significant.

It was later that afternoon when the detectives arrived at Stuart's office. Police technicians had followed them, prepared to go over the car with a fine-toothed comb. If there was anything inside or outside to tie the vehicle to any of the murders, they would find it.

Stuart was more than cooperative, walking them to the garage where the car was parked.

"This whole thing is crazy," he protested mildly. "You can't find something that isn't there."

"Let's hope not, Wolfe," said Ray menacingly. "For your sake."

But it wasn't his sake that Ray was really worried about, he knew deep down inside.

It was Carole's. If she could be tied to the car in any way, she would be in big damned trouble.

The techs got to work right away while Ray and Nina observed closely, alongside a stoic Stuart.

He gave Ray a hard look. "Carole really likes you, man, you know. I hope to hell you don't end up stabbing her in the back for something she couldn't—and wouldn't—have done!"

"Give it a rest, Wolfe." Nina tried to interject her two cents. "Playing the guilt trip won't work—not this time."

But Ray had to speak for himself. He faced Stuart man-to-man. "You seem to know a lot about her."

"Yeah, so what's your point?" Stuart said smugly.

Ray's nostrils flared. "My point is that if there's any backstabbing here it will come from *you*—if it's found that you were withholding information in a criminal investigation."

Ray seriously wondered if he could have betrayed Carole of his own accord, had Nina not stepped up to the plate, forcing him to do so as well. It was something he didn't want to think about at the moment, much less the future implications for him and Carole.

Stuart knitted his brows together. "And just what type of damned information do you think I'd be foolish enough to withhold, Detective?"

Ray glared at him. "For starters, knowledge that your car was being used in the commission of one or more murders."

"That's ludicrous! This whole thing is a sham. We both know it."

Before Ray could respond, one of the technicians said, "I think we may have found something. . . ."

Cliff Featherstone was a thirty-two-year-old Native American and eight-year veteran of the force. He climbed out of the car, plastic gloves molded to his hands, his tall, angular body righting itself. His long, shiny black ponytail contrasted with a beige complexion. He held up what appeared to be a bracelet.

"Found this wedged in the front seat," he said, looking from Nina to Ray. "Appears to have blood on it."

"Looks like a woman's bracelet," said Nina. "Hmm . . . cultured pearls. Expensive stuff." She looked at Stuart suspiciously. "Does your wife own a pearl bracelet, Mr. Wolfe?"

Without prelude, he answered convincingly, "No, she doesn't. Vivian hardly ever wears jewelry. Certainly not something so ostentatious, even if we can afford it."

"Maybe you bought it for someone other than your wife?" Nina questioned. "Someone who likes to wear expensive bracelets?"

Stuart shook his head vigorously in denial. "I have no idea where that came from. I've never seen it before in my life."

Ray studied the stunning bracelet as Featherstone held it up to his eyes. It was rose-toned, with a heart-shaped toggle. He had seen it before.

Or at least something like it.

Ray suddenly felt his stomach churn as if he were about to throw up. Carole had worn such a cultured-pearl necklace and matching earrings the night she came to his houseboat. He had found them captivating. He recalled her saying they were family heirlooms.

Did the set include a cultured-pearl bracelet? Ray wondered. Had Carole worn it the night Blake Wallace was killed? And somehow lost it in the shuffle?

Nina had observed his reaction. "What's the matter, Ray? You look as if you've seen a ghost."

Ray wished to hell he had. He might have been able to deal with the supernatural, or some other mystical phenomenon.

Instead, he knew that he could be looking at the one piece of evidence that could nail Carole as a murderess. Especially if the blood on the bracelet proved to be a DNA match for Blake Wallace's blood type, or any of the other dead batterers.

Ray didn't even want to think about the possibilities. Yet he had little choice, he realized, for there they were staring him squarely and frighteningly in the face.

40

Carole took advantage of the overcast, cool afternoon to run. It also gave her time to think about the direction her life was headed in. Things between her and Ray had reached a point where she believed they might actually have a future. One that could include a committed relationship, love and devotion, or possibly even marriage—though both had been down that road before and were not likely to jump into something on a whim.

Even children could not be ruled out, Carole reflected.

She considered that Vivian and Stuart had lost a child before ever having it. She had gone to visit them the day after the miscarriage and found that Vivian appeared to have all but recovered physically, though her mental state was still somewhat fragile.

"I never knew it would hurt so bad," Vivian had cried. "The baby was a part of my body, growing inside me. I don't know if I can deal with this."

"You will," Carole told her, "because you have to,

R. Barri Flowers

Vivian. Life goes on, no matter what awful things happen. You'll get another chance to have a child. Probably many more."

Vivian fixed her with sullen eyes. "I could never go through that again," she declared. "I'm just not strong enough."

"It'll take some time," Carole said feelingly. "But you'll be fine, honey. You're stronger than you think."

Was she really? Carole wondered. Or would Vivian be on a downward slide for the rest of her life? She could picture her never quite recovering from her loss.

Which begged the question: Had Vivian really wanted to have her baby? Or had the doctor been right in his suspicions that she had found a way to avoid giving birth to a child that Stuart wanted far more than she did?

Carole had watched as Vivian fell asleep, then left the bedroom and headed down a solid-oak spiral staircase and into the sunken living room with its Ethan Allen furniture and wall paintings that Stuart commissioned young local artists to do. She had found Stuart standing near the window drinking a beer.

"How is she?" he had asked.

"She's still trying to come to terms with what happened."

"So am I," Stuart muttered, eyes bloodshot from lack of sleep. "I wonder if I'm somehow being punished for talking Vivian into something she wanted no part of. Maybe it would have been easier if she had gone through with the termination on her own. At least I wouldn't have gotten my hopes up."

"Don't, Stuart," Carole scolded him as one might a child. "You're not being punished; neither is she. You both made this decision together and fate intervened. There's nothing you can do about it, other than use this as a positive step to move forward."

Stuart put the bottle to his mouth. "It's hard," he'd said, a bitterness to his voice. "You should know that better than anyone. How positive did you consider it when your old man took away your mother's life with his fists? This wounds me every bit as much."

Carole leveled her eyes at him. He had hit her where it hurt most. She had confided in him her most painful secret at a time when she needed to tell someone. Now he had shoved it in her face, as if to maliciously break her down. She could hardly compare the way he had lost his unborn child with the violent way she had been robbed of her own mother. Yet Stuart had managed to believe the two were equal in their sheer agony.

Realizing what he had done, sensing her thoughts, Stuart said regretfully, "I'm sorry, Carole. I didn't mean that."

"Didn't you?" she snapped. "I trusted you, Stuart. I thought you would understand. Now I'm beginning to wonder if you ever really did."

"I do understand everything you've gone through," he promised, and put his arms around her protectively. "I'm so sorry, baby. I don't know what the hell came over me. I guess I was only thinking about myself and reacting like a jerk when you were only trying to help. You know I'd never do anything to hurt you intentionally. Forgive me."

In spite of herself Carole knew it wasn't in Stuart's nature to strike out at anyone who only wanted to be there for him as a friend. But it hadn't changed the facts any. He had used against her what she had given him when the opportunity presented itself. She was not sure she could—or should—ever trust someone in that way again.

Including Ray.

Caught in the whirl of past and present traumas, Carole had allowed herself to be held by Stuart longer than she should. Before she could break away, Vivian was standing there looking at them. The look in her eyes was one of dark despair, fresh pain, and stark betrayal.

Now Carole ran in steady strides alongside the river, feeling the tension in her legs and the rapid pumping of her heart. She recalled Stuart trying to reassure his wife that nothing was going on, while at the same time trying to make apologies, as if there were anything to apologize for.

As for Carole, she had wanted only to get out of there as fast as she could, feeling herself unable to breathe or think straight. But not before she made it perfectly clear to Vivian that *Vivian* was the love of Stuart's life. What Carole had had with her husband was strictly in the past.

Indeed, as though to hammer this point home to all concerned, Carole had announced unceremoniously that she was in love with another man.

Now she wondered if it was true. Had she really fallen in love with Ray Barkley?

Did he love her?

Would it be enough for either of them?

Or maybe I'm only fooling myself, she thought.

Carole began her cooldown. She considered whether she was prepared to deal with her past.

Could she ever feel comfortable telling Ray things that she'd never wanted to tell anyone, but had told to Stuart in a moment of weakness? That was something she now regretted.

Might she feel the same way afterward in confiding to Ray?

If things continued to progress between them, could they actually have a family of their own that was not marred by domestic violence, homicide, and a lifetime of agony?

By the time Carole returned to her condo she was exhausted, but felt better about things, including the future and its interesting possibilities.

She stepped into the shower and cleansed herself before putting on a silk mock halter and Bermuda shorts.

The phone rang, giving her a start. She answered it in the bedroom.

"Hello?"

"It's Stuart. Thank goodness I've finally reached you."

She could hear the quaver in his voice. "What is it?"

Carole listened as Stuart spoke of his meeting with Detective Parker. "I had to tell her some things I didn't want to . . . about you . . ." There was a break in his voice. "She didn't leave me much choice. You've got to believe that if there had been any other way—"

Carole felt numb. It was as if she had managed, if only briefly, to block out all that hurt her. Now it seemed to be coming back with a vengeance. She wondered if her secrets would finally cause the world she'd made for herself to crumble down around her like a house of clay.

"I think Parker and your boyfriend may be coming your way next," Stuart warned. "I just didn't want you to be caught off guard."

Those last words were distant to Carole as she considered the information he had shared with the police about her past, their suspicions, and what might happen next.

She heard the intercom ring, further drowning out what Stuart was saying. Walking to it, she punched the button. It was Ray.

"We need to come up, Carole," he said in a voice absent of emotion.

We? she thought.

Not just him? Meaning Detective Parker was downstairs too.

Were they planning to confront her with past sins?

Could they have found something incriminating with respect to the vigilante on the loose? Something that would point the finger directly at *her?*

Fear raced through Carole in that moment like a tornado passing through town, destroying everything in its path. She suddenly felt as if she were being victimized all over again. Only this time not as a child, but as a sitting judge.

And perhaps a murder suspect.

She put the phone up to her ear and said glumly to Stuart, "I think I may need an attorney."

41

Ray and Nina rode up the elevator in silence, as if neither wanted to be the first to speak. For Ray's part, there was nothing left to say that hadn't already been said in one way or another. The blood on the cultured pearl bracelet would have to be tested to make sure it was human. It would take additional DNA tests to link it to any of the victims of the so-called Vigilante Killer; and consequently to get a judge to sign a search warrant against a fellow judge—if it was proven to be necessary.

Ray had chosen to bypass the search warrant for now, believing that if it was in fact Carole's bracelet, there might be a rational explanation for why it was in Stuart Wolfe's car. This in spite of the fact that the brother had actually insisted that Carole had never been in his BMW.

Ray had been forced to take that with a grain of salt, all things considered. He knew only at this point that he wanted to keep it as informal as possible with Carole, hoping they could still somehow salvage whatever relationship they had left.

Or would have left after today.

Nina looked at him skeptically. "Are you sure you're okay about this, Ray?"

He rubbed his head. *Hell, no, I'm not okay about it*, he thought. But what other damned choice did he have? He couldn't sit on what might be crucial evidence in a murder spree that had taken five lives. Not even when it could blow his personal life up in his face.

Nina, who had managed to connect Carole to the serial killer case, had insisted she be present for any questioning, on or off the record. And Ray couldn't blame her, or object. This was her case as much as his.

And she was far more objective at this stage than he was, Ray had to admit reluctantly.

He looked at her and kept his voice level. "Yeah. I'm fine."

"Good," she said concisely. "You know, we have to talk to her and see what she says."

"I know."

"If push comes to shove, we can probably get a warrant by tonight."

Ray wrinkled his forehead. "Why don't we wait and see what happens and take it from there?" His muscles felt tense.

"Your call," Nina said respectfully. "For now."

The elevator doors opened and they got off, walking down the long hall till they came to Carole's door. It opened as if on cue, and Carole stood there as if she were part of a welcoming committee. Ray could see that she now viewed him with caution and apprehension rather than as a friend and lover.

"May we come in?" he asked politely, noting that

she was dressed in a stylish silver suit and gray pumps, as though on her way out.

She acquiesced without a word, stepping aside.

The three stood in a triangle in the living room. Planting her eyes directly upon Ray, Carole asked in a controlled voice, "So what's this all about, *Detective* Barkley . . . ?"

He swallowed the lump in his throat. Pulling out a plastic bag from his pocket containing the bracelet, he held it before her. "Do you recognize this?"

Carole needed only a moment to study the bracelet. She looked at him, as she knew instantly where he had first seen the cultured-pearl jewelry.

"Yes," she responded with resignation. "It looks like the matching bracelet to a necklace and earrings I own."

Ray flashed Nina a quick, uneasy look. To Carole, he said, "This was found in a car owned by Stuart Wolfe."

Carole lifted a thin brow. Ray wasn't sure if it was in surprise that she had been associated with Wolfe or that the bracelet had been in his car.

"I'm not sure what to say," she uttered, flushed. "Stuart and I are friends, yes . . . but I haven't been in his car in recent memory, if ever." She paused. "Certainly not wearing that bracelet."

Nina stepped forward. "But you don't deny it's your pearl bracelet?" she asked point-blank. "Do you, Judge?"

Carole peered at her, then at Ray, asking him innocently, "Maybe *you* could tell me what's going on here? Am I being accused of something? If so, I'd damned sure like to know what."

Ray averted his eyes, then looked back at Carole

again, sighing. "We have reason to believe that Stuart Wolfe's BMW may have been driven by the person who killed Blake Wallace." It pained him to have to draw her into this cloud of suspicion, but there was no other way at this point. "All leads, no matter how remote, have to be checked out. I'm sure you understand."

"Yes, I think I'm beginning to."

"Look, if you'd rather have your attorney present," Nina said patronizingly.

Carole shot her a scathing look. "I'm a criminal court *judge*, Detective Parker! I think I understand the law and my rights." To Ray she stated frostily, "This whole mix-up could have been straightened out with a simple phone call."

She marched abruptly toward her bedroom. Both detectives watched, then followed, Ray leading the way. He saw the bed upon entering the room and remembered how soft it felt. And how Carole had felt even softer on it. He wondered if he would ever get to make love to her again. It irked him that their relationship now hung in the balance, surrounded by the specter of murder.

Carole went to a cherry-colored jewelry box atop a Queen Anne dark-oak dresser, yanking open a drawer. She dug around in it haphazardly but came up empty. Her eyes popped wide at Ray as she stammered, "I can't seem to find it. The bracelet was in here, along with the necklace and earrings. I'm sure of it." She lifted the cultured-pearl earrings and necklace to show them, as if for effect. "I know I put the pearl bracelet back the last time I wore it."

"And when was that?" asked Nina bluntly.

Carole looked up thoughtfully. "I really can't remember for sure. . . ." Her voice faltered.

Nina narrowed her eyes. "Maybe I can refresh your memory, Judge. Maybe you wore the bracelet when you beat Blake Wallace to death with a bat?" she pressed accusingly. "Or Eddie Jackson . . . ?"

"That's enough, Parker!" Ray blared at her. But the damage had already been done. He could see it in Carole's face, which was now etched with fury—at him.

"How dare you!" Carole retorted bitingly, glaring at Ray before settling in on Nina. "You don't know what the hell you're talking about!"

"We do know that your father battered your mother to death." Nina's voice was caustic, unapologetic. "And that you witnessed it."

Carole locked eyes with Ray. Once again he found himself unable to meet her gaze head-on, hating that they both were put in such an unenviable position. Instead he focused on the expensive jewelry box with the even pricier missing cultured-pearl bracelet that may have been the one in his pocket.

"We also know that you testified on behalf of Esther Reynolds in her trial for killing her abusive husband fifteen years ago," said Nina.

"So what!" Carole snapped, tossing her hands up in the air. "My family skeletons and friendships hardly make me a murder suspect . . . much less a cold-blooded killer!"

"I think they do," Nina responded bravely. "Especially if the blood on the pearl bracelet that we both know is yours, which you seem to have conveniently misplaced, matches that of one of the victims of the Vigilante Killer."

241

Carole shook her head in disbelief. "This whole thing is totally absurd."

Ray made himself face her. "Are you and Stuart Wolfe lovers?" he asked in a throaty voice, the question having dual implications.

"No, we are not!" Carole's voice seemed to echo throughout the room. "I already told you, we're just friends. . . ."

"Friendly enough that Wolfe would allow you to use his car while he was lecturing?" Nina asked with a catch to her tone. "To commit murder?"

"I won't even bother to dignify that with an answer." Carole snorted derisively.

"Mind if we look around a bit?" Nina peeked at Ray, then gave Carole her full attention. "Just routine, you know. We can get a warrant—"

"Go right ahead!" Carole practically did a 360-degree turn of her slender body in disgust. "I'm not sure what you expect to find, but I have nothing to hide."

When Nina left the room Ray approached Carole, not sure what to say—or how to say it without sounding like an asshole who'd just stabbed his girlfriend in the back . . . and twisted the knife a bit for good measure.

"Look, baby," he managed, placing a hand on her shoulder, "you have to believe I never wanted to—"

She whirled away from him as though he were her worst enemy. "Don't!" Her voice was filled with indignation. "This is not the time and certainly no longer the place to hear your sorry-ass lies."

"Carole," Ray said regretfully, "this has nothing

to do with us. . . ." The words sounded hollow even to him.

"Like hell it doesn't," she lashed out. "It has *everything* to do with us. Do you really think I'm that big a fool that I can't see through you? It's obvious that whatever we had was nothing more than a sham. You used me, just like other bastards, and now you're trying to bury me for something I had nothing to do with."

You have it all wrong, Ray thought miserably. But how the hell could he get through to her while at the same time remembering he was a cop with a job to do? No matter who got hurt in the process—including himself.

Nina got their attention. She came in, a gloved hand holding a wooden bat. "Look what I found."

Ray gazed at the bat, then Carole.

"Where did you get that?" Carole asked, sounding just as shocked as Ray felt.

"Found it in the spare-bedroom closet," Nina said. "Is it yours?"

"I've never seen it before," she claimed, wide-eyed.

Nina shot her a skeptical look. "Oh, really?" She held it up toward the light. "Looks like there might be dried blood on the bat. It also looks just like the bats the killer left behind after battering her victims to death—right down to the same manufacturer. Now you wouldn't know anything about that, would you, *Your Honor?*"

Carole was speechless and looking for all the world, thought Ray sadly, like a guilty person whose life was beginning to unravel before her very eyes.

And he too was shocked into an uncomfortable and fearful silence.

First the pearl bracelet.

Now a bat.

What the hell next?

A body stuffed in the basement?

Studying this disturbing chain of coincidences and possibly damning evidence, Ray knew it didn't look good for Carole.

But did that make her a calculating, coldhearted serial killer?

He thought uneasily about the question.

42

The bat was immediately confiscated as possible evidence. It was also confirmed to be the same make and size of the other bats used by the Vigilante Killer.

Two days later, preliminary DNA tests showed a match between the blood on the bat's handle and Roberto Martinez's blood. Other tests conducted on the cultured-pearl bracelet linked blood found on it to blood taken from Blake Wallace. This constituted more than enough hard evidence to issue a warrant for Judge Carole Cranston's arrest.

Nina made the arrest, along with a couple of uniformed officers. A shell-shocked Carole, accompanied by her attorney, Stuart Wolfe, went without incident. She was booked and fingerprinted at the Portland City Jail and separated from the other inmates in a holding cell.

Carole sat in a near trance on a cot that bore the stench of stale urine. She had never known such humiliation till now. The press had a field day in labeling her "the Honorable Judge Vigilante Killer." She had been branded a serial murderess, avenging her own mother's death at the hands of her abusive father. After years of committing herself to justice there seemed to be precious little left for her. She had already been tried, convicted, and sentenced by many.

Carole wondered if her judge and jury included Ray Barkley. Just like nearly all the men in her life, he had betrayed her. He had hurt her so much and the wounds ran so deep that she could not imagine the pain ever leaving.

They had been lovers, and Carole had thought she loved him. Even marriage and children seemed distinct possibilities. *I was prepared to give my all to that man and a life together,* she told herself.

Now there was no future to look forward to. No plans to make for a lasting, loving relationship. Her fate had been sealed, partly because of her being so trusting and naive. And partly because of the ghosts of the past that had come back to haunt her just as she had known instinctively they would someday.

No matter what, her life would never be the same again, Carole truly believed.

Ray sat across from Carole not as an investigator, per se, but as a man who still cared deeply for her. She was stone-faced, sullen, tight-lipped, and likely as scared as hell, he thought. Who wouldn't be in her position?

But she was still beautiful and desirable, even under the worst of circumstances. He had given her a part of himself that he thought was too far buried ever to rise to the surface again. He had found someone to believe in. To make him feel like a real man. To want to treat and cherish like a real lady.

Now she was the primary suspect in the vigilante killings. And Ray couldn't be sure if he was looking at the woman he might have fallen in love with or a brutal killer.

A search warrant had allowed them to enter Carole's condo and search for any other possible evidence that could link her to the murders. They had come up blank. No other bats hidden in the closet. No clothes with victims' bloodstains. No bodies in the attic. No visible indication that they were dealing with a madwoman, let alone one of the worst serial killers the city of Portland had ever known.

Yet the evidence they had was indisputable and injurious, Ray mused, if not just a little too convenient, as far as he was concerned. The bat was conspicuously in the closet, as if waiting to be found, while the bracelet was stuffed inside the front car seat of Stuart Wolfe's black BMW like it was put there rather than left accidentally.

To Ray this smelled like a damned setup. Either that, he thought, or the woman before him was not half as bright as he believed her to be.

Especially if she truly was a killer.

It left more than a little suspicion in his mind.

"I suppose you're here to gloat," hissed Carole. She wore standard bright-orange jail garb, as if to wipe away any hint of her judgeship in the face of her possible savage crimes. "Take the gullible judge to bed while screwing her left and right behind her back—figuratively speaking."

"Stop it, dammit," Ray said, peering at her sorrowfully. "I never meant for any of this to happen."

"Didn't you?" she said doubtfully. "You've been after me from the very beginning. And I don't mean to get in my pants, though probably that too. Now you've got me. So why not just leave me the hell alone?"

"Because I want to believe you're innocent."

Carole gritted her teeth. "Is that why you never bothered to get in on the big arrest, Ray?" she asked. "The big, bad, bald, black brother detective suddenly turned gutless when it came to showing up to see his girlfriend handcuffed, humiliated, and taken into police custody like a common criminal? You shouldn't have missed it . . . complete with a media entourage fit for a queen. So now you come here as the good guy, hoping I'll say I'm as guilty as sin and make some elaborate confession with a motive dating back to my childhood? Well, you know what, Ray? I'm not going to do that. I may be a little screwed up—even a lot—but I am *not* a killer! Whether you choose to believe it or not, that's your damned problem!"

"Any idea how that bat wound up in your closet?" Ray drummed his fingers on the metal table separating them, resisting any desire to turn his back on her—on them. No matter how much she tried, he would not allow her to push him away.

She looked him in the eye while responding levelly, "None whatsoever. I don't play baseball or softball and have never purchased a bat in my life. Not even to use as a weapon . . ." Her words drifted off, as if into a deep fog.

"So you're saying it was planted there?"

Carole thought for a moment. "It's the only possible explanation," she said definitively. "How else would it have gotten there?"

Ray asked himself the same thing. Especially with the blood of Roberto Martinez smeared on it. He too didn't have an alternate answer, aside from the real possibility that it had been an inside job. Meaning someone who knew Carole like a book and had access to her place had managed to set her up.

His muscles tensed. "Let's talk about the bracelet," he said. "Any thoughts on how it could have ended up inside the front seat of Wolfe's car?"

Carole squirmed in her chair. "No," she admitted, perplexed. "Like I told you, I can't even remember if I've ever been in Stuart's car. If I had, it would have been from the courthouse to a nearby restaurant or coffee shop. And I certainly would not have worn a bracelet that I saved for special occasions."

"You're sure about that?" Ray questioned, locking eyes with her.

"Positive," Carole asserted. "Besides, I know I saw the bracelet in my jewelry box the last time I wore the necklace and earrings."

"And when was that?" he asked thoughtfully.

Carole wet her lips and said in a conspiratorial undertone, "When I came to your houseboat. Or have you forgotten so quickly?"

Ray felt the lump in his throat, and all the wonderful memories come flooding back, as if it had happened only this very day.

"I haven't forgotten, baby."

"Well, neither have I, *Detective*," she said angrily. "I can't explain how the bracelet ended up where it was found—other than that someone obviously put it there. I do know, though, that bracelets do not simply fall off. Particularly in strange and unlikely places."

Ray chewed on his lower lip contemplatively. "Have you had a break-in recently?" he inquired, trying his damnedest to find a loophole. Anything that could point the finger elsewhere. Anywhere else.

"No," Carole uttered without thought. "Not that I'm aware of. The building has an excellent security system . . . so does my condo."

"Does that include people you know?"

She narrowed her eyes. "What's that supposed to mean?"

He sighed. "Stuart Wolfe," he said tentatively.

"What about him?"

Ray grew uncomfortable, but went with it. "The pearl bracelet was found in the brother's car, Carole! If you weren't in it that means someone else had to put the damned thing there. Someone in a position to take it from your jewelry box without being suspected of doing so. He seems the logical candidate at this point, unless you tell me different. And if Wolfe did do it, then he sure as hell wouldn't have had much problem making sure that bat could be easily found at your place by anyone who was looking for it."

"This doesn't make any sense," protested Carole defiantly. "Stuart wouldn't have tried to frame me. For what possible reason?"

Ray leaned forward, lips pursed. "I was hoping you could tell me?"

She regarded him unevenly. "There's nothing to tell." She paused for a long moment. "Or is this your way of asking me if we were ever lovers?"

Carole hung on that note, and Ray realized it was something that surprisingly bothered him. He had never been the jealous type. Had that changed when Carole entered his life? Did the notion that she had been with other men make him a little crazy?

Carole seemed to read his thoughts as she said candidly; "The answer is yes, we were intimately involved once. It ended a long time ago, but we've remained friends ever since. Nothing more than that. I'm even friends with his wife, if it makes you feel better. Stuart would never do anything intentionally to try to hurt me."

"What about the wife?"

Carole's nostrils expanded. "She just had a miscarriage, for heaven's sake. Vivian Wolfe is not my enemy, and not serial-killer material either." She sighed. "I can't imagine her and Stuart somehow conspiring to make me out to be this so-called Vigilante Killer."

Ray met her eyes. "Well, someone sure as hell wanted to make it seem like you were this killing bitch." He knew in so saying he was more or less exonerating her of guilt. But he was strictly in the minority at this stage. Proving Carole's innocence would not be as easy.

"But who?" she asked herself out loud. "I don't have any enemies that I know of specifically."

"You're a judge, Carole," he noted. "That gives you enemies on the inside who get out. And enemies on the outside who may blame you for not putting all batterers away."

"That could make it almost anyone," Carole said bleakly.

"More like *someone*," Ray said pensively.

She furrowed her brow suspiciously. "I'm not sure I can trust you, Ray—not anymore. . . ."

251

He took a breath and said tensely, "You don't have much choice, baby. Right now I may be the only one you can trust in this whole damned city."

Ray only hoped he could trust his own instincts that told him Carole Cranston did not belong in jail. And she didn't deserve to be branded as the female counterpart to Wayne Williams, Gerald Gallego, Ted Bundy, or any other serial maniac out there killing people.

Not if the woman he'd grown to really care for was truly innocent, as he believed . . .

Carole met with Stuart in an interview room. She had not hesitated to ask him to represent her when it became apparent that she was in big trouble. Aside from being a friend, he was a fine defense attorney who had won a number of high-profile cases aside from Esther's. Carole feared that she just might need all his skills and expertise to get out of this one.

"How are you holding up?" Stuart asked with concern while sitting at the table.

Carole, already seated, sneered. "How do you think? I'm a damned judge, not a murderer. I don't belong in here, Stuart—with people I put away! When can you get me out?" There was desperation, yet hope in her voice.

Stuart's tired eyes betrayed the stress he was under. "I'm doing everything I can to make that happen as soon as possible, Carole. We have a bail hearing this afternoon. With any luck, you could be out shortly thereafter."

"Could they deny bail?" Carole asked.

As a judge she knew that in most instances involving violent crimes, bail was difficult, to say the least. Where it concerned multiple murders, bail was all but impossible. Which made her cringe. The thought of spending even one night in jail unnerved her, much less weeks, months, or even possibly the rest of her life, she thought gloomily.

"They could," Stuart said, seeming to read her thoughts. "But given that you are a sitting judge with no previous criminal history, and that the evidence against you is highly circumstantial at best, I doubt that will be the case. A tainted bat that appears out of nowhere, thanks to your cooperation with the authorities? A bracelet smeared with blood from a victim that just happens to be found in my own damned car, for crying out loud? Your own history that someone is trying to use against you—not to mention your current profession? I mean, c'mon, who's kidding whom here? Anyone in his or her right mind can see that this is obviously a frame-up."

Carole wondered if anyone could really see this, aside from him and her. The police apparently did not, including perhaps Ray. And certainly not his partner, Nina Parker! Would she have seen it herself so clearly had it been someone else in her shoes? Carole pondered.

She fixed her eyes on Stuart. "What's your theory on how the bracelet got into your car?"

Stuart sat erect in his stiff brown suit, meeting her gaze. He took a deep breath, then said, "I've been giving that some thought. All I can think of is that you either dropped the bracelet somewhere and someone picked it up—or it was stolen from you or your place. This person obviously then placed the bracelet where he or she fully intended for it to be found—in my car. Probably while I was at the uni-

versity. I have a bad habit of leaving my doors unlocked or my windows down, especially when it's as
hot as it's been lately. Guess that will have to
change . . ."

"But whoever did this would have to have known
about us," Carole surmised. "Otherwise, why plant
evidence in your car, of all places? It's hardly the
first place the police would have thought to look."

She thought about Ray's suspicions regarding
Stuart. Even Vivian. Was there any merit to them
whatsoever?

"It is when they were apparently looking for a
black BMW," said Stuart, "which I just happen to
own. Think about it."

Carole did, and only found herself more mystified
and unsure. *I can't allow myself to believe you were
somehow behind this*, she thought. *But I can't dismiss
the notion outright either. I'd be a fool to, as long as I'm in
here for something I'm innocent of.*

Stuart reached out to her, their hands touching.
"Listen to me, Carole, if this lunatic killer wanted to
know all there was to know about you—or me, for
that matter—it wouldn't be very difficult to make
the connection between us. A little bit of research on
the Internet would give the person a running start.
She or he could probably figure out the rest with half
a brain." He paused. "My guess is that it's someone
who's sat in on your trials dealing with these batterers, and she figured that sooner or later the police
would tie us together. The killer made sure they
wouldn't come up empty-handed with the well-
placed bat and bracelet—likely as a means to get
some of the heat off herself."

It made sense, thought Carole. Except for those

who believed she had somehow engineered her own setup to make it appear she was being framed, while really being this sister from hell who killed men almost for sport.

Who would do such a thing to her? Carole mused angrily. Where did she possibly start in narrowing down the list? And how could she do anything as long as she was behind bars?

"This whole thing is really starting to freak me out, Stuart," she said suddenly, feeling the heat as if she were already being burned at the stake.

"I know, baby," he muttered sympathetically. "Which is probably what the killer wants. What better way to gain some vicarious, sick thrill than to know that the judge herself who's letting these creeps go free is getting a dose of what she should be giving them?"

"Well, I'm getting the message loud *and* clear!" Carole voiced of her wake-up call. "I'll be damned if I'm going to be a target for some crazy woman who's out to destroy me and my reputation for what she falsely believes is my inability to put away the assholes who beat up on women—"

Stuart drew his brows together. "Whatever you're thinking, Carole, forget it! This bitch is not a person to play around with. She's dangerous, deadly, and *definitely* unstable! Leave the detective work to people like your boyfriend—or should I say *former* boyfriend . . . ?"

Carole blinked involuntarily. She was not sure what to think where it concerned Ray. The jury was still out on whether he was the person she hoped he'd be. Or one he could never be.

A man she could trust with her life?

Or the one person who could put her to death by lethal injection?

"I haven't decided yet exactly where we stand," Carole told Stuart as much as herself. Something told her, though, that she should keep an open mind and not quite give up on Ray Barkley just yet.

43

"It's the least I can do," offered Vivian, behind the wheel of her Lexus. "You've certainly been around when I needed someone, girl."

Carole sat beside her. Forcing a smile, she said, "I think I'm only just beginning to realize who my friends truly are." *And who would just as soon hang me out to dry,* she thought, for all their lack of support.

Vivian had been waiting when Carole stepped outside the Criminal Court Plaza after posting bail. Stuart had guided her through a throng of reporters to the car before dashing back to the building to be with another client.

The judge, Harvey Winston III, was not a friend, but a colleague and acquaintance of Carole's. The sixty-year-old African-American former Portland city councilman had clearly been torn in his decision on bail. Finally he compromised between the prosecutor's wishes for no bail with his own inclination for a significant but not unattainably high bail in setting it at five hundred thousand dollars.

Carole had been required to put up 10 percent, along with her personal guarantee that she wouldn't skip town for as long as this case was pending. She had gladly agreed to such, tapping into her savings and being willing to beg, borrow, or steal, if necessary—anything to avoid spending one more second behind bars as a murder suspect.

Carole felt sick to her stomach that she had been demeaned this way. All her adult life she had stood for fair and honest justice. Now with one calculating move someone had managed to put a serious dent in her accomplishments and integrity, with no guarantee that she could ever right the wrongs—or repair the great damage that had been inflicted upon her character.

"Do you want to get something to eat?" Vivian broke into her thoughts. "There's a new Caribbean restaurant not far from here. Stuart took me there last week."

"I don't think so," Carole told her. "I just want to go home, take a nice long, hot shower, and go to bed."

Carole almost expected Vivian to argue that she had to eat—but Stuart's wife did not.

Instead she said, "I can understand that. It must have been awful in there."

Carole bristled. "*Awful* doesn't even begin to describe it," she grumbled. "Try a living hell." Actually she knew she had been treated better than the typical jail inmate. Being a prominent judge who had put many others away had allowed her at least that much. But that did little to keep her from feeling like a damned caged animal during her short stay.

"I hear you, girl," Vivian said. "Especially for

something you didn't do." She turned the corner a little too sharply, causing the car to tilt. "Sorry. Sometimes I drive a little crazy."

Carole had on her seat belt, but was startled nonetheless, gripping the seat impulsively. Her mind went beyond the unsteady driving, more piqued by Vivian's words: . . . *for something you didn't do.* She wondered how Stuart's wife could be so sure of her innocence.

Could Vivian have actually stolen the bracelet from her condo when she dropped by . . . and planted it in the front seat of Stuart's BMW? If so, why?

Could this possibly be about my past with Stuart and some sort of insane animosity? Carole considered nervously.

Or might it have more to do with her as a judge, and vindictiveness related to abusers who walked from her court as free—but still far from innocent—men?

Carole regarded Vivian thoughtfully. "I'm not guilty of these crimes," she affirmed. "But someone is. . . ."

"Yeah," Vivian muttered in agreement. "I just hope the police get real smart before this sister—if it is one—has everyone in town accusing one another while she remains free to keep killing these dudes."

Carole managed to sound nonchalant when she said, "Stuart and I were trying to figure out how on earth someone got my bracelet then put it in his car without the alarm going off or anyone being seen."

Was this about jealousy? Carole wondered, recalling Vivian's apparent outrage when she saw her and Stuart embracing. Could Vivian have misinterpreted Stuart's show of friendly concern for romantic feelings?

But the question of most concern to Carole at the moment was whether or not Vivian could have resorted to murder.

Five times . . .

"If you ask me," said Vivian with a catch to her voice, "someone clever and daring enough could have broken into your condo and stolen the bracelet. I've read that most locks can be picked in a matter of seconds, if you know what you're doing. Of course, the person would also have to know your schedule—like when you wouldn't be home." She stopped at a light. "It wouldn't take a genius or pro to plant evidence in Stuart's car to try to set you up. I'm always getting on him about keeping it unlocked with the alarm off. But he never listens. He also likes to park away from other cars so his pretty BMW doesn't get scratched. Can you believe that?"

Carole shuddered. "Sounds like you've got it all figured out," she said without inflection.

Vivian shrugged. "Hey, it's just a theory." She pressed down on the accelerator. "I suppose every armchair detective has one."

Am I overreacting? wondered Carole, getting a bad feeling about Stuart's no-longer-pregnant wife. Had Carole been influenced by too many mystery novels or movies?

Or was Vivian speaking more from actual knowledge than theory?

"I still haven't figured out why this bitch would try to frame you." Vivian shifted her eyes. "Must be someone has it in for you, representing the system and men who beat their women half to death and seem to get away with it almost every time."

"So it would seem," mused Carole unsteadily.

Vivian drove up to the building. "I'd watch my step if I were you," she said, concern in her voice. "Something tells me that this vigilante broad may not stop here. Carole, you could become a target next."

A target?

The thought unsettled Carole. *Is she warning me about herself as a perpetrator?*

Beyond that Carole contemplated the notion that a serial killer of male batterers was really targeting her. What for? She answered the question herself: *To punish me for their sins, real or otherwise.* Hadn't she already been punished enough for what her own father had done to her mother?

Now even another victim is going after me for only doing my job, Carole mused bleakly.

When would all the madness end?

She unfastened her seat belt and glanced over at Stuart's young wife, wondering if Vivian was capable of orchestrating this entire thing.

Or was she looking at the wrong suspects, Carole asked herself, simply because they were in the right place with the right opportunity?

With a forced grin, she told Vivian, "Thanks for the advice and ride. I'm sure I'll be fine."

She got out of the car and waved as Vivian drove away.

There was much to think about, Carole knew, heading toward the building, ill at ease. One was getting back her good name.

Another was seeing if what she and Ray had was real or just a figment of her imagination—and her body's reaction to his touch.

Most of all, Carole mused, she had to try to figure out who hated her enough to want her to take the fall for the vicious and malicious murders of abusive men.

44

"You're pissed at me, aren't you?" Nina asked.

"Would it make you feel better if I said I was?" responded Ray from the other side of the table. They were at a coffee shop in the heart of downtown Portland.

"I'd just rather hear it from you, Ray, than speculate that my partner hates my guts because I caused his judge girlfriend to go down on this one."

"I don't hate your guts, Nina," he told her sincerely over the rim of his coffee cup. "You did your job the way you thought it had to be done. As far as Carole is concerned, I wouldn't put this down as a done deal just yet."

Nina raised her eyes. "Oh, really?" she said skeptically. "Why not? She's got motive, opportunity, and working knowledge of the dead batterers and their living victims. Not to mention her association with both the court and the shelter. Throw in some strong circumstantial and direct evidence with the sister's signature all over it, and I'd say it looks pretty damned convincing to me."

"It looks anything but that to me," Ray countered, realizing he was going out on a limb here. He was confident it was with just cause. "We've got a bat with no fingerprints tying it to Judge Cranston that could have been put there by anyone. It just happens to conveniently have Roberto Martinez's blood on it, though we both know that the bat that was used to kill him was left at the scene. Add to this a cultured pearl bracelet, which Carole never denied was hers, that mysteriously shows up inside the seat in a car both she and the car's owner claim she's never even been in. If this doesn't smack of a damned setup, I don't know what does."

Nina curled a corner of her top lip upward into a sneer. "Don't fight me on this one, Barkley," she offered him a stern warning. "You'll lose."

Ray gripped the table. The last thing he wanted was to screw things up between them. Put in jeopardy what had been for the most part a good partnership as well as friendship. But even that was not as important to him as righting what he saw to be a terrible wrong. He wasn't about to sit idly by and watch Carole take the rap for something he felt certain she was innocent of.

"I went to see Carole," he admitted, knowing it was not advisable under the circumstances.

"You what!" Nina's head snapped back as if she had run into a door. "Have you lost your damned mind, Barkley? The lead investigator in a serial-killer case does not play footsies with the lead suspect . . . not at this stage of the process, anyway. You know that, Ray! What the hell's gotten into you anyway? This can't be all about falling for the judge to the point that you've lost all perspective?"

Ray stiffened. "It's far from that, Parker!" he insisted, even knowing that feeling as he did about Carole had definitely figured into his thinking. "My gut tells me that Carole's not the Vigilante Killer! I don't give a damn what the evidence suggests. . . ."

"And how can *you* be so sure of that?" Nina's voice had a cynical lilt to it.

How can I be so sure of anything these days? Ray asked himself. Including the judgment of his partner. Maybe Nina had lost some objectivity in her pursuit of Carole at all costs, he thought. Whatever else he didn't know about Carole Cranston, in his heart of hearts he could not believe this lady was capable of one murder, let alone multiple homicides.

Ray met Nina's unblinking gaze. "You'll just have to trust me on this one."

"Can't do that," she said dismissively. "I'll go to hell and back for you, Ray. You know that. But I won't jeopardize this case—my career—for a lovelorn whim of yours."

"It's more than just a whim, Nina," he told her firmly. "Whoever is killing these men is someone who has no respect for the justice system. And not a hell of a lot for men either. Carole doesn't fit that profile. She's spent much of her adult life trying to make the laws work for people like you and me. She definitely respects males who earn her respect. I also seriously doubt that Carole would somehow find a way to lose her pearl bracelet in the seat of a car she may never have been in, much less driven."

"Now you're starting to piss me off," growled Nina disapprovingly. "Why don't you just leave well enough alone, Barkley, and quit overpsychoanalyzing things?"

Ray's brows descended. "Because you don't really want that any more than I do," he responded, an edge to his voice. "Especially if it means letting the real killer off the hook—in favor of one you simply hope is the culprit."

Nina peered into her cup of cappuccino. "I'll pretend I didn't hear that last part, okay? The only thing I'm hoping for is to stop this madness and bring the murderer to justice—whoever she is."

"Yeah, all right." Ray drank more coffee, conceding that they weren't getting anywhere by attacking each other and their motivations.

After a moment or two, Nina said, "So if the judge isn't our killer—and I'm not saying I'm buying this hypothesis of yours—then how do you propose we find the *real* killer?"

Ray pondered the question pensively. "I've felt almost since the beginning that the key to this case was the Rose City Women's Shelter," he said frankly. "Or, more specifically, Esther Reynolds. I think she knows a hell of a lot more than she's said. Maybe it's time we turn up the heat on her—all the way. . . ."

Esther Reynolds lived in a small, dull white wood clapboard house with black shutters not far from the shelter. An attached garage was open and filled with boxes, as if it were a storage facility. Lights were on in the house when the detectives rang the doorbell.

Esther opened the door, shock registering on her face, as if she were seeing her late husband raised from the dead. She was dressed more casually than her professional shelter attire, in a sea-foam v-neck cardigan, cropped denims, and grommet thongs.

"We need to talk to you," Ray told her in a not-too-friendly voice.

Esther adjusted her glasses nervously. "I'm busy right now. Can't this wait till tomorrow?"

"Afraid not," Nina responded. "It's about your old college chum who once graciously testified on your behalf. Carole Cranston . . ."

Esther reacted, her voice faltering as the detectives exchanged glances.

"Come in . . ." she finally uttered.

She walked them into a living room with sage carpeting and African furniture. The acrid stench of cigarette smoke permeated the air.

"What about Carole?" Esther asked, her hand planted firmly on hip.

Ray gazed at her. "Well, unless you've been out of town for the last couple of days, you know she's been arrested on suspicion of being the Vigilante Killer."

Esther lowered her eyes. "I heard about it."

"You don't seem surprised?"

She raised her head. "Of course I'm surprised. There's been a big mistake here. Carole could never have killed anyone."

"Not even if he battered her?" asked Nina.

Esther flung her a wicked stare. "Carole would sooner walk away than kill the bastard. Just like she did when her father killed her mother." She paused, as if she'd given away a family secret. "I think that's partly why she became a judge—so people like the man I was married to could get what they deserved without making the victims become perpetrators."

"But it doesn't always work out that way," Ray said thoughtfully, "does it?"

She sighed. "No. Not always."

"And so someone other than Judge Cranston has decided to be the judge she hasn't been in punishing these batterers. Someone who's trying to set her up to be this killer." He tilted his head but maintained a fixed gaze. "I think *you* know who this person is. . . ."

Esther's lower lip trembled. "Think what you like. But you're wrong."

"Am I . . . ?" Ray could feel the blood pumping through his veins. This sister was lying through her teeth. "If anyone at the shelter is in a position to know all and hear all, it's you! Carole Cranston's life and freedom may rest on your shoulders. She helped you out once when you needed it most. Maybe it's time you do the same before someone else is killed and the wrong person gets blamed. We need a name, Esther."

She put her hands to her face, as if to hide a tremendous burden. Taking her glasses off, Esther was teary-eyed.

"I only know her as Monique," she said in a voice barely audible.

"Monique," repeated Ray almost to himself.

"She's been coming to the shelter for a few months now," Esther stated. "I never kept an official record of her visits because she begged me not to. She said her husband was an important man and would kill her if he ever found out."

Ray and Nina looked at each other, their interest piqued.

"How long have you known about this Monique?" Nina asked searchingly.

"I suspected she might be involved after the first murder," admitted Esther shakily. "There was something about the way she knew all the details." She drew a long breath. "I only wanted to try to help her. I hoped she would stop at one. Then two. But it became like cocaine to her—the more she killed the greater the urge to kill again. It got out of control. Monique lost whatever sanity she had started out with."

"And you just let this go on?" Nina's mouth hung open in disbelief at what she was hearing.

Esther wiped tears from her cheeks. "I couldn't stop it . . . stop her. I was too deeply involved to go to the police. I didn't want to end up losing the shelter and maybe going to prison in spite of myself."

"Maybe you won't have to," indicated Ray, "if you cooperate with us fully. . . . Where can we find this Monique?"

"I-I, uh, I don't know where she lives," Esther stammered. "I only know that she's involved somehow in the legal profession . . . or maybe her husband is."

That would help explain the killer's intimate knowledge of the goings-on in Carole's courtroom, Ray thought. *And place her in direct contact with the shelter.*

But where the hell was she now? What was her next move?

He wondered what she hoped to gain by setting up Carole to take the fall for her killing spree. Did she really think she would get away with it?

Ray turned his thoughts to this important man the

woman might be married to. A cop, maybe? he considered. Or even another judge?

And who the hell was she behind her killing mask?

They not only needed to find this serial-murdering bitch, but it had better be damned quick, Ray told himself. Before she went after someone else and took deadly batting practice on him.

Ray looked at Esther with some compassion. "We'll need a good description of Monique," he ordered. "And anything else you can think of that might help us find her . . . and soon."

45

"I thought that name sounded familiar," Nina said, sitting at her desk. She looked at the statement from a crime witness. "A Jacqueline Monique Davis was at the scene of the Blake Wallace murder. She was the one who gave the description and partial license plate number of the car that allegedly left the scene."

"Let me see that." Ray hovered over her like a big brother. He studied the statement and frowned. "Looks like Jacqueline Monique Davis, if that's her real name, calculated all her moves like a general in the military. Spoon-fed us what she wanted us to know, and we swallowed it like candy."

"Now wait a minute." Nina looked up, one brow cocked. "The judge isn't off the hook yet. We still need to talk to this Jacqueline Monique Davis and see if her story jibes with Esther Reynolds's account of the suspect—assuming the two women are one and the same."

"It all fits perfectly from where I stand," Ray said, studying the suspect's physical description. "Tall, shapely, attractive, light-to-medium-brown skin, dark pixies . . . Esther pretty much described the same person you interviewed. Which is also damned close to the woman described at the bar the night Roberto Martinez was murdered, minus the blond wig and shades. I'd say that *this* is our woman."

Nina rose. "Well, let's check her out," she said noncommittally. "She gave us an address. Meanwhile I'll have records run a check on the name Jacqueline Monique Davis and any possible criminal background."

"Good idea." Ray had the feeling that this Monique broad was still one or two steps ahead of them—making her that much more dangerous.

The address the suspect had given was a vacant lot surrounded by tall weeds and littered with everything from beer cans to used condoms.

"The lady was a witness," Nina spoke defensively. "There was no reason to suspect that she was feeding us a bunch of bull."

"No one's blaming you," Ray told her, driving back to the station. "She's been playing all of us like a piano. We've seen it before. Killers get some kind of sick gratification out of being so-called innocent bystanders, while manipulating the police and press right under their noses."

"You think she could be a lawyer? Or even a judge?" Nina looked at him keenly. "And who the hell is her husband?"

"Well, so far she's a battered woman, a witness to a crime, and currently a missing woman," Ray said. "Yeah, I think it's possible she could be a judge, lawyer, or some other public servant. Or none of those. The husband, if there is one, could be any one of these as well." He shifted his eyes to Nina. "What seems pretty clear is that this bitch is a very unstable woman. Which scares the hell out of me."

He thought about Carole. Had her life been placed in danger by her release from jail?

Would Monique go after her?

Ray wondered if Carole even knew the woman. Or was this more of a guilt-by-association thing? Who knew what this psychopath used to justify her actions? he thought.

More distressing news came that afternoon from the records department. There was nothing on a Jacqueline Monique Davis. Which meant she did not exist, technically, insofar as police files. At least not by that name.

"Could Davis be her maiden name?" Nina asked.

"Maybe." Ray twisted his lips. "Or maybe she just made it up in that sick head of hers."

Ray ran a hand across his baldhead. "Why don't you see if we can get the sketch updated to include the greater details on Jacqueline Monique Davis, or whatever the hell her real name is? We can distribute it in legal circles and on the streets. Someone might recognize her."

"I'm on it."

"I'll go see Carole," he said, dispensing with the formalities when referring to her around Nina. "She may know Monique under a different name. It's obvious that Monique knows her—which could spell trouble once she learns that the plan to set Carole up has backfired."

46

Carole struggled in trying to decide upon chicken or pork chops for dinner. In the end she went with the pork chops, picking up the package and putting it in her cart. She envisioned breaded pork chops, along with broccoli and brown rice. She often turned to eating when struggling to deal with weighty issues, and was thankful that her metabolism and exercise regimen kept the pounds off.

The supermarket was busier than usual with shoppers, and Carole wondered if it was a holiday she wasn't aware of, or just other people looking for some escapist food, like her.

She was still trying to come to terms with the various things that had happened in her life of late and what they meant in the larger picture.

Her thoughts centered on Ray Barkley. Were she and Ray destined to be like two ships passing in the night, never to truly connect? Or find everlasting love and commitment?

There were more pressing matters that stood in

the way of any thoughts of romance, Carole mused. She could actually have to face a multiple murder trial as a defendant rather than judge. And with the press looking to sensationalize it, she couldn't possibly hope for a fair trial in Portland. Or anywhere else, for that matter, as the so-called Vigilante Killer.

She imagined herself being vilified as a seriously disturbed female serial killer of men. But knew there would likely be at least some public sentiment in support of her as an avenging angel in ridding the world of men who abused women and children.

Stuart and Vivian entered Carole's head as she gazed absentmindedly at a row of cereal boxes. It seemed to Carole that if she had to point the finger, it would have to be at Vivian, whom she hardly knew, in spite of the circumstances that had brought them together on several occasions.

Carole had been so deep in her thoughts that she never even saw the cart that she plowed into—or the woman on the other side of it, who went sprawling backward into a shelf, knocking a few boxes over. However, she showed remarkable agility in maintaining her own balance.

"Oh, I'm so sorry," Carole stammered, embarrassed that this should happen. "Are you all right?"

"I'm fine," the woman said in a sure voice, a smile raising her already high cheeks. "No broken bones."

She straightened out a marine-blue pantsuit that matched her strap heels. The woman, about Carole's height, build, and complexion, had long brunette Senegalese twists and wide almond-brown eyes. Carole imagined her to be in her mid to late thirties.

"I'm usually not that clumsy," Carole told her, feeling foolish. "I was distracted."

"I think it was more my fault," the woman surprised her by saying. "I have a bad habit sometimes of looking up rather than straight ahead."

Carole suspected she was just being kind. She noted that the attractive woman's cart was empty, as though she were rolling it around just for effect. *Kind of odd*, she thought.

"I guess we had both better try to avoid any more accidents," Carole told her. "At least today."

The woman smiled, gazing steadily at her. "Yes, you're right."

Carole found herself also studying the woman. She almost detected familiarity there.

Was it her well-defined face? The somewhat throaty voice? Carole homed in on the smile that almost seemed to be at her and not with her. The way the woman stood with an air of overconfidence. The way that she wrung her hands, as if a habitually nervous person.

"Is it possible that we've met somewhere before?" Carole asked impulsively.

The woman did not flinch when she responded. "I don't think so. I'm usually pretty good with faces. I'm sure I'd remember yours."

Carole nodded, wondering if everything that had happened was starting to get to her wherever she went. Including diminished cognizance and perception. She was imagining knowing people she'd never laid eyes on before. Was this part of the price of being falsely accused and put under the microscope by peers, police, and the general public? What other things would she have to endure along the way?

"Well," Carole said politely, "I guess I'd better finish my shopping. Good-bye."

" 'Bye," the woman responded, favoring her with a cool smile before walking past Carole and leaving the empty cart there.

By the time Carole had paid for her groceries and left the store, she considered the issue behind her. Right now she hoped to get home and enjoy a quiet evening alone, away from all the distractions that had converged on her lately like a tidal wave.

The woman watched from a distance as Carole went up to the checkout counter. The judge had nearly recognized her. *Damn.* But the bitch had not been certain, not believing her own eyes and mind. She would have to be more careful next time. . . .

She couldn't have her plan derailed. Not now. Not by anyone.

Judge Cranston had been responsible for those abusing assholes being set free. After all, she was the presiding judge in every instance, and therefore had the final word. Didn't she?

So it was only fitting that she be given the sentence they should have been dealt had the judge been stronger and more determined to see that justice was properly served. Life behind bars, if not death by lethal injection. The bitch deserved no less.

First, though, there was one more bastard to be punished, while Carole Cranston was out on bail and capable of being blamed. This one would not only serve notice to the world about the evils of abusive men, but would be the final straw for making certain the judge got her own just due.

The woman, calmly sidestepped shoppers, casting an artificial smile here and there. She left the store just in time to see Judge Carole Cranston climb into a cab.

She watched as it drove off, its occupant guilty of allowing scum to walk away scot-free from their abusive crimes against women. For that she would pay dearly. Just as they had.

The woman sucked in a deep, calming breath and walked away contemplatively.

47

Carole saw the detectives' familiar car parked in front of her building as the cab dropped her off. Ray was leaning against it. He looked at her with penetrating eyes that gave no clue as to his purpose for being there.

Had Ray come to arrest her again? mused Carole worriedly. Or tell her he loved her with all his heart and that this whole thing was nothing more than a bad nightmare? She didn't allow herself to think too optimistically, for fear of yet another letdown.

Carole tightened her grip on the bag and felt her heart skip a beat. "What do you want?" she asked cautiously.

Ray moved toward her. "To talk," he said in a low voice.

She eyed him with misgiving. "Should I have my attorney present?"

"Not necessary," he assured her. "Let me carry that bag for you."

He reached his arms out, but Carole involuntarily stepped around him.

"No, thanks. I can manage."

Carole had mixed feelings about being alone with Ray, as though they hadn't already been together in the most intimate ways. She decided to hear him out, then show him where the door was. No matter what her sentiments for him were, she refused to let herself be manipulated by a man Carole felt unsure she could trust, much less depend on. Or even love.

In the condo, Carole placed her bag on the kitchen counter, intending to put the items away afterward, expecting this to be short, if not sweet.

"There's been a break in the case," Ray told her, a hint of expectation in his voice.

"Oh . . . ?" She was all ears.

"We may have found our killer," he said. "Or at least tentatively identified her."

The way Ray shifted his eyes at her face, for an instant Carole wondered if he was referring to her. Then she thought of Vivian.

"So who is she . . . ?" Carole asked with a sharp intake of breath.

Ray ran long fingers across his mouth. "We're looking for an African-American woman named Jacqueline Monique Davis. Trouble is, we're not sure that's her real name. She's been a volunteer at the Rose City Women's Shelter, according to your old friend Esther Reynolds."

Carole listened intently even as she replayed the name Jacqueline Monique Davis in her mind.

"Appears she is the same Jacqueline Davis who was at the scene of Blake Wallace's murder," Ray informed her. "It was her statement that led us to Wolfe's car and eventually to you."

Carole didn't know whether to be elated or angry. The fact that he and the whole city had all but convicted her before the facts could come out left her a bit numb and more than a little disillusioned, not to mention pissed off.

Ray gazed at her studiously. "We're hoping you can tell us who Jacqueline Monique Davis is," he uttered. "My guess is that she's someone you're acquainted with as a judge, if not outside the court."

"Jacqueline Monique . . ." Carole thought out loud, trying to recall the name. "Hmm . . . Doesn't ring a bell."

Ray began describing her. "About your height, build, and skin shade; long, darkish individual pixies, good-looking . . . maybe in her late thirties . . . ?"

The description made Carole think instantly of the woman she had all but knocked over at the store. Only her hair was in Senegalese twists. She had seemed eerily familiar, Carole remembered thinking.

"What is it?" Ray asked.

"Jacqueline Lewiston . . ." The words rang out of Carole's mouth almost in song. "She was a temporary court stenographer for me about six months ago while my regular stenographer had some personal problems to attend to."

Ray reacted. "When did you last see her?"

Carole stared into his face. "I may have just seen her a short while ago . . . today."

After she explained her brush with the woman at the store, Ray said worriedly, "Hell! She must be stalking you. Or at the very least she's toying with you while she plays out this deadly game of setting you up as a murderer."

Carole found her legs growing wobbly. She might have fallen had Ray not grabbed hold of her, wrapping his strong arms across the small of her back like a lover.

"Are you all right?" he asked, concern etched across his face.

"I think this whole damned nightmare is just starting to catch up with me," she admitted, her hands trembling. "As a judge, I'm used to just about everything you can imagine in a courtroom. But lately my real life has been a soap opera all its own. Having a sociopath out to ruin me just tops it all."

Ray continued to hold her, their bodies pressing together. "I'm sorry, baby," he spoke tenderly. "Hopefully the nightmare will soon be over for us all."

Then what? Carole wondered. Would life ever go back to normal for her again?

I'm not even sure what normal is anymore, she told herself. Or if she wanted things to go back to exactly the way they were.

That included having a sexual relationship with Ray.

"You wouldn't happen to have an address for Lewiston," he asked, "would you?"

"I'm sure it's on file at the courthouse," she told him.

"Feel up to a drive?" Ray asked her.

"Try to stop me," Carole dared him, just as anxious to get to the bottom of what had turned her life upside down.

* * *

At the Criminal Court Plaza personnel office, an administrator gave Ray and Carole access to the employment file on Jacqueline Monique Lewiston. It listed her as a temporary court stenographer, age thirty-six, along with dates of employment. For further information it referred to the Legal Temps Agency.

"I hope I'm not leading you on a wild-goose chase," said Carole as they headed for the agency. She was beginning to wonder if this actually was the same woman she had seen at the store. The woman had given no indication that they had ever met before. Or that their run-in was anything more than a coincidence. Just the opposite, in fact.

But then, Carole thought, even a madwoman—or especially one—could orchestrate a convincing setup and play of innocence.

Ray seemed to read her mind. "I don't think so," he said knowingly. "This psycho broad's certainly clever and daring, but also very dangerous. If there is a goose to be caught, she's the one."

The Legal Temps Agency was in downtown Portland. They supplied temporaries for virtually all support functions in the legal field, including courtroom staffers. The office was large and sectioned off into cubicles with desks and computers. Phones rang off the hook as employees tried to keep up with the demand.

The manager was a short, heavyset white woman in her fifties named Rosalyn Bradford. Ray used his police ID and a commanding presence that betrayed his sense of determination to get what they wanted.

"Here is Ms. Lewiston's personnel file," Rosalyn said. "What type of trouble is she in?"

"Right now we just need to find her for questioning, ma'am," said Ray evasively, taking the folder.

"Actually, Jacqueline hasn't worked for us for some time," she remarked. "We called her about jobs but there was no answer. It was like she just dropped out of sight."

"But not out of mind," muttered Carole thoughtfully.

Ray studied the file. It included a phone number and home address, an apartment in Portland. Jacqueline Monique Lewiston's marital status was listed as single, he noted. Was that true?

He glanced at Carole, wondering if things could ever be right for them again. Once this was all over, he knew he had his work cut out in regaining her trust.

Her affection.

And whatever else they'd had going on, till he had destroyed it.

Favoring Rosalyn, Ray handed her the folder but kept the documents. "I'll need to hold on to this for a while, if you don't mind."

"Not at all," she said nonchalantly. "Everything's on computer these days. If we need another file on Jacqueline, we'll simply print it out."

Ray imagined that should they ever get their hands on Jacqueline Lewiston, her employment history and everything before, during, and after would be no doubt be useful in a psychiatric case study of the crazy woman.

"Do you have a gun?" Ray asked Carole during the drive.

"No," she responded tersely. "My late husband

collected guns. And I saw firsthand the results. I have no burning desire to keep one, thank you."

"Maybe it's time you reevaluate that," he strongly urged. "At least so long as a serial killer is on the loose who could come after you."

Carole bit her lip. "If this woman had really wanted to kill me, I'd probably already be dead. I'm sure she's had her opportunities. I doubt that I fit the profile of the type of person she's targeting."

"Profiles can change," Ray warned. "If she thinks for a minute that you're no longer a serious suspect, then she just might decide you're expendable in much the same way as she did the batterers."

Carole certainly did not take the threat to her life lightly. But she refused to dramatically alter her view on guns. Too many people died needlessly when possessing one, including a man she once thought she could save from such a fate. She would not be intimidated into arming herself by a mentally unbalanced woman who blamed her for something she had no control over.

"I'll make sure my doors are locked and alert building security," she compromised. "I also keep pepper spray in my purse and condo."

Ray cleared his throat and suggested, "You could stay at my place until we get her. . . ."

The offer was admittedly tempting to Carole—in more ways than one—but she wasn't sure it was for all the right reasons. She needed more time to sort out her feelings—and to allow him to sort out his.

"I don't think that's such a good idea," she told him succinctly. "Besides, if it is Jacqueline Lewiston, hopefully we'll find her, and my safety will no longer be an issue."

Ray faced her with a raised eyebrow. *"We'll* find her?"

Carole held his gaze. "Damned right," her voice snapped. "If you think I'm going to just sit around and be a potential target while someone tries to frame me for murder or make an attempt on my life, think again!"

Ray did think about it. He could have insisted she stay out of it as official police business. But he knew Carole had a right to at least be there when they snapped the cuffs on the suspect. He'd make sure she was well out of harm's way.

Perhaps this would also be a way to try to make amends to her, he thought, and salvage what they had. If the damage was not irreversible.

48

"Looks like Jacqueline Monique Lewiston just might be our killer," Nina said humbly, her gaze straying regretfully to Ray and Carole. They were standing around Nina's desk. "Found out some rather disturbing things about her . . ."

"Such as?" Ray prompted her.

"Nine years ago she snapped after being battered one time too many by her renowned civil-attorney husband, Derrick Lewiston. She literally beat him to death with a wooden bat. She was charged with murder and found guilty, but by reason of insanity. Spent nearly eight years in a mental hospital before being declared sane again. She was released six months ago."

Ray looked stunned, as did Carole.

"She must have really done one hell of a con job on those shrinks at the hospital," said Ray in disbelief.

Nina nodded in agreement. "Yeah, I'd say they screwed up big-time on this one. I guess I did too," she said with an eye on Carole. "I'm really sorry, Judge Cranston, for putting you through this."

Carole managed a smile. "Don't worry about it, Detective Parker," she said diplomatically. "What's done is done. You were only doing your job. Some people—or at least one person—seem to think I screwed up in allowing some accused or convicted batterers to go free. I too was only doing what my job called for. I suppose the downside comes with the territory for us both."

"So we're cool then?" Nina asked hopefully.

"Yes, Detective," responded Carole evenly, peeking toward Ray, "we're cool."

A smile of relief spread across Nina's face.

"Now that we've made peace among ourselves," Ray said between them, "I think it's time to focus our attention on the person behind the vigilante murders. Let's go pick up Jacqueline Monique Lewiston."

There were no dissenters.

They drove to an address on Philmore Street in the Hayworth District of the city. Backup units accompanied them. The suspect was considered armed and dangerous, but they still wanted to try to take her alive.

So long as no one's safety was compromised.

The cottage-style apartments were surrounded by well-kept shrubbery and walkways resembling a college campus. Ray and Nina led the assault on the first-story unit in question, leaving Carole at a safe distance in the car. Guns were drawn and in ready position.

The lights were on inside, indicating that someone

was home. On the porch was some rotting leftover wood from winter and a couple of half-soaked newspapers.

Ray knocked once on the door, then yelled, "Police! Open up!"

Moments later the door opened and an elderly, frail white man appeared, looking as if he were about to have a heart attack.

"What is this about?" he asked in a frightened voice, with a thick German accent.

"We're looking for Jacqueline Lewiston," said Ray, wondering if they could have the wrong address but not taking any chances. He kept his gun pointed at the man, who was trembling badly.

"There is no Jacqueline Lewiston here anymore," he stated. "She moved out two weeks ago."

Ray regarded his partner, who hunched her shoulders as if stumped.

"My wife and I just moved in last week," the man stammered. He scratched his wide pate. "What did she do—rob a bank or something?"

"If only," Ray muttered to himself.

It took them about two minutes to verify the man's story and vacate the premises, realizing that Jacqueline Monique Lewiston was still very much on the loose. She had, to no one's surprise, left no forwarding address.

While seemingly remaining one step ahead of everyone else.

"You want to do *what?*" boomed the voice of the man in charge of the homicide/robbery division. Lieutenant Vernon O'Neal was a twenty-five-year veteran of the Portland Police Bureau. At five-eleven, he was built like a brick house and had a gravelly voice from years of smoking cigars.

"I want to act as a decoy," repeated Ray tonelessly.

They were gathered for a strategy session aimed at capturing Jacqueline Monique Lewiston, now unanimously believed to be the psychopathic Vigilante Killer.

"You've either lost your damned mind, Barkley," growled O'Neal, standing in front of the room, "or you're one brave son of a bitch."

A spatter of uneasy chuckles went around the room.

But Ray was not laughing. He had given this some serious thought. It seemed the best way of flushing this killer out into the open, without putting others at risk. Worse, he believed, if she suspected they were on to her, Jacqueline Lewiston would probably disappear into the woodwork of any big city in America and continue her self-appointed mission. Or never be heard from again. Either way, it would be disastrous to the department—not to mention men across the country.

"It makes sense," he said confidently, eyeing Nina, who had been vehemently against the idea. So had Carole. "If I'm set up as an abusive creep who gets off with a pat on the back, I know she'll come after me. We can go the whole nine yards, including a rap sheet, a convincing battered wife or girlfriend, and a trial—anything it takes to make it seem legit. If we're lucky we'll spot Monique in court or hanging around the building, and nab her ass right then and there."

"And what if we're not?" O'Neal's brow creased.

"Then I'll make myself a target," offered Ray succinctly. "When the bitch thinks she's luring me into a trap, it'll really be the other way around. It can work, Vernon."

At least I hope to hell it will, he thought. In truth, Ray knew it could just as easily blow up in his face. But he considered it worth the risk in trying to catch an elusive and maniacal killer.

O'Neal hesitated. "I don't know, Barkley. If we keep this thing under wraps and she kills someone else instead of being taken down, it'll be *my* ass on the line." He peered. "Not to mention *yours!*"

Ray sucked in a deep breath. "If we publicly identify her, it may drive Jacqueline Lewiston over the edge even more. She could strike out at anyone who happens to be male. Even a female, if she gets in her way. Hell, Lewiston could even go underground, aided and abetted by people who believe she's doing the right thing. I say we try it my way. If it doesn't work we still know who our suspect is."

"Knowing who Jacqueline Monique Lewiston is and finding her are two different things," Nina pointed out, two chairs over in the front row. She glared at Ray. "This is my case too, Barkley. I say we put out the word to our informants and the media that we're looking for Lewiston. We can go house to house, door to door, if we have to. Even offer a reward. Someone would come forward. Once Monique knows she's been identified, there will be too much heat for her to try to kill someone else—except maybe herself."

Ray knew this was Nina's way of looking out for his ass. Not to mention the sister's own damned stubbornness coming out in full force. He was not deterred.

"But why take the chance she might kill again or commit suicide?" he argued. "Why send the public into a panic and maybe a killer as well when there may be a better means to bring her to justice?"

O'Neal shuffled his feet. "Barkley's right, Parker." He angled his eyes on Nina. "Besides, we already tried things your way once, and look what it got us—an innocent judge whom we had all but locked up and thrown away the key."

This silenced Nina, and Ray felt for her, just as he did Carole. He wished to hell it had never happened. Carole had simply been in the wrong situation at the worst possible time, making her a perfect suspect.

But all they could do now was look ahead, he thought. No one said it would be easy to mend fences. He wondered if Carole realized just how much he missed having her in his life.

Maybe after this was all over . . . he mused.

O'Neal turned his attention to Ray, grimacing. "One shot at this," he said tersely. "We do it all by the book. No stepping out of line, Barkley. We don't need any more dead heroes. Do I make myself clear?"

"Perfectly," Ray responded, already putting the plan into action in his mind.

49

The cab dropped Carole off in front of the Rose City Women's Shelter. The day was dreary and drizzly, the sky dark and threatening.

Carole made her way up the cobblestone walkway. The shelter reminded her of an old English castle that had been renovated. She could see faces peeking out of windows, as if fearing their men had come to take them back into an abusive environment.

She had received a call from Esther asking her to come. The call came after they had spoken on the phone briefly for the first time in months. Their friendship had been strained in recent years, as both had put more focus into their jobs and less in strengthening the bond they had developed so long ago.

Neither had spoken much since the trial about Esther killing her husband. Both knew that it did no good to harp on what had happened. To Carole, her friend had been left with no choice, other than to be killed herself.

Carole had often wondered if she should have had the courage to fight her own father, maybe saving her mother's life. That image of her mother's beaten, bloodied, lifeless body lying broken on the bed beside her drunken father would haunt her forever. Years of therapy had more or less convinced her that there was little a seven-year-old girl could have done against her brute of a father, aside from feeling the sting of his fists herself. And perhaps be permanently silenced, like her mama was. He had confessed to the crime, sparing her from testifying against him. He died in prison from a heart attack.

It had been years before Carole had been able to cry for the man out of love and pity. For as much as she wanted to hate him, she couldn't. In spite of what he had done and how, he was still her father— the only one she'd ever have.

Her mother must have felt the same way, she'd imagined. She wanted only to have her family whole, willing to sacrifice her own life to make a home for her daughter and be a good wife.

Family was something Carole had run away from like the plague ever since. First settling on a substance-abusing, unstable husband, then being in a few mostly meaningless, short-term relationships designed to disintegrate. Her work had become her family, and she'd poured herself into it as though nothing else in the world mattered.

Only with Ray Barkley had she finally felt as if something else did matter. He had given her cause to actually think she might want to be with someone long enough to create a life together with a family of her own.

But that too had come under fire recently, leaving

Carole with doubts. Could they survive the strain placed on their relationship? Or would it prove to be their undoing at the end of the day?

Ray had urged Carole to stay behind locked doors as long as Jacqueline Lewiston was still at large. She had rejected this insofar as it would make her essentially a prisoner in her own home. Having already known what it was like to live in fear of someone, she refused ever to be placed in that position again.

Not even if it put her life in jeopardy.

Carole entered the shelter. She had always felt that its warm ambience set it apart from other shelters and helped give battered women hope and encouragement that they didn't have to be victims.

But one of the women had managed to veer way off course and slip through the cracks of sanity and social behavior. She had become the person all battered women feared existed within them, waiting to be brought to the surface by violence perpetrated against them by their male lovers.

Which then made such a woman even more dangerous, she considered.

And deadly.

"Hello, Esther." Carole looked at her friend, who appeared tired and overburdened. She wore a purple-and-gold African skirt suit and saddle-brown leather toe sandals.

"Hi, Carole." Esther licked her lips nervously, eyeing Carole tentatively in her buff crepe suit with a sable mesh shell and black leather mules.

After a moment of awkwardness like strangers, the two women embraced warmly.

"I've missed you, girl," Esther cried.

"I've missed you too," Carole said, choking up.

"I know I should have called sooner, but . . . well . . . I just didn't know what to say or do."

"Maybe neither of us did." Carole pulled back and smiled at her. "I think I could do with a good strong cup of coffee, if you have any."

"I sure do." Esther pushed her glasses up.

They went to Esther's office, where she made two cups of coffee, spicing her own with a shot of gin.

Carole sat down, wondering how Esther could have gotten mixed up with the likes of Jacqueline Monique Lewiston. Of course, she knew the answer. Jacqueline had been touched by violence in the same way that Esther had, as well as most of the women passing through those walls.

It wasn't hard to imagine that Esther would feel a sense of loyalty to such a woman, even if she had gone over the edge. What was harder, thought Carole, was the feeling that in some strange way it was she who had let Esther down rather than the other way around.

Esther handed Carole the cup and sat beside her. "I know what you're thinking, girl," she said, her voice hollow. "That I should have called you, if not gone straight to the police, the moment I began to seriously suspect that Monique might have been a killer."

Carole raised her chin. "I'm not here to criticize you, Esther. I'm sure you had your reasons for what you did or didn't do. I just need to try to understand what went wrong."

"Wrong . . . ?" Esther slurred as if in a trance.

"Yes," Carole said. "Since when has it ever been a sound idea to kill off our problems—or men?"

"Since they wouldn't stop ramming our damned heads through brick walls," Esther retorted snappily.

"What you did was in self-defense," Carole reminded her. "A jury agreed. But being a vigilante killer of alleged, or even proven, abusers indiscriminately . . . that's going too far. And it does nothing to solve the problem of battered women in this society. It only takes the lives of a few male batterers, while leaving their women with the responsibilities of taking care of their children, debts, chores, and even themselves. Does that really sound like true justice to you?"

Esther's face darkened and tears formed in her eyes. "No," she uttered weakly. "All I've ever wanted here was a place where women could feel protected. Then Monique came along and I felt an instant bond with her. Kind of like I have with you. I could feel her pain and somehow made myself justify what she was doing." She sighed. "I wanted to come to you from the beginning, but . . . you're a judge, Carole. I didn't want to get you involved in this. By the time things got out of hand, I felt as if I had nowhere to turn."

Carole took a deep breath. "There was always somewhere to turn," she said lamentably. "And I became involved. Monique saw to that. Maybe if you had trusted yourself more we might have been able to avoid what's happened."

Esther wiped at her eyes and sobbed. "I'm so sorry, Carole. I haven't been nearly the friend to you that you've been to me. I've brought this whole thing down on myself."

Carole suddenly felt like a mother and put her arms around Esther, much as her own mama used to do when she needed to be comforted.

"What's going to happen to me?" Esther asked fearfully.

"I'm not sure," Carole told her honestly. "First they have to find Monique. If you can assist them, please do. Aside from that, so long as you cooperate, chances are the authorities will go easy on you."

Esther faced her. "What about us?"

Carole mused and said, "As far as I'm concerned, nothing has to change—except for the better. We've been through far too much in our lifetimes to turn against each other. Especially now."

And she meant that with all her heart and soul, Carole thought. When all was said and done, she could scarcely afford to abandon the few friends she had. Not even those who, at times, seemed determined to abandon her.

50

Monique watched as Carole left the shelter and got into the cab. She followed it.

She wondered what Judge Cranston and Esther had talked about. That bitch had probably sold her out, she thought angrily.

She knew about Esther and Carole's longtime relationship. How Carole had testified for Esther after she killed her old man, and then began sleeping with her attorney. She'd wormed this out of Esther when she had gotten her drunk. Esther had resented their intimacy, having secretly had her eye on Stuart Wolfe right up until he married Vivian, preferring younger stuff to someone closer to his own age, like Esther.

She even found out about Carole's daddy beating her mama to death, mused Monique. Then her husband blowing his gutless brains out and leaving her to clean up the mess.

They were all in the same damned boat, Monique

convinced herself. Men had abused them all in one way or another.

Yet they were also different, she knew. She was the only one with the balls to make those bastards pay for their sins in the only way they could appreciate what it meant to feel helpless, vulnerable, and get an ass whipping and their face smashed in.

And no one would stand in her way.

Not Esther.

Not the detectives on the case.

And certainly not *Her Honor*, Judge Carole Cranston.

Monique watched as the cab let Carole out in front of her building. Carole was soon inside, back to her protected, sheltered world.

Don't feel too comfortable in there, Monique told the judge with a mental chuckle.

"I know right where you are, bitch," she said aloud. "I can get you anytime I want. I've been in your place right under your cute little nose and you never suspected a thing."

She had stolen the cultured-pearl bracelet from Carole's jewelry box and put some of that asshole Blake Wallace's blood on it that had splashed onto her clothing after his head exploded from her pounding it with the bat. It had been easy to plant the evidence in Stuart Wolfe's car, particularly after she had given the police a description of the brother's BMW and a partial license plate number. She knew it would be only a matter of time before they discovered the bracelet and linked it to Carole.

Especially since she was sleeping with the lead detective on the case. It didn't hurt matters that his spunky partner stayed on his ass, pointing the finger at the judge.

Monique had counted on this sister-rivalry thing in putting the bloody bat in Carole's condo, and waiting till the detectives discovered it—further assuring that the honorable Judge Cranston would be charged with the crimes she had failed to prevent by putting those sons of bitches away.

"Enjoy the freedom while you can, Judge," she sang satirically. "Because you're going down! Just like the others—only to prison, where your black ass can rot away for the rest of your stinking life!"

But not before she made sure another battering bastard went down with her, thought Monique. It was the least she could do for the judge while she was out on bail.

Not to mention for the women of America who were fed up with having their noses broken, teeth knocked out, faces caved in, and bodies used as punching bags and objects to slam against walls and toss down stairs.

Violence begat violence.

Live by the sword, die by the sword.

Or in this case, she thought wryly, *live by the fists and die by the bat*. What could be more appropriate payback for those who liked beating up women?

Monique drove off, suddenly feeling triumphant. Yet she was also unsettled, as if her own shoulder needed to be looked over.

51

The headline read, MAN GOES ON TRIAL TODAY FOR BEATING WIFE. Monique gazed at the article with interest. *Richard Kendall, a thirty-seven-year-old journeyman, was charged with brutally assaulting his wife, Whitney, two months ago. She suffered mild brain damage from the attack and faces years of physical and mental therapy.*

"Bastard!" Monique screamed, and muttered a few more expletives. He had to pay for what he did. Like all batterers.

She looked forward to the trial and trusted that someone other than Judge Cranston would take the appropriate measures to punish the dickhead.

If not, then she would.

The bald defendant, with several days' beard growth, wore a cheap blue suit and a certain smugness about him. He was a tall, lighter-skinned black man, and in fairly good shape. A fat lawyer with a graying horseshoe-shaped hairline sat beside him, appearing as if he would rather be anywhere else.

The prosecutor was a tough-talking, slender black woman named Althea Payne. She laid out her case before the jury as though she were running for political office. She promised that there would be no room for doubt when it came to convicting the defendant. Her chief witness was to be the victim herself, who Althea promised would give a chilling testimony.

The jurors listened intently, seven women and five men.

The trial was taking place in the courtroom of Judge Carole Cranston, her duties on indefinite hold while under criminal investigation. The replacement judge was the honorable Phyllis Dubois. She was African-American and in her early forties. Her dark hair was in an updo. She was on the heavy side, with a strong voice to match.

When the defense attorney's turn came for opening statements, he outlined an entirely different case. He insisted that his client was a law-abiding citizen and completely innocent of all charges. He even hinted that the alleged victim may have been having an affair at the time and that such person, if anyone, was the one who should really be on trial.

Jacqueline Monique Lewiston watched on Courtroom TV as the lawyers called their witnesses and experts. She cringed as she listened to the victim describe the horrors of her life with the defendant, including that horrific night in question when he damned near beat her to death and left with brain damage and still visible scars.

"Asshole! Son of a bitch!" Monique shouted at the screen. "You need to be taught a lesson you won't forget!"

The defendant himself later took the stand. He denied everything in a toneless, smug voice, almost daring anyone to prove otherwise.

"Lying bastard!" Monique shrieked. "Anyone can see that you're as guilty as hell, Kendall! Just like the others."

The trial lasted only three days. The jury took four hours to deliberate. They came back with a hung jury. The judge declared a mistrial.

The defendant was ordered to be released on bail pending a new trial—*if* the prosecution bothered to file new charges.

"No!" Monique screamed at the TV in total disbelief, rage building in her like steam in a freight train. "How could you let him off? The brother is *guilty* and deserves to rot in prison! If not be put to death for his heinous crimes against poor Whitney."

But Monique knew that her words had fallen on deaf ears. Judge Dubois had proven to be as inept as Carole Cranston.

It would be up to her to see to it that justice prevailed, Monique told herself. Richard Kendall would pay dearly for what he had done.

And then he would rot in hell.

Like his fellow abusers.

Including the asshole who had robbed her of her dignity and anything resembling a normal life.

52

Dressed in a charcoal leather bomber jacket, short-sleeved linen shirt, well-worn jeans, and sneakers, Ray sat at the bar, casually surveying the premises. Undercover detectives occupied half the seats, including Nina, who insisted she be part of any operation as his partner and friend. Others were in place at various locations outside, ready if needed to help snare a killing, calculating cobra.

The club, Alder Street Bar & Grill, was chosen because of its location and surrounding nooks and crannies. Ray was banking on the fact that it would be too irresistible to the woman who, no doubt, wanted him dead and dismembered.

The trial had gone like clockwork. The DA's office had fully cooperated, even supplying a jury composed of their staff. The victim, a vice squad detective, had given a performance worthy of an Oscar. Courtroom TV had agreed to show the trial in its entirety, increasing the probability that Monique had seen it. There had been no sign of her inside the courtroom or the building.

But Ray felt her presence, even if he saw no one who resembled her in the bar, which had more detectives and undercover police than patrons present. And most of these were men or women who didn't fit the general profile of Jacqueline Monique Lewiston in age, race, or physical build.

Had she been able to disguise herself so that she no longer fit her own description? he wondered. The woman had already proven to be somewhat of a chameleon in her ability to easily move in and out of different circles without being detected, for all her lethal intentions.

Perhaps she was lying in wait outside, away from their dragnet? Ray considered.

He ordered another drink from an undercover detective doubling as a bartender. The drink was only colored water made to look like the real thing.

Five minutes later Ray went to the bathroom, signaling others with eye contact. In his shoulder holster was a Glock .40-caliber pistol.

In the restroom he checked underneath the stalls for any signs of occupancy. He saw no one.

He washed his hands as a man entered wearing a rumpled suit and scowl on his face. They gave each other a long stare, and for an instant Ray wondered if Jacqueline Lewiston might have had an accomplice. . . .

Could she actually have a male partner helping her as a setup man, if not an actual killer himself?

But the man quickly dispelled such theories as he disappeared into a stall, giving no indication that he wanted a piece of the undercover detective.

Ray made his way back to the bar, where he downed a couple more fake drinks and made his presence known, as if inebriated. On cue he left the bar, without having seen the suspect, but almost feeling as if she were there.

Somewhere.

Close enough that he could practically feel her.

He moved clumsily down the sidewalk, hoping that Monique would emerge and his team would converge on her like ants on a piece of rotting fish.

It didn't happen.

Ray made his way to a cheap motel, where he was registered as Richard Kendall. Detectives occupied rooms on either side of him and on floors above and below. Others manned the front desk and doubled as maintenance workers.

The room was dingy yellow with a single-size bed and a table, with a tiny bathroom off to the side. It had been wired for sound, so as not to take any chances on a surprise attack. A window overlooked the street. Below was a delivery truck with officers inside. On the other side of the street was an unmarked police sedan with two plainclothes detectives in it.

Ray lay down on the bed, waiting as if a lamb to be slaughtered. He knew he had a hell of a lot riding on this venture. It was his idea, his baby. If Monique did not show up, he would have to deal with the fallout.

That might even include his job.

His camaraderie with Nina.

And even whatever he might still have with Carole.

It made him wonder if it was time to take stock of his life. Maybe after this, Ray thought, no matter what, it was time to hang it up. Try something different. He was getting too damned old for this crap.

Crimes had become more violent and bizarre than he could remember, this case being a good example.

Maybe the time was right to seriously think about settling down. Having a family. Children he could call his own.

Maybe he and Carole could talk about that.

First, he thought, they had to talk about each other again. And reigniting the passion and flame that had seemed to have all but been extinguished with the recent chain of events.

He only hoped it wasn't too late.

The short but crisp knock on the door made Ray immediately spring up and go for his gun. On his feet, he crept to the door on a squeaky floor. There was no peephole. He could hear his heart beating wildly as he asked, "Who is it?"

"It's me, O'Neal," the lieutenant said, a pointed edge to his voice. "Open up."

Recognizing his authoritative voice, Ray put his gun away and opened the door. O'Neal barged past him, his face contorted with indignation.

"It's been over three hours, Barkley," he huffed.

"Hang in there," Ray said "Give it time. She'll show up. I know it. The sicko sister wouldn't want to see me get away with beating my wife senseless."

"Looks like you already got away with it," O'Neal declared without humor. "If she saw the trial, she wasn't impressed. Your plan backfired!"

"Why don't I go back to the bar?" Ray said, a note of desperation in his voice, unwilling to give up. Not when he was this close to nailing her ass. "Maybe she was being extra cautious. I can start the whole thing over—"

O'Neal shook his head so hard it seemed like his

neck would snap. "Nope. I don't think so. I've already sent everyone packing. Now I'm telling you to go home, too, Barkley. It's over."

"Not until Monique's either behind bars or dead, man," Ray tossed at him defiantly.

"Yeah, right," O'Neal shot back. "And because of you we've lost ground on that objective." He fixed him with crinkled eyes. "I want to see you in my office first thing tomorrow!" With that he stormed out.

Ray stood motionless for a moment. He had been so sure this would flush Jacqueline Monique Lewiston out of the woodwork like the rodent she was. But it hadn't. She had remained as invisible as she had been since the murders began. Except when she wanted to make her presence felt. Then it was too late for some hapless bastard. It was as if the killing sister was working with someone on the inside, keeping her one step or more ahead of the game.

Where the hell is she? Ray wondered in frustration.

He considered that Monique could have recognized him beneath the hair on his face as Detective Sergeant Ray Barkley of the Portland Police Bureau's homicide division. Could she have remembered him from the night of Blake Wallace's death?

Could it be that she had been tipped off that they were on to her . . . ? Ray thought. In which case, she might already have left Portland for greener pastures.

He hated to think that Jacqueline Monique Lewiston had managed to escape the net they had placed around the city and was headed to unknown parts to continue her self-appointed mission.

Ray left the room, wondering if their window of opportunity on this killer had closed for good.

53

Ray unlocked the door and stepped down into the houseboat. The moonlight shone into the passageway, and the illumination was enough that he avoided turning on the foyer light. Instead he headed directly to the bedroom. It had been a long day, and all he wanted now was some sleep in his own bed.

Ray had phoned Carole on the way home and told her about the botched plan. She had expressed sorrow and, he detected, uneasiness that they were unable to capture the serial murderess tentatively identified as Jacqueline Monique Lewiston. He offered to come over, but Carole hesitantly assured him it wasn't necessary, noting that she had locked her doors and wasn't planning to go out till morning.

They left it at that.

No talk of reconciliation, renewed romance, or even maintaining a friendship.

He didn't even want to think about what that meant. Not tonight. Maybe tomorrow, when the light of day might cast a brighter perspective on things.

Ray entered the bedroom. More moonlight filtered through the vertical cellular shades. He removed his jacket, tossing it on a chair. Then the gun and holster came off, which he set on the dresser.

Ray thought he heard the slightest sound, causing him to swivel around. Out of the corner of his eye he detected movement.

A woman's harsh voice said, "Bastard! Did you really think you could get away with what you did to Whitney?"

Without saying a word, Ray immediately pivoted to go for the gun. But the intruder was quicker, more determined than he, to his surprise. He felt the blow slam into his side and he knew that it had cracked several ribs.

"Asshole!" she taunted him. "Did you think I was so stupid as to fall for a dumb trap? It's you who has to die—not me!"

Ray had barely a moment to regard the woman. Even in the low light he could see that she was tall, statuesque, and wore a short blond wig. She wore black gloves and held a wooden baseball bat up at her side. Wearing a menacing look, she swung the bat at his head like a home-run slugger.

Ray, sensing it was coming, dove at the last instant. But not before it grazed the side of his head. The pain was staggering, made worse when he crashed to the floor. It left him dazed.

"That's right, Kendall," she ridiculed him, "try to get away. Just like the others. Won't do you a damned bit of good. You can crawl, dickhead, but you can't hide. Not from this sister!"

She raised the bat and struck him flush on the leg. Ray let out a piercing scream as the bone snapped just above the ankle. He felt like a trapped and wounded animal, defenseless against the likes of a madwoman—and running out of time. He ached all over and suspected that unless he made some sort of move now, the next blow would be the one that took him out permanently.

"Wait, Monique," Ray gasped in a voice he didn't recognize. "Jacqueline Monique Lewiston, isn't it?"

Ray saw the shock in her face that he actually knew her name. Maybe that could work in his favor, he thought, trying to push out of his mind the throbbing pain he felt from head to toe.

But the look was quickly replaced by pure, unbridled hatred. "So you get bonus points, asshole, for knowing who I am," she cursed. "It won't make one bit of difference. You'll never survive to tell a living soul. Or a dead one, for that matter."

"I'm a cop, Monique," he managed, and thought, *Have to buy some time with this bitch or else I'm done.* "So was the woman you saw in court as the victim, Whitney. The whole thing was a setup designed to flush you out into the open."

Monique flashed him a look of confusion. "You'd say anything to save your own black ass, scumbag. But it won't work!"

She slammed the bat again on the same leg. More bone shattered like glass. Ray had never felt such pain. He ached too much now even to scream.

"I'm telling you the damned truth," he groaned, trying to maintain consciousness. "I'm Detective Sergeant Ray Barkley. You knew about the trap. Do you think they would use a real batterer to trap you?"

Monique pondered this. She considered that he really was not an abuser. That the brother really didn't deserve to be beaten to death. That the trial had been nothing more than a cheap trick.

But her mind was too far gone to accept this. Even if she had, Monique felt that this man didn't deserve to live. He was no different from the rest: a user who got his kicks out of humiliating and battering women.

"Nice try, Richard Kendall," she hissed, "but it won't work, baby. I didn't just get out of the loony bin. Not today anyway. Your time for screwing with me—and your wife—is over!"

Ray's life literally flashed before him, as if he were watching a home movie. Everything he had achieved and hadn't. Everything he had worked for and hoped to have. Everything he meant to do but never got around to. Every dream he still had, including a life with Carole.

It was all about to end in a way he had never imagined. Unless he could somehow avert disaster.

But I'm quickly running out of options here, he mused.

Summoning up every ounce of strength he had left—and it was fading fast—Ray managed to use his one good leg to ram into his assailant's stomach as hard as he could, taking her by surprise. She doubled over in agony, and he tried to crawl away for his life.

But she recovered quickly and cornered him like a rat.

"Just like the rest of them, no balls to take pain," she snarled with a derisive chuckle. "Hurting women, but sissies when it comes to taking like a man what you dish out. Well, it won't work this time! You're the one who will feel real pain when I'm through with you."

Ray watched in horror as Monique raised the bat above her head. It was aimed squarely at *his* head, and he doubted he would be able to ward off the attack with the force she would exert in bringing the bat down upon him. He said a prayer at this point and hoped that the end was swift, but didn't count on it. Even after death, he knew that she planned to work him over so that what was left would barely pass for a man, much less Ray Barkley.

Without prelude, the lights suddenly came on, temporarily blinding both victim and perpetrator. A voice boomed, "Drop the bat, Monique! Now . . . !"

Ray squinted and saw Nina standing there, legs spread, gun aimed squarely at Jacqueline Monique Lewiston's chest.

Monique, startled, glared at Nina, the bat still hovering perilously over her head. "This ain't about you and me," she said. "It's about *him* and what he did!"

"No, Monique," blared Nina, never taking her eyes off the killer, "it is about *you* and what you've done. Now I said drop the bat! I won't say it again!"

Monique seemed to weigh her options for a moment or two before saying tartly, "Go to hell, bitch."

She looked down at Ray and, tightening her grip on the bat, began to lower it toward his head.

He covered up defensively, but the blow never came.

Nina fired twice at Jacqueline Monique Lewiston, driving her backward as the bat flew from her hands, landing two feet from Ray. Monique went sprawling onto the floor. The blond wig she wore sprang loose upon impact, revealing dark Senegalese twists tied up underneath. As blood spurted from her mouth and chest, she attempted to get up. But Nina now hovered over her like a gladiator, planting a foot solidly on Monique's outstretched arm. The gun was pointed at the Vigilante Killer's face.

"Don't even think about it!" Nina shouted at her with asperity. "Believe me, I will kill your black ass, if I have to—assuming you survive. . . ."

Monique glowered and groaned, spitting out, "Bitch."

"Takes one to know one," Nina tossed back sharply.

Monique's eyes rolled to the back of her head, then slowly closed. She became silent.

"What the hell are you doing here?" Ray tossed at his partner, struggling even to speak.

Nina glanced at him while still standing above Monique. "Had a hunch," she said matter-of-factly. "Figured Lewiston wasn't as dumb as we wanted her to be, even if insane. Then, wouldn't you know it, I got stuck in traffic. Didn't think I'd make it."

Ray winced, fighting back the pain that enveloped him like a dark cloud. "Damned good thing for me that you did," he sputtered. "Otherwise I'd be one dead brother about now."

Nina glanced at Monique, who had lost consciousness, two gaping bullet holes spurting blood from her chest. Satisfied she had the killer under control, she put her gun away and rushed to Ray.

"You look pretty banged up to me, Barkley," Nina uttered, wide-eyed with concern. "Man, she did one hell of a job on you. Hang in there, partner."

Ray saw the fear in Nina's face and tried to reassure her, if not himself. "It'll take a hell of a lot more than a few broken bones and cracked ribs to do me in, Parker. Afraid you'll have to put up with my bossing you around for a while yet." Just how much longer, he wasn't sure.

"Wouldn't want it any other way," she said emotionally. "I'll call for help."

"You do that," he muttered in agony. "I don't think I'll be going anywhere."

Ray shut his eyes and began to feel his head spin like a wheel. Once again his life seemed to come to him in distorted images. The pain that racked his body almost seemed to disappear.

He thought about Nina and all they'd meant to each other over the years.

Then Jacqueline Monique Lewiston and the abuse that had turned her into a killing machine.

Then Carole and the short time they known each other that would always be with him no matter what happened in the future. He could only hope there was a future. That they were able to pick up where they left off, and much more.

Then there was nothing but darkness. . . .

54

Carole was there when Ray came to. So was Nina. They were in his room at the Portland Medical Center. Carole saw that he was about as pale as a brother could be, swollen, and weak-looking. He had tubes extending from all parts of his body. A cast went from just below his right knee to his foot, suspended several inches above the bed. He had suffered a contusion on the side of his head, broken ribs, and multiple fractures of his right leg.

But he would live. She thanked God for that.

In fact, doctors expected Ray to make a full recovery in time. For that Carole was grateful. The thought that he could have died without their having ever settled their differences made her feel faint.

"Am I dreaming," Ray asked groggily, "or am I really in the company of two beautiful sistas?"

Nina blushed, as did Carole.

"Compliments will get you everywhere, Barkley,"

quipped Nina. "At least so long as you're on vacation in this hospital."

Ray forced a smile. "So am I going to pull through, or what?" he asked hesitantly.

"Afraid so." She feigned disappointment. "There's no easy way out for you, Ray. You're too bullheaded to die."

"Apparently some people will do anything to get their name in the paper." Carole grinned at him, trying not even to think about what almost was.

Ray furrowed his brow thoughtfully. "What about Monique?"

Nina's lips were a flat line. "She didn't make it." There was a moment of contemplation all around. "It was either you or her. I chose you."

Ray counted his blessings, considering just how close he had come to meeting his Maker. "Must have been my lucky day."

Nina's eyes grew. "I think it was Portland's lucky day. We located a storage locker Monique had rented. It was filled with wooden baseball bats, as if she were just getting started on her murder campaign. Or maybe she had been planning to start a major-league baseball team in the Rose City." She sighed. "Her crib wasn't much better. Left behind practically a library stocked with books and magazines on everything you ever wanted to know about battering, domestic violence, and the inadequacies of the criminal justice system. Not to mention more evidence tying her directly to the murders."

"It's likely we'll never know for sure just what put her over the edge," Carole suggested. "Spousal abuse is nothing new. Responding to it as she did seems to be. A scary thought."

"At least for some of us," muttered Ray, wincing.

"For *all* of us," she insisted. "Who knows where such unpredictable, vigilante violence could lead?"

"One thing I know for sure," he remarked dryly. "This town will never be the same again."

Nina wrinkled her nose at Carole. "I think the brother's been watching too many B movies. Either that, or those painkillers are really starting to kick in."

Both women chuckled.

"It's not the town I'm worried about," Carole joked, turning serious. "It's the people in it who can cause trouble!"

After a moment or two, Nina said, "Well, I'll leave you two alone for a while. I have some paperwork to finish up. You take care of yourself now, Ray. I'll check in on you later."

She kissed his cheek, smiled at Carole, gently squeezing her arm, and walked out.

Ray flashed earnest eyes at Carole. He couldn't help but think how fine she looked, even from the vantage point of a hospital bed. He imagined she had this effect on most men, in and out of the courtroom.

"Tell me about you," he said, remembering that she had faced all sorts of legal troubles before this case was brought to a head.

Carole was thoughtful in looking at him. "All charges were dropped," she announced happily. "I've been completely exonerated and deluged with apologies and regrets. I return to the bench next week."

The expression on Ray's face betrayed his relief and satisfaction. "I'm glad to hear that," he said. No other words seemed necessary, though there was still much more he wanted to say.

Carole moved closer to the bed, taking Ray's hand. It was damp but warm. "You know, you really had me worried for a while there, Detective Ray Barkley."

He met her gaze. "Oh, yeah. How worried?"

She licked her lips. "Worried enough that I couldn't imagine my life without you in it in a big way."

Ray looped his fingers through hers. "So you think we might have a future then?" he asked hopefully.

"I'd certainly like to discuss the possibilities," Carole said eagerly.

"So would I." A broad smile parted his mouth. "I was thinking that a real family might be nice."

She smiled back. "It might be."

"Just promise me one thing," Ray said, not letting her out of his line of vision. "If I ever get out of line, can we just talk about it, please? This damned physical-violence stuff can be hazardous to my health."

Carole chuckled warmly. "Of course," she said teasingly. "Wouldn't have it any other way, darling."

Neither would I, Ray thought. As far as he was concerned, there was only one way—and that was making a life together and not letting the past stand in the way of the future. He fully intended to make this happen, relishing the possibilities almost as much as he did the lady herself.

55

Ray Barkley was still laid up on his back with limited movement. The grunts and moans he heard were music to his ears, and his aches were anything but painful. He gripped Carole's slender waist, assisting as she delicately lifted up and down atop him. Her full breasts bounced greedily upon his face, begging him to put her nipples in his mouth. He did so ravenously and immediately felt them tauten with her rush of breath. This turned him on, as though he hadn't already been, and for an instant he thought about flipping them over and assuming control of their lovemaking.

Then Ray thought better of the idea. It had been a few months since he had come face-to-face with Jacqueline Monique Lewiston and gotten his ass whipped by the bat-wielding, crazy vigilante bitch. Although he had more or less recovered from his injuries, there was still some lingering soreness in parts of his body that reminded him that a bit more time was needed to get back to 100 percent.

But 95 percent was more than enough to make love to his sexy judge girlfriend. Or be made love to by her.

Carole sensed that things were building up to a heated climax in Ray's bed. They certainly were for her. She replaced her nipples in his mouth with her lips, sticking her tongue inside his mouth, enjoying the taste of him and the remnants of the bottle of pinot noir they had shared before turning their attention to more carnal interests.

She felt a certain peace and lots of joy at being able to shed her judge's robe in his company and be herself. Ray clearly felt the same in leaving his badge and detective persona outside the bedroom, allowing them to work at this relationship on an even footing. There was something about nearly losing one's freedom and very life that gave a person a whole new perspective on what was truly important. Or, at the very least, what deserved equal time.

Carole pondered that thought for a moment before returning her attention to Ray's hard body, which he'd worked diligently on getting back into tip-top condition. They kissed passionately, and his mustache tickled her mouth. She felt Ray actually grow inside her, compelling her to bring him in even deeper. She lifted slightly, moving astride him with a sense of urgency.

"Oh . . . Ray," she murmured, having nearly reached the point of no return.

"Yeah, I'm with you, baby," he grunted. "Every step of the way . . ."

Ray wrapped his arms around Carole, holding tightly as they both trembled wildly with their orgasms coming in full force. It must have lasted for a full minute, and even afterward he was still seeing stars and already thinking about the next time.

Those thoughts had to be put on hold as the phone rang. *Oh, hell*, mused Ray, hating the timing, though they had already reached the main goal. That didn't mean he wouldn't have been happy just holding Carole for a while.

"That mine or yours?" he asked, their chiming cell phones virtually indistinguishable.

Carole lifted her face from his shoulder, looking weary and slightly irritated. "Think it's yours. I made a point to cut mine off the moment I stepped onto your houseboat. Didn't want to be disturbed this night."

"Why the hell didn't I think of that?" Ray felt a twinge of guilt, though he knew damned well that his job didn't allow him the luxury of having time off—even when off duty with a very special lady whom he'd come to know and love.

He rolled off the bed and rifled though his pile of clothes on the floor till he found his pants and the phone.

The caller ID told Ray that Nina was the intrusive caller. Had it been anyone else he would have been pissed. But ever since she saved his life, he had remembered what he first saw and admired in her and would be ever grateful to have her as his partner, friend, and ex-lover.

"Hey, Parker." Ray tried to lower his voice, as if Carole wouldn't hear. The truth was, she knew about him and Nina—or what they once had and still did to some extent—and was cool with it. She and Nina had gained a mutual respect for each other and coexisted just fine. "What's up?"

"Big trouble, I'm afraid," Nina said tensely.

"I'm not liking the sound of that." Ray glanced at Carole, who was hanging on his every word. He tried not to think about how hot she looked in the nude after sex.

"Yeah, well, it gets worse. The mayor's daughter has been abducted."

This news caused Ray to react, but he recovered quickly. "Sorry to hear that, but the last I knew we were in homicide."

"Her boyfriend was shot to death during the scuffle that led to the abduction. Everyone will be expected to bust their butts on this one."

"Damn," Ray muttered under his breath.

"I know," Nina said. "Me too." She paused. "So see you at the office . . . ?"

"Yeah, I'll be right there."

"Hope I didn't catch you at a bad time."

"Is there ever a good time for stuff like this?"

He never gave her a chance to answer, clicking off the phone and facing Carole.

"What is it?" she asked, her brow furrowed.

"Looks like the mayor's daughter has just been kidnapped."

The Taker watched with glee as the pretty young woman with the long, dark hair didn't look so pretty anymore. She was tied down naked to the table he'd prepared for her arrival. Those big, bold blue eyes batted rapidly with fright. A moaning sound tried to escape her lips but ran into the double layer of carpet tape he'd strapped across her mouth.

"Scream all you want, bitch," the Taker said.

"Won't do you a bit of good. Not even the mayor himself can save you now!"

He laughed at her as she squirmed and tried to somehow free herself from the rope that held her arms and legs spread-eagled.

Using his video camera, the Taker recorded these precious moments of life for his captive. Just as he would record her first moments of death. The mere thought sent chills of satisfaction up and down his spine.

"Consider yourself lucky," he told her. "You're the first one to be an honored guest of the Taker. But you sure as hell won't be the last. Look at it this way, honey: the mayor will thank me for doing what I'm gonna do to you. Bad girls need to be punished. And you will be punished in a manner you'll never forget. Or, for that matter, remember, 'cause you'll never live to reflect on it."

The Taker felt himself become aroused, as the person chosen to put him on the map was now scared out of her wits and helpless to do anything about it.

But prepare to die.

IDENTITY

STEVE VANCE

The Madison Facial and Cranial Surgery Center is famous throughout the world for helping victims of birth defects and traumatic injuries. The world doesn't know, however, that the center does very special work for the government as well— providing new identities for select patients, creating perfect assassins for clandestine "wet work."

When butchered bodies begin turning up, FBI agent Russell Montgomery immediately recognizes the handiwork of serial killer Calvin Peter Bryant—the Prince of Darkness. Impossible—Montgomery shot and killed him. Can he somehow still be alive and killing? Montgomery can only find out by following the trail of victims—leading right to the Madison Center.